Author's Note

If you are sensitive to topics such as police brutality, social injustice, racism in America, etc., this is a fair warning that this may not be the book for you.

It happens all too often; you hear about a police officer abusing their power; whether it be brutality, shouting racial slurs, or shooting and killing an unarmed person. Many of these cases involve a White police officer and a Black civilian, but how often is it that you hear about a Black civilian shooting a White police officer? Could the argument of self-defense sit in court?

Would it be considered justified in the eyes of America? I decided to take on this topic only because the opposing situation happens way too frequently, and there needs to be a conversation about this. I want to be the one to spark the much-needed conversation in this country... no, the world.

I'm not saying this book is going to change the world, but if I can at least spark a much-needed conversation, mission accomplished.

Dedication

I truly want to say thank you for supporting me on this journey. It has been nothing short of amazing; I love telling stories and writing is one of my passions, so I must keep going and pushing the limit. This piece touches on sensitive topics, so I'm prepared for the pushback; this book may not be for everyone, and that's okay. I just hope it brings some awareness to what's going on.

I dedicate this piece to all my fans, as well as anyone who may have ever experienced police brutality or have (or have had) family members that have fallen victim to this treatment. I don't expect this to bring you closure, but I hope this brings some awareness and sparks a much-needed conversation. I greatly appreciate your love and support, as it is what motivates me. So many things inspired me to write this piece, including the thought of releasing another work to satisfy you all, my fans. I would like to take a moment out to thank my family and friends for their consistent words of motivation, as those play major factors in me moving forward.

Finally, I would like to dedicate this work to my strong, loving mother, who despite all adversities, has continued to push forward and fight; I guess that's where I get my loving and fighting spirit from.

-For Cherrie-

1

"Junior, can you come here for a minute?" Keisha called from the kitchen.

"Be right there," he replied before turning off the television.

He left his room and walked to the kitchen.

"Yes, Ma?" he asked as he put his locs into a ponytail.

"C.J., have you heard from your father?" she asked.

"Not since he left," Junior replied. "I think he said he was running by the gun range to speak with Alex."

Junior opened the refrigerator. He pulled out a bottle of water before closing it.

"Ah, so that's where he ran off to," Keisha spoke aloud as she started taking the groceries from the bags.

"Need some help?" he offered and picked up one of the shopping bags.

"Thank you, babe," Keisha said.

Junior looked in the bag and began unpacking the items.

"How was school?" Keisha asked.

"It was okay," he shrugged his shoulders. "Took my test in my Social Justice class."

Keisha raised her eyebrow.

"And how did my star student do?" she asked.

"Ma," Junior looked at her sternly, "it's me we're talking about," he chuckled.

"So, that means you got 100, huh?" Keisha chuckled.

Junior smirked.

"I don't want to brag, but," he wiped off his shoulder and laughed. "On another note, I had to go to practice for basketball at lunch. Coach had us running a few drills. You know we're going to the championship."

"I know. I'm so proud of you, babe," Keisha smiled at her son's accomplishments. "Don't let anyone *ever* take your focus."

"Thanks, Ma," Junior smiled as he put the bread in the cabinet.

Keisha closed the refrigerator and saw a picture of Christian in his uniform. A tear came to her eye and Junior noticed.

"Ma, what's wrong?" he asked before noticing the picture she was looking at.

He pulled his mother close for an embrace.

"Man, oh man," she started, "not a day goes by where I don't think about how life used to be."

Junior heard this story before, and he never got tired of hearing it.

"Your dad got his job back after the trial; same rank and everything. And to apologize, all they did was pat him on the back and gave him a hundred-dollar gift card to Olive Garden."

Junior shook his head.

"How was it when he went back?"

Keisha shook her head slightly.

"I think that is a question for your father," she answered.

"Understandable."

Junior looked at his father in uniform.

"So," Keisha cleared her throat as she squatted and opened the cabinet. "After he got out, he was paid restitution, took a year off," she looked at the spice label, "went back, and has only gotten three promotions in 18 years," she chuckled. "I think the department is retaliating against him."

The two of them emptied the bags.

"I keep talking to him about going on and retiring, but he's so persistent about working and making a difference."

Keisha smiled.

Junior was silent as his mother spoke.

"Do me a favor, Junior," she started as she looked at him.

Junior looked at his mother.

"Be careful when you're out there," she stated. "America has no place for an educated black man. And these cops today," she continued, "they will shoot first and ask questions later."

Junior nodded his head.

"I understand, Ma," he replied. "I'll be safe."

Keisha embraced her son and kissed his cheek.

Once the embrace expired, the two of them finished unloading the groceries.

Christian entered the home and put his keys on the table. He unloaded his weapon and put it on top of the refrigerator.

"Hey, Babe," Keisha kissed him.

"Hey, Queen," Christian replied to his wife. He looked at his son.

"Come here, little man," he chuckled as he embraced Junior.

"Little man?" Junior asked. "Dad, you realize I'm as big as you, right?" he chuckled.

"C.J., no matter how big you get, you'll always be my little man."

Junior shrugged his shoulders.

"What are we eating?" Christian asked her. His arm remained around Junior.

"What do my men want to eat?" she smiled as she looked at the two.

"Whatever you're cooking," Junior answered his mother with a smile.

"That's my boy," he walked over to the counter and grabbed the remote.

Christian turned on the television.

"*Bernard Smith, the father of Benjamin Smith, has officially announced his bid for the 2040 gubernatorial race.*"

"Unbelievable," Christian spoke aloud.

"As you all remember, Benjamin Smith was shot and killed by Miami P-D Lieutenant, Christian Tate, nearly 19 years ago. Tate was acquitted of the charges and he retained his rights as a sergeant of the force."

Christian shook his head as the reporter spoke.

"If elected, Smith has announced that one thing he will do is reassess all members of the Miami P-D for mental health and stability, to ensure all officers are medically cleared and able to perform their jobs."

Christian loosened his tie.

"Isn't it funny?" Christian started. "Even after the evidence has come out and proven that Benjamin was a threat, I'm still the bad guy."

Keisha looked at her husband in shock but didn't say anything.

"Meanwhile, people like Zimmerman are still walking around free, even though everything was laid out in black-and-white, no pun intended, that showed he was as wrong as two left shoes."

Keisha touched her husband's shoulders.

"Don't pay him any attention and you just keep being great," she smiled.

Junior studied the image of Benjamin on the screen.

He noticed the image displayed was a graduation photo.

"Pops," Junior started.

Christian looked at his son.

"When you went back to the force, how was it?"

"Elaborate on the question, young bull," Christian spoke.

"I mean," Junior started, "how did they treat you at the office? Was there any form of remorse that they'd put you through that?"

Christian sighed.

"Once Andrew helped to clear my name and helped me get my job back, I received all kinds of looks from the force," Christian spoke. "And I could tell the respect that I'd once earned from the officers was no longer there."

"What do you mean?" Junior asked.

Keisha kissed Christian on the cheek and motioned towards the stove.

"Go on, babe," he spoke to Keisha before continuing the conversation. "Son, I'd just been arrested and tried for first-degree murder," he laughed lightly. "Add that on top of me being a Black man at the top of the force; it created chaos. Hell, America already doesn't like us," he explained to his son.

Junior nodded his head.

"I'll be real with you," Christian continued. "A Black man has no business in White America."

Christian rose to his feet and grabbed a bottle of water from the refrigerator.

"So, when I got back, they did all they could to try to get me to quit; I didn't budge," he sipped the water, "and a lot of that has to do with the love and encouragement your mother was giving me."

Junior scratched his beard.

"Three promotions in twenty years," Christian shook his head. "Don't be like me, son," he cleared his throat.

"Dad, why did you stay?"

Christian took a short pause before answering.

"I guess I was just comfortable," he admitted. "After the trial, receiving the restitution, retaining my rank, and everything," he looked at Keisha, "I wanted to make sure that you and your mom would always be set."

"Pops, you don't have to worry about us anymore," Junior looked his father in the eye. "I'm going to show you that you've raised a man. I got this," he slightly nodded his head.

Keisha smiled at her son as she turned on the stove to boil the water.

Christian chuckled lightly.

"Man, the only thing you need to worry about having is making sure that jumper stays wet," he laughed. "Come on, let's go shoot a few at Ottoman's Park."

Christian rose to his feet and touched his son on the shoulder.

"You sure your back can take it?" Junior laughed.

"Yeah, a'ight," Christian chuckled. "I'm going to hit up your Uncle Ray and see if he and his son can come through. Going to take you all to school with some two-on-two."

"Get ready, old man," Junior retired to his room to put on his apparel.

Christian picked up his phone and dialed Raymond's number.
He answered on the first ring.
"Yo," he answered.
"What's good, Ray?" Christian spoke. "You and Marcus good to meet me and Junior at Ottoman for a little two-on-two?"
"You know I'm down," Raymond laughed. "When are you trying to do this?"
"Man, we can be there in about twenty. Junior's in his room getting ready and I'm gearing up."
"Bet. See y'all there," Raymond spoke.
Christian ended the call and put on his shorts and Kobe Bryant jersey.

The two emerged from their rooms and walked into the kitchen.
Keisha smirked.
"Look at my two handsome men," she started.
She walked to the refrigerator and handed each of them two bottles of water.
They put the water in the gym bag.
"Yeah," Junior started, "make sure you have the heating pad ready for the old man," he laughed.
"Baby, would you tell this youngin' that I was the man back in the day," Christian put his arm around Keisha.
"Yeah, but Pops, the game has changed since 100 years ago," Junior joked. "Must I remind you this is what I do."
"You think because you're my son, I'm going to take it easy on you?" Christian raised an eyebrow. "Nah, I'm about to take you to school."
"Pops, no disrespect, but just because you have that jersey on doesn't give you Kobe's powers," he laughed heartily. "The new face of basketball will be C.J. Tate," he smirked.
"Look at this boy," Christian smiled. "He gets it from his old man."
"You taught him well," she replied with a grin.

"Ray and Marcus are going to meet us over there," Christian spoke to his son.

"You all better head on out then," Keisha responded.

Christian kissed Keisha before heading to the door.

Junior embraced his mom.

"We'll be back, babe," Christian spoke.

"Stay safe out there," she called to the two as they headed out the door.

"I got you, babe. I love you," he added.

"Love you, Mom," Junior shouted.

"I love you all, too," she replied as she closed the door.

Junior held the basketball in his hands as the two got into Christian's car.

"Junior," Christian spoke with a serious tone, "I need for you to stay safe out here."

Junior inspected the ball.

"I will," Junior replied. He noticed the look on his father's face. "What's up?"

"As you know, there are a lot of people gunning for me," he shook his head. "Although I was acquitted, White America can't stand the fact that a Black man shot and killed one of them and walked on it."

Junior shook his head.

"It's a shame. Here we are in 2039, and we still have to live like this."

"It's not fair," Christian drove towards the park, "but it's the way it is." Christian adjusted the temperature in the car. "And so, as my son, your name is on the same hit list. Pedestrians and cops alike."

Junior was silent for a few moments before speaking.

"Don't worry, man. I'll be safe," Junior responded as he looked at his father.

"My boy."

Christian pulled into the parking lot and parked next to Raymond. Christian and Junior exited the vehicle.

"I thought you all weren't coming for a minute," Raymond spoke.

"Man, this young bull was talking so much crap that I figured that we could teach them a lesson."

Christian clapped hands with Raymond.

"Hey Uncle Tate," Marcus spoke firmly.

"Hey Marcus," Christian spoke as he shook Marcus' hand.

"What's good, man?" Junior did his signature handshake with Marcus. "You ready to teach these old souls a lesson?"

Marcus laughed.

"They ain't ready."

"Save that shit talkin' for the court," Raymond chuckled as he shook Junior's hand.

"Bet it up," Junior spoke as the four walked into the park.

***

Christian and Raymond sat on the ground and held the towel around their necks.

Junior and Marcus both leaned over with their hands on their knees.

"See what happens when the student challenges the master?" Christian chuckled.

He and Raymond fist-bumped and laughed.

"Yeah, yeah," Junior chuckled as he stood erect. "Run it back."

"Nah," Christian sipped his water. "I'm going to retire undefeated."

"You damn right," Raymond laughed.

Raymond sipped the water.

"But you boys have skill. Keep applying the pressure and watch it'll take you places," Raymond spoke to both of the gentlemen, but was more so speaking to Junior.

"Thanks, Unc," Junior remarked.

Junior heard the story about how his father and Raymond met and it was a little shocking to him that a two-timer made friends with an officer.

Junior looked at the tattoos on Raymond's arms.

"Unc, what went down when you got out?" he questioned.

Raymond chuckled lightly and sipped his bottle of water.

"Man, how much time do you have to spare?" he questioned.

Junior raised an eyebrow.

Raymond continued.

"Long story short, after Andrew helped me get out, it was and still is hell," he admitted. "Once you have a record, whether it's big or small, it affects *everything*," Raymond stressed.

Christian stretched and popped his shoulder.

"It's hard to find a job. I was fortunate that Andrew pulled a few strings and got me in at his firm as security, but I know brothers with a much smaller rap sheet who can't even land a fast-food job."

"Damn," Junior spoke.

"Yeah, man," Raymond wiped his arms with the towel. "That's why we're on you all so much. Don't get mixed up in the life of crime," he reminded Junior and Marcus. "Shit ain't fun."

"You have nothing to worry about, Dad," Marcus replied. "C.J. is gunning for a scholarship for ball and forensics, and I'm pursuing law," he chuckled. "We won't disappoint you all."

Christian cleared his throat.

"For real, be smooth out here. For us as Black men, we have a different set of rules than the rest of the world. Let Benjamin had shot and killed me, the judge would have given him a slap on the wrist because 'he's a good student and has a bright future ahead of him' and all that bullshit," Christian remarked. "It's a bullshit system; take it from a Miami-Dade police lieutenant," he chuckled.

Christian sipped his water.

"Look at how they treated the man in New York who raped his classmate, but the judge said he should be given leniency because of his 'potential bright future'."

Christian became furious at the thought.

"Aye, on some real shit, I was thinking 'here we go with this bullshit' when I saw the headline," Raymond responded.

"It's messed up," Christian shook his head. "But, anyway," he redirected his attention, "we're telling this to you all because you're young men and it's *very* different for those who look like us."

Junior and Marcus both nodded their heads.

Raymond looked at his phone.

"Looks like we'd better be getting back, Marcus," he spoke. "Your mom is going to kill us if we miss dinner," he laughed.

Marcus laughed at his father.

Christian and Raymond both rose to their feet.

"Yeah Junior, we should be getting back as well."

"I'm set, Pops," Junior replied.

"Ray, it was good seeing you and balling with you, man," Christian spoke. "Marcus, stay focused and stop chasing these girls," he joked.

Marcus chuckled.

"C.J., good game," Raymond responded. "Work on that jumper and keep your arm tucked," he coached Junior. "Christian, I'ma fuck with you," he and Marcus walked to their vehicle.

"One," Christian chuckled as he and Junior walked to the car.

Once they pulled off, Christian spoke to Junior.

"Man, did you see that last shot?" he laughed as he boasted to his son.

"Blah, blah, blah," Junior replied.

"Man, that was a bounce pass, between the legs, oop. Don't be like that," Christian laughed.

Junior chuckled.

"40 to 32," Christian continued. "Don't worry, maybe you guys will get us next time," he grabbed his son's neck and smiled.

"You old-timers just got lucky, Pops," Junior responded. "Plus, we didn't want to hurt you."

"Yeah, yeah, yeah," Christian remarked as he pulled into his driveway.

They both exited the vehicle and retired into the home.

2

Junior met with Marcus after class the next day.

"What's good, bro?" Marcus greeted Junior.

"What's good, man? Yo', you did that shit yesterday," he responded.

"Man, I wouldn't have been able to do a thing without your facilitation. We all know you're the basketball guru around here."

Junior chuckled at his friend.

"I wouldn't be anything without my teammates," he humbled himself. "Our old men just got the best of us," Junior admitted.

"They didn't play too bad for some old-timers," Marcus walked to the school's exit with Junior.

"Yeah man, one thing I'll always do is give props where they're due."

Junior and Marcus walked outside with their bookbags on their backs.

The two walked towards the train.

"What's your week looking like?" Marcus asked.

"Got a meeting with this recruiter from U.C.L.A. tonight," Junior spoke. "After the game, she wants to discuss my potential basketball future."

"Damn man," Marcus spoke. "You've got it made."

"Man, I'm just trying to make it. I don't have it made," Junior shook his head slightly.

He kicked a crushed can of soda as they walked.

Marcus lifted Junior's chin. "Chin up, we don't have time for negativity," he kept one hand in his pocket.

"You're right," Junior remarked. "Gotta be at the stadium at six for warmups."

"I'm gonna be in the front row egging you on, bro, right alongside Bianca and Sierra," Marcus remarked. "And the recruiters are going to be there," Marcus chuckled lightly. "This is the championship game! You're going to need a manager," he suggested.

Bianca was Junior's girlfriend and they'd been dating for two years. Although the road wasn't always easy, they'd managed to pull through.

Marcus and Sierra had been dating for the same length of time and had been through equally as much. The two couples nearly did everything together and it wasn't often that you'd see one without the other.

Junior laughed. "Let's cross that bridge once we get there, bro."

The two of them entered a convenience store.

Junior and Marcus split and walked down two separate aisles.

Junior opened the walk-in refrigerator door and retrieved two Gatorades and three bottles of water.

Junior and Marcus regrouped at the front of the store.

The clerk rang up the items and looked at Junior. Junior noticed him staring.

"Is something wrong, my man?" Junior asked.

"You look *very* familiar," the clerk spoke.

"Maybe you know him as the next big thing in ball. The Lebron James protégé," Marcus hyped his friend's skills.

The clerk shook his head. "Nah, that's not quite it," he remarked.

The clerk continued to scan the items.

Bernard's image appeared on the television screen. He was wearing a suit and the news broadcaster was discussing his gubernatorial run.

The screen switched to Christian's body camera's footage of the shooting of Benjamin.

Following the footage, it showed Christian's mugshot.

Junior shook his head. "So, out of all the things they could show, they choose to display the image of him in his darkest moment," Junior spoke to Marcus.

"You already know they're going to do whatever they can to keep the Black man down," Marcus spoke. "Plus, it's a story for them," Marcus added. "It's the only way they can make people care about Bernard running for governor. No one knows who he is," Marcus shrugged.

The clerk turned his head slightly and looked at the screen. He saw Christian's image.

He scoffed.

"That's who you remind me of," the clerk added. "Christian Tate!"

Junior was silent as he remembered what his father told him about people being after him.

The clerk chuckled.

"It's a shame he killed that little boy," he began to bag the items. "He had such a bright future ahead of him."

Junior was getting annoyed. "Bruh, you have the evidence in front of you. Clearly, it was self-defense."

The clerk became anxious. "Buddy, no need to get hostile with me," he moved his free hand underneath the counter.

"Nah, man, no need to push that button. Just because you see an upset Black man doesn't mean you need to be petrified," Junior smirked as he put his hand in his pocket.

He pulled his hand out of his pocket and laid the money owed on the counter. Junior didn't want to touch the cashier's hand.

Marcus put his hand on Junior's shoulder. "Not the place," he reminded his friend.

Junior grabbed the bag and walked out of the store with Marcus.

"These White folks got a lot of nerve," he shook his head as they continued the walk home.

"Don't even let that bother you," Marcus uttered. "You need to take that anger and passion that you're feeling and put it into your game tonight."

"It's just frustrating me," Junior added. "But you're right. I'm not going to give too much thought to it. I got a game to prep for."

***

"And, at guard, number 22, C.J. Tate!" the basketball announcer called.

Junior performed his pregame ritual with his teammates.

Christian, Keisha, Raymond, and Marcus all cheered loudly.

Junior raised a hand and displayed the peace sign towards his family.

Junior said a small prayer after spotting the recruiters.

He huddled up with his team and listened to the coach's motivational speech to the team.

"They are here in *our* house. We are in charge of this game," the coach projected. "As I always tell you, they don't matter. You are playing against yourselves; they don't even exist. You are your biggest opponent."

Junior nodded his head as he listened to the coach.

"We start this game off running. Egan, you're our big man," he spoke to the tallest player on the team. "Crash the boards and secure those rebounds, just like we worked on."

Egan nodded his head.

"When on defense, we are running man-to-man. Lock them down with pressure and force them to get the ball out of their hands," the coach continued. "Nothing good will come to them when they have to force the ball away. When running offense, space the floor. Keep them on their toes. Pick-and-rolls will be our best friends in this game. If they go for it, we use the matchups to our advantage. Cut to the basket and get the easy score. Do not force a shot," he stressed. "If it's not there, don't take it!"

The coach was shouting so his team would hear him over the crowd and music.

"This is the championship game, gentlemen. All that putt-putt BS is behind us. It's either all or nothing at this point."

Junior put his hand in the middle and everyone put their hand on top of his. "Soldiers on three!" Junior shouted. "1-2-3."

"Soldiers!" the teammates shouted.

Junior adjusted his shorts and walked onto the court.

Junior took his place in the backcourt alongside his teammates and opponents.

Egan stood parallel to the opponent's center and jumped for the ball.

He won the tip and Junior collected it.

"Spread out," he shouted and directed the team with his right hand.

The shooting guard ran to his right and the power forward set a screen for him to get open.

"Let's go, Tate!" Christian shouted from the sideline.

"Watch your right!" Marcus shouted.

Junior crossed his defender over and looked to his right.

He saw the shooting guard, Anthony, had little spacing between him and the defender. Junior could tell Anthony's defender was paying more attention to the ball than to Anthony.

Junior dribbled aggressively and went towards the basket. The defenders swarmed in to guard him and he passed the ball out to Anthony, who was now wide open. He shot the ball from behind the three-point line and it went through the hoop; nothing but net. The crowd cheered ferociously at the shot.

"Anthony Miller!" the announcer shouted over the PA system. "Assist by C.J. Tate."

"Get back, get back," Junior directed his team as they played defense.

Junior tightened the pressure on his opponent. As his opponent approached half-court, Junior poked the ball into the backcourt.

He chased the ball down, gathered it, and performed a layup.

"Yes!" Christian shouted.

The ball went through the net once again and the audience cheered loudly once more.

"C.J. Tate!" the announcer shouted.

"M-V-P, M-V-P, M-V-P!" the audience chanted.

Junior made eye contact with his mother and she blew him a kiss.

He continued to apply pressure to his opponent and kept his focus on the game.

***

"You keep balling the way you're doing, there may be a spot for you at U.C.L.A.," the recruiter spoke with a smile after the game.

Christian, Keshia, Marcus, Raymond, Bianca, and Sierra all stood behind Junior as the recruiter spoke.

Christian looked at the scoreboard and smiled at the score.

97-72. The Soldiers had won the game and Junior finished with a 13/17 shot ratio, 34 points, 10 assists, 4 rebounds, and 7 steals.

"Thank you, Mrs. Tucker," Junior smiled.

The recruiter passed Junior her card.

"Tell me," she began, "what was your approach to the game tonight?"

"Just playing the game that I love," Junior replied without hesitation. "I couldn't have done any of it without my teammates," he finished.

The recruiter whispered to her assistant.

She looked at Junior and continued.

"We'll be in touch," she smiled. "You got skills, kid. Impressive showing tonight," the recruiter patted Junior on the back.

When the recruiter stepped away, Christian touched Junior's shoulders.

"My boy's going to U.C.L.A. to ball," Christian smirked.

"Baby, you did so well," Keisha smiled.

"Keep hooping like that, me and Christian are going to have to triple-team you next game," Raymond chuckled.

Junior looked at the scoreboard and smiled.

Marcus picked up the duffle bag for his friend.

"Outstanding, bro," he uttered as he patted Junior on the back.

"Thanks, guys," he humbly spoke.

Bianca embraced Junior and kissed him on the cheek. Sierra held Marcus' free hand.

They all headed toward the exit of the gymnasium.

"Where are we celebrating?" Marcus asked gleefully.

"It's still surreal to me," Junior replied as he held the Naismith Prep Player of the Year trophy.

They walked to their vehicles.

"Let us know, son," Christian spoke. "As you say, we're getting old now," he chuckled, "and it's getting late."

Junior laughed. "I'm craving seafood," Junior spoke as he opened his car door.

"Let's hit up a broil," Christian suggested. "There's one over on Flager St."

Christian, Keisha, and Raymond got into Christian's truck.

"Dad, I'm going to ride with C.J.," Marcus spoke.

"That's cool," Raymond responded.

"I'll meet you all over there," Junior shouted.

"You all coming with?" Marcus asked Sierra and Bianca.

"We're going to sit this one out," she chuckled. "Gonna head to the house and get some things done."

Junior walked over and embraced Bianca. "I love you, babe. And thank you."

She smiled and kissed Junior on the lips. "I love you, too."

Marcus embraced and kissed Sierra before the girls got in Sierra's vehicle.

The girls left the lot and the boys got in Junior's car.

"Let's go lover boy," Marcus teased Junior.

Junior chuckled and started the vehicle.

"I actually did it," Junior smiled and spoke aloud.

"I knew you had it in you," Marcus put his hand on his back. "Man, you're going far in life, I'm telling you."

"Thanks, man," Junior spoke as he rolled down the windows and connected his phone to his car's audio system.

"Once you get in U.C.L.A., you know that these NBA recruiters are going to be flocking to get you on their teams."

Junior laughed. "Let's take it one step at a time," he rebutted.

He turned on some music and drove away from the lot.

"I'm proud of you, bro," Marcus thought about Junior's future. "And I'm proud to call you my brother."

"That means a lot," Junior drove with his left hand atop the steering wheel. "Real friendships are hard to come by, and so for you to say you feel that way is monumental. It's not often that we build each other up."

"It's time to change that stigma," Marcus immediately replied. "Me, I give credit where credit's due," he professed and smirked.

Junior extended his fist and Marcus connected his fist with Junior's.

Junior made a right turn and increased the volume to the music.

He and Marcus rapped along with the song.

Their rap session was soon interrupted with red, white, and blue flashing lights.

Marcus looked behind them. "The fuck, man?" he groaned.

"Nah, it's all good man," Junior pulled over to the right of the road. "We haven't done a thing wrong."

"As our fathers said," Marcus began, "the rules are different out here for us as Black men. And," he continued, "with you being your father's son, me being the son of an ex-con, and Bernard running for governor, I have a bad feeling about how this will play out."

"Don't worry, man," Junior assured him.

He positioned his trophy on the dashboard so that it was in plain sight.

"Hand me my wallet out of the glove compartment," he motioned towards the panel in front of Marcus.

Marcus sighed and shook his head slightly.

He retrieved the wallet and passed it to Junior.

Junior removed his license and registration card from his wallet. He placed the cards on the dashboard.

"Ellie," Junior spoke to his phone.

His phone responded with a chime.

"I'm getting pulled over," he finished.

"*GPS location sent,*" the phone started. "*Now recording. Calls, S-M-S messages, and notifications will be silenced until the wake word is spoken,*" his phone spoke.

Junior looked in his side mirror and saw the officers exit the vehicle.

"Two of them," he spoke softly to Marcus. "Both White."

Marcus put both of his hands on the dashboard; all ten fingers extended. Junior followed suit and placed open hands above the steering wheel.

The driving officer approached the window with his flashlight and shined it into the window.

Junior squinted his eyes.

The passenger officer approached Marcus' side of the vehicle.

"License, registration, and proof of insurance," the driving officer spoke.

"Good evening, Officer," Junior spoke. "What seems to be the problem?"

"Didn't come to a complete stop at the light back there before completing your right turn," he spoke sternly. "What are you all doing out so late?" the officer questioned.

"Just had a game," Junior remarked. "Going out for a celebratory dinner."

"Have you all had anything to drink tonight?" the second officer asked.

"We just came from a game," Junior reiterated. "There's been no drinking from *anyone*," Junior stressed.

"Here we go," Marcus whispered under his breath.

"And what about your partner over there?" the officer asked.

Marcus didn't respond to the officer.

The second officer spoke at Marcus' window.

"Do you have your ID on you, my man?" he questioned.

"I do, it's inside my coat pocket. I will have to reach inside to get it."

The officer waved him on. Both officers kept one hand on their weapons.

"I'm reaching for my identification card," Marcus spoke aloud as he slowly put his hand in his pocket.

Marcus pulled out his ID card and passed it to the officer.

"Christian Tate," the driving officer spoke with a chuckle. "Wasn't your daddy the one who shot and killed Benjamin Smith almost twenty years ago?"

Junior didn't reply.

"Marcus Farris," the second officer read from the card.

"You boys sit tight," the driving officer spoke.

He nodded his head and the second officer followed the first to the vehicle.

"They're already starting with the shit," Marcus whispered.

"Just keep your head, man," Junior responded.

Marcus reached in his pocket and pulled out his phone.

Junior shook his head.

"Not yet, man. Let's let these officers finish."

The officers returned to Junior's car slowly.

"Christian Tate, Jr., son of Miami P-D Lieutenant, Christian Tate," the officer began.

Junior read his name tag: Officer Whitley.

"And here we have Marcus Farris, son of ex-convict Raymond Farris," the second officer spoke.

Junior and Marcus kept their hands visible and didn't make any sudden moves.

"Now, you know what I find peculiar, Officer Montrose?" Officer Whitley spoke to his partner.

"What is that?" Officer Montrose asked.

"What are the odds of having the two cell neighbors of the inmates who caused the most noise, riding around together at this time of night," Officer Whitley chuckled.

Officer Montrose shined the flashlight in the car on the trophy.

"What are you all? Some kind of 'ballers'?" he taunted.

"Don't say anything," Marcus mumbled to Junior.

"Officer, we're running a little late. Respectfully, will you please just give me my ticket so we can go?"

Officer Whitley sucked his teeth and looked at Officer Montrose. He passed Junior his license and registration card.

"We're going to let you off with a warning," he tapped the top of the vehicle. "Make sure you come to complete stops at those lights."

Officer Montrose passed Marcus his license and they stepped away from the vehicle.

The two officers walked back to their car and Junior drove off.

Junior shook his head.

"Some things will never change," he huffed.

"Driving off," Marcus announced to the phone.

"*Recording ended, media message sent. Restoring notifications for calls, messages, and alerts.*"

"I wonder if they ever get tired of the bullshit," Marcus returned his license to his pocket.

He extended his hand and Junior gave him the license and registration card.

Marcus returned the cards to Junior's wallet.

"And my dad explicitly said they would be picking on me because I was his son."

"Man, you heard how it was going to escalate. You see how they tried to make it seem like we were up to no good since we were the children of the inmates who made a difference."

Junior became more irate and drove into the parking lot of the restaurant.

He and Marcus exited the vehicle and entered the restaurant.

Junior looked around and saw their parents seated across the room.

"Over there," he spoke to Marcus and nodded his head towards the adults.

Marcus followed Junior with his hands in his pockets.

"What the hell happened?" Christian asked as his son sat down.

Junior figured he'd seen the video recorded by his phone.

"Officer pulled us over. I supposedly ran a light and didn't come to a complete stop. But we kept cool and got out of there alive," Junior shook his head.

Christian displayed a serious expression on his face.

"I saw where you were pulled over; this is my district's jurisdiction," he started. "Did you catch their names?"

Keisha motioned for her son to come close to her.

Raymond rose to his feet and Marcus walked by him.

"Officer Whitley," Junior spoke as he walked over to his mother. "Officer Whitley and Officer Montrose," Junior emphasized.

"I know those two," Christian shook his head.

Junior and Marcus took seats next to each other after embracing their parents.

"What's going on, Pops?"

Christian shook his head.

"They have a reputation for staking out certain vehicles and presenting specific infractions," Christian cleared his throat after speaking. "Did they give you a ticket?" he questioned.

"He gave me a warning," Junior remarked.

"Who was the driver?"

"Officer Whitley."

Christian sipped the water.

"I'll handle it," he responded.

3

Christian looked at his computer screen and typed notes into his system.

He was overseeing a robbery-homicide case and wanted to ensure the evidence and suspect list was properly documented.

Christian looked at his watch and saw a picture of Keisha and Junior on his desk. He groaned and rose to his feet.

He exited his office and looked around.

Francesca approached him.

"Sergeant Gaines," Christian greeted her.

"Lieutenant Tate," she greeted him.

Francesca passed him a coffee.

"I figured you probably needed one," she smiled. "How's everything going?"

"Same shit, just a different day," Christian chuckled as the two walked. "Junior won his championship game yesterday," he boasted.

"Did he?" Francesca asked excitedly. "I know you're proud of him."

"You're damn right I am," he confirmed. "My boy finished 13 for 17 and had 34 points, 10 assists, 4 rebounds, and 7 steals," he smirked as he sipped the coffee. "I think he was showing out for the recruiter."

"Wow, he's playing like he's in the NBA," Francesca chuckled. "Tell him Auntie Frankie says hello and to keep pushing," she sipped her coffee. "He's going to make it."

Christian nodded his head.

"Yeah, I can see he's determined, and I don't want for him to lose that focus; over anything."

Francesca could tell he was on a mission. She could see the fire in his eyes.

"What's going on, Boss?" she asked as the two walked.

"Last night, on the way to the celebration dinner, he and Marcus were pulled over by two of our own."

"Well, you know him being your son doesn't put him above the law," she tried to make light of the situation.

Christian stopped in his tracks and looked at her.

"It's not that, Frankie. It's the reason they were stopped in the first place. And it's the officers that initiated the stop that I want to speak with."

Christian continued to walk, and Francesca followed.

"What's going on? Why did they stop him?" she inquired.

"Failure to stop at a red light before turning right," Christian spoke. "The two officers in question: Officer Whitley and Officer Montrose," he finished.

They reached the computer that kept the record of every officer and the shifts they worked.

Francesca realized why this was an issue.

"What do you need from me?" she questioned.

"Well," Christian logged in to the system, "since you're here, just back me up when I talk to them," he instructed. "If they really violated the law, the red-light camera would have captured their plates, or the pursuing officer should have issued a citation. Since neither of the two occurred, I need to speak with them," Christian shrugged his shoulders.

"Understandable," Francesca uttered.

Christian viewed the shifts for the evening around the time and location of the stop.

"Officer Brian Whitley and Officer Hubert Montrose," he confirmed the two were on duty and around the location of the stop.

He clicked on a link to view license plates of any violators at the intersection.

Junior's plates weren't on the list.

"Not even here," Christian spoke with a slight chuckle to Francesca. "Come on, their shift ends in fifteen minutes," Christian walked towards Brian's cubicle.

Christian assumed Brian would be at his desk finalizing the necessary paperwork before the end of his shift. Christian tapped on the cubicle's glass.

"Officer Whitley, you got a minute?" he questioned.

"Lieutenant Tate," Brian spoke. "Just finishing up some paperwork from last night. It was a pretty quiet evening," he had a slight smile on his face.

"Glad I caught you when I did," he started. "Last night, around 9:45 on 107th and Flager, you and Officer Montrose initiated a traffic stop on a black Mustang with gold trim," Christian straightened his tie.

Brian looked over at Francesca. Hubert was standing beside her.

Brian cleared his throat.

"Yeah, the driver failed to come to a complete stop at a traffic signal before turning right."

"Did you issue the infractor a citation for doing so?" Christian asked.

"Let him off with a warning," Brian spoke. "He informed us," he nodded to Hubert, "that he'd just won a championship game or something like that, and we didn't want to ruin his evening," Brian clicked his pen.

"I'm certain that you knew that was *my* son," Christian spoke. "And while I'm not saying he's above the law, you know he committed no infraction," he continued firmly. "There was a traffic camera at the intersection, and it didn't flag his car as having committed any violation."

"Lieutenant Tate, you know yourself that those cameras aren't always accurate," Hubert interjected.

"Yeah, man, the city is talking about taking them all down anyway," Brian added.

"Officer Montrose, I haven't even started with you yet, so I suggest you don't say a word," Christian warned.

Hubert glared at Christian.

"Officer Whitley, do you have dashcam footage of the alleged infraction?" he questioned.

"It wasn't recording until the time of the stop," Brian replied.

"So, if he were to take this unlawful stop to court, we wouldn't even have minute evidence to defend the decision to pull him over."

Brian was silent.

"Officer Whitley, I know we have history, but you will not take any of your aggression out on mine or Raymond Farris' children, or anyone else for that matter if they haven't committed any unlawful acts," Christian spoke firmly. "You understand?"

Brian sighed.

"Yes sir," he responded.

"And the same applies to you Officer Montrose. Those boys did nothing wrong last night besides being Black in a White neighborhood, and you all pull them over to throw a bogus traffic violation at them," Christian shook his head. "You both should be ashamed. If this happens again, I will place you both on suspension and then termination; do I make myself clear?"

"Yes sir," they spoke simultaneously.

Brian and Hubert both looked at each other.

Christian laid two pieces of paper on Brian's desk.

"Here, I need for you two to sign on the line, verifying that I've given you both this verbal warning," he spoke.

Francesca looked over the divider at the paper. She smirked at the paper.

Brian raised an eyebrow.

Brian and Hubert both signed on the lines.

Christian collected the papers.

"You gentlemen have a better day," Christian remarked. "Sergeant Gaines," he nodded his head.

Christian and Francesca walked away.

"Christian, why did you have to scare those boys like that?" she chuckled as they departed the cubicle and approached the front desk.

"That fear they're feeling right now," Christian began, "is the same fear my son and his friend felt when they saw the lights behind them. It's the same fear all my people feel when they see police," he continued to stand tall.

Francesca nodded her head.

"That fear that you speak of, my people feel the same thing," she sighed. "We still have people being detained and children locked in cages at the border due to the previous presidents' laws," she shook her head.

"I'm going to make a difference one way or the other," Christian spoke. "Things can and will not remain the way they've been going."

"Looks like you need to get on that ballot for governor," Francesca joked.

Christian thought about what she mentioned.

"You're laughing but maybe I do need to look into running," he uttered. "But you know I'd be up against Bernard Smith."

Francesca shook her head. "Man, that would be something," she spoke aloud. "It would definitely catch some buzz. But," she continued, "if you feel like you can make a difference and change this state and have a drawn-out plan, I say go for it," she affirmed.

"I'll run," he looked at Francesca, "if you'll run as my lieutenant governor."

She looked at him in awe. "It would be a huge switch from what we're doing now," she chuckled.

"Well, we're not getting any younger," Christian laughed. "May as well run and try to make a difference."

"Let me think about it," she responded.

Christian knew he had her thinking about this.

It was her fault for putting the idea in his head. He laughed at the idea.

"Don't take too long," Christian uttered. "If running, we have work to do," he reminded her as they approached his office.

"I'll let you know," she said with a slight chuckle.

"Sounds good," he remarked. "Get back to work, Sergeant," he snickered.

Francesca walked to her office and Christian looked at the picture of his son and wife.

"Yeah, I'm going to make a difference — one way or another," he touched the image.

4

"I heard about your pops," Marcus spoke to Junior.

"Yeah, man, it's official now. The old man is running for governor of Florida," Junior bragged. "All signs are pointing up as of now."

"Imagine if he wins. He'll be the first African-American male governor in the state of Florida."

"Man, I would be livid. Pops would have a high rank, I would be in L.A. on a scholarship, looking to play in the NBA. Life is good right now," he smiled as he walked from school with Marcus.

"I know I keep telling you man, but I'm extremely proud of you. You're going to make us all proud."

"Thanks, man," Junior smiled. "I'm proud of you as well. You just landed a full scholarship to Stetson's University College of Law. Dawg, that's huge," Junior remarked.

"We're destined for greatness," Marcus spoke. "We're going to bring the change we need."

Junior and Marcus continued the walk to his house while laughing and talking. They kept a keen eye on their surroundings, especially since Junior's father was a larger icon now.

They walked in the home and learned they were the only ones there.

"Pops," Junior called out. "Ma."

There was no reply.

"Must be out getting things in order," Marcus remarked.

Marcus placed his bag on the floor and took a seat on the couch.

He turned on the television.

"In other breaking news," Christian's image appeared next to the reporter, *"since the announcement of his run for governor, the city has seemingly been divided."*

The camera switched to a recorded video.

In the video, there were people of different ethnicities on two sides of the street. On one side, there were primarily African Americans, Hispanics, and other minority groups, and on the opposing side were primarily Caucasians.

The two sides were arguing.

"Christian Tate was acquitted of the murder of Benjamin Smith nearly twenty years ago, and with Christian announcing his gubernatorial run, it's brought the trial outcome to the forefront of the race."

The camera switched back to the reporter.

"Christian Tate currently serves as the Police Lieutenant of Miami-Dade County and feels that this state needs to undergo restoration, and he says he will bring that change. Tate also went on to say that the state has been divided long enough and it's time to come together and understand that we are not enemies."

Marcus muted the television.

He clasped his hands together.

"Bro, it's been rough out here. And it's even rougher now," he admitted. "We gotta keep a low profile; you see how divided these people are," he continued, "man, those Whites want blood and revenge."

Junior gave thought to what he was saying.

"And if they can't get to Lieutenant Tate, guess who they are going to target."

Junior's eyes widened as his friend spoke.

Marcus nodded his head.

"Let's keep our focus," Junior replied. "I don't wanna be spooked into not even going outside," he laughed.

"You know I got your back," Marcus uttered. "I'm just saying."

"I appreciate that, man," Junior replied.

The two of them changed their attire and Junior grabbed his basketball.

They exited the home.

Junior ensured the house was locked before they departed for the basketball court.

After their game, Junior and Marcus sat at the bench.

"I got a question for you, man," Junior spoke as he took a drink from his water bottle.

"Yeah, what's up?" Marcus asked.

"What do you think happens after we die?"

Marcus looked sternly at Junior. Marcus rose to his feet.

"Why are you asking me this, man?" he questioned.

"I don't know," Junior started. "I guess with everything going on and the discussions going on, it makes me think of Benjamin and what he's up to in the afterlife."

"Man, whatever it is," Marcus held the ball with two hands, "I can assure you it's not something that we have to worry about for a long time." Marcus tossed the ball in the air. "We can't live our lives in fear due to what others may say, think, or do. The only people that we can control is ourselves," Marcus said, "and the sooner we come to terms with that," he scoffed, "man, I guarantee that we'll live our lives to our best potential. It's all about living in the moment."

"Bruh, you're a philosopher now?" Junior laughed lightly.

"Nah, you know it's the truth. The only person you have control over is yourself. There's no use in living life in fear or worrying about what the next person is going to do. That's not living."

Junior clapped hands with his friend. "You just know how corrupt this shit can be, especially in law enforcement. Shit man," Junior scratched his goatee, "both of our fathers were incarcerated due to crooked cops."

"Yeah, I remember my pops told me that one time an officer planted some coke in the back of his car and booked him for possession with intent to sell."

Junior shook his head. "Damn, man."

"Yeah, that shit set him back," Marcus shook his head. "Imagine doing a bid for something you didn't even do. And then to have a drug charge with intent to sell," Marcus scoffed, "that shit sits on a nigga's record and isn't going anywhere."

Junior looked at the basketball rim.

"I hope Andrew was able to settle that shit," Junior remarked. "That's fucked up," he sipped his water bottle.

"My dad said it wasn't easy, but he got it expunged before he got booked for the robbery. So, it was before he met Andrew," Marcus added. "But that's why I keep saying we gotta set the example and make sure we stay on the right path. We don't have time for the bullshit."

"You're right, man. We must be the ones to bring this change; no one else will. Shit, it may sound cliché as hell, but we *are* the future," Junior concluded.

The gentlemen rose to their feet and walked to Junior's vehicle while speaking.

He saw his father's picture plastered seemingly everywhere to promote his campaign in the election.

Some of Christian's posters were defaced by people who didn't support him.

Junior shook his head and Marcus put his hand on Junior's shoulder.

Junior and Marcus got into Junior's vehicle and Marcus reclined his chair a bit.

"Time to unwind, bro," Marcus spoke.

Junior laughed at his friend.

Junior started the vehicle and increased the volume of the radio. He heard his father speaking to the host.

"It's quite simple," Christian uttered. *"Next week when we have the debate, I'm going to present the change I'm going to bring to the state,"* he eloquently spoke.

"Elaborate," the host remarked.

"The state of Florida needs major reform to the educational system, the overall economic state; there's a lot that needs to be changed." Christian

cleared his throat. *"But, like my opponent, there's one thing that we definitely agree on and that's to bring reform to the law enforcement."*

"I think a large amount of the population would agree to that. Now, Lieutenant Tate," the host said, *"what makes you feel confident that you can run for governor. You don't have a political background, and this is your first time running for any office."*

Christian laughed lightly.

"My good man, I have knowledge, faith, and confidence," Junior could hear that his father had a smile on his face. *"Tell me, do you set an alarm every night?"*

"Yes," the host answered.

"Even though you don't know for certain that you will wake up the next day. You're doing it because you have faith, right?"

The host didn't respond verbally.

"Have some faith in me. I love my state and I know we all want the same thing. You're right, I don't have a political background, but I do have knowledge. And I feel that I can pass on this wisdom to all of the inhabitants of this great state so this can be the best place to reside."

"Damn man, your dad is deep," Marcus drank from his water bottle.

"Yeah, the man can get pretty philosophical at times. I can see him taking this state and transforming it," Junior replied.

"Well, you have a bias," Marcus chuckled. "That's your dad."

"True," Junior laughed, "but you can't tell me you don't feel the same way."

"Yeah, he a'ight," Marcus chuckled. "Just remember, you're under a microscope now. I mean, you always have been, but now, it's even a tighter focus," Marcus pulled out his tie and tied his locs.

"Don't I know it?" Junior uttered as he continued the drive.

Junior arrived at his house and the two walked inside.

"Mama," Junior called out.

"I'm in my room, babe," Keisha responded.

"Is Pops here?" Junior opened the refrigerator.

"No, he hasn't made it in yet."

"Must still be at the station," Junior remarked.

"Hey Mrs. Tate," Marcus called.

"Hey Marcus," Keisha walked down the stairs.

Junior walked over and embraced his mother.

She kissed him on the cheek.

"How was your guys' day?" she asked them.

"Same old, same old," Junior replied.

"No one bothered you, right?" she questioned.

Keisha often worried about her son and Marcus, especially since Christian started his gubernatorial run. Christian's past didn't sit well with many inhabitants around the country, but more importantly, the state.

Keisha feared someone would seek vengeance for the death of Benjamin Smith.

"No problems, Ma," Junior laughed lightly.

He noticed the serious look on her face and took her hands in his.

"Don't worry Ma, I got this," he smiled.

Junior's smile reminded her of Christian's.

"You are truly your father's son," Keisha remarked. "That confidence and assurance screams 'Christian Tate'," she spoke with joy.

"Well, that is my name as well," Junior laughed. "So, I guess it's fitting."

Keisha chuckled and walked to the kitchen.

Junior fist-bumped with Marcus, who was now teasing him.

"Yeah, babe, the last time I spoke to him, he was leaving the radio station and heading home. He probably got held up in traffic or had to run into the office for a second," she shrugged her shoulders.

Junior and Marcus took a seat in the kitchen.

"We heard Mr. Tate on the radio," Marcus spoke. "He's got my vote," he laughed.

"I'm almost certain that's a biased vote, but we appreciate it none-the-less," Keisha laughed at Marcus. "How's your dad, baby?" she inquired.

"He's doing okay, Mrs. Tate," Marcus answered. "I think he said something about your husband hiring him as his security intel when he wins the race."

"See, I told your dad things would work out when he got out," she smiled at Marcus. "I think it was a blessing that your father and Raymond met," she directed to Junior.

"If they hadn't, I wouldn't know this homie," Junior laughed.

Keisha smiled and heard her phone ring; it was in her room.

"Let me go get that," she spoke.

"Ma, we're going to head out for a bit," Junior remarked before she walked away.

"Okay, babe. Stay safe out there," she gave her son and Marcus a hug.

"See you later, Ma," Junior called out.

"Bye Mrs. Tate," Marcus shouted as she to the stairs.

"I'll have your dad call you when he makes it in," she shouted from the top of the stairs.

Junior looked at Marcus.

"You ready to go get into something?" Junior chuckled.

"Shit, I gotta ask you if you're ready for what's coming," Marcus laughed.

"I'm ready for anything," Junior joked.

5

Christian adjusted his tie and Keisha looked at him in awe.

"Keep your notes with you," she began, "and go out there and win this debate. It's been a few months since you announced your entry into the race, and you have so many supporters," she remarked. "Including your biggest supporters, me and Junior."

Christian looked at the crowd from behind the curtain.

"You know he wishes he could be in the front row cheering you on," Keisha remarked as she adjusted his sports coat.

"Yeah, I know," Christian remarked. "He has this thing with school, right?"

Keisha chuckled.

"He, Bianca, Marcus, Sierra, and a few other friends are at the school studying for their exam they have coming up," Christian smiled at his wife. "He'll be watching it from school though, right babe?"

Keisha's phone rang and she pulled it out.

It was Junior.

"Look at that," she chuckled before answering the phone. "We were just talking about you, babe," Keisha spoke with excitement.

Her smile never left her face as she spoke to Junior.

Christian felt a little relieved.

"Yeah, he's right here babe. Yeah, I'll let you speak with him."

Keisha handed Christian the phone.

"My boy, what's going on?" Christian answered.

"What's going on, Pops? Just wanted to give you a quick call to let you know that I wish I was there. But me, Bianca, Marcus, Sierra, and a few others will be watching from one of these computers in the computer lab."

"Who's all at the school?" Christian questioned as some of the debate coordinators approached him and adjusted his clip-on microphone.

Christian held his chin up for them.

"Got some security guards and the principal is still here. Several students and a few teachers as well," Junior remarked. "Exam week is the worst," Junior laughed.

"I remember how that was," Christian laughed. "Look, son, they're about to do some tests on the mics and such, so I'm going to let you go. I love you, man."

"Love you too, Pops," Junior replied. "Go on and kill it."

Christian ended the call and handed Keisha her phone.

Francesca approached Christian and Keisha.

"You all ready?" she asked Christian.

"Ready as I'll ever be," he laughed lightly.

"Your wife is looking beautiful, as always," Francesca commented. Keisha smiled at her.

"You better be ready," Francesca finished.

"Five minutes, folks. Gotta run these mic checks," the coordinator spoke.

"You better get out there, babe," Keisha remarked. "And let these people know who Christian Tate is and who his terrific running mate is. Let them know your plan and show them you mean it!" she energized her husband.

Francesca smiled and patted Christian's shoulder.

"You got this, Lieutenant Tate," she addressed him.

Christian gave Keisha a quick kiss on the lips and walked from behind the curtain to the podium.

He looked at the crowd of people awaiting the debate.

Bernard approached him with a blank stare. He extended a hand for a handshake.

Christian accepted the handshake.

"You may as well throw in the towel now," Bernard spoke in a low tone to Christian.

"Bernard, I'm sorry about your son," Christian replied. He could see the anger in Bernard's eyes and Christian knew Bernard's anger towards him was because of what happened with his son.

Bernard chuckled deviously.

"Benjamin Smith will be the last White teenager to die at the hands of a Black cop."

Christian looked at Bernard sternly.

"How about we just keep it cordial?" Christian spoke as he jerked his hand back from Bernard.

"As you wish, 'Lieutenant'," Bernard walked over to his podium.

Christian shook his head at Bernard's comments. He figured Bernard's campaign had an agenda behind it, and his words just confirmed it.

Christian side-eyed Bernard as the coordinator counted down.

Christian and Bernard both put on a smile for the camera.

"Welcome everyone to the 2039 gubernatorial debate," one of the announcers spoke.

The audience applauded and cheered.

Christian stood tall and kept both of his hands atop the podium.

"I am Laurence Holder, and I'm one of your moderators for this evening. I'm joined alongside Ms. Sabrina Wexler and Mr. Michael Wallace," the announcer continued.

The audience applauded again. Once the applause subsided, the announcer spoke.

"Joining us onstage are your nominees for the 2040 race: Lieutenant Christian Tate and Mr. Bernard Smith. Welcome gentlemen," the applause started again.

Christian and Bernard both stepped to the side of their podiums and walked over to each other.

They shook hands for the camera.

"Game on," Bernard whispered.

***

"*Lieutenant Tate, your actions in the past make it hard to process when you say you want to bring reform to the prison system,*" Laurence spoke. "*Can you elaborate on your plans to bring change to the system?*"

Junior laughed as he listened to the question posed by the host.

"They're going to keep on bringing up the old shit because they have no other intentions for the Black man."

"They can't stand to see us win," Marcus chuckled. "It literally scares them."

Junior crept to a halt and put the car in park; he turned down the volume to his radio.

"A'ight, y'all," Junior spoke to Bianca and Sierra.

The ladies were having a sleepover.

Junior and Marcus both exited the vehicle and hugged their girlfriends.

Junior laid a kiss on Bianca's lips and retreated.

"I love you," he spoke.

"I love you, too," she responded. "Drive safely," Bianca put her hands around his neck.

"I'm straight," Junior spoke. "We're going to the debate. They still have roughly an hour to go, so me and Marcus are going to swing by there."

"His dad is up there too?" Bianca asked.

"Yeah, he's working O-T as security for my pops during his campaign."

Bianca moved her hands to Junior's chest. "I'll be waiting for you to call me and let me know that you've arrived."

"As soon as I drive in, you'll be the first one I call," Junior kissed Bianca once more.

Bianca smiled and turned her head.

"Sierra," she called, "you ready, girl? Let's let these men get to the debate," she smiled at Junior.

Sierra kissed Marcus on the lips once more and she walked over to Bianca.

Marcus licked his lips after the kiss, and the women walked to the house before opening the door and disappearing inside.

"Alright, lover boy," Junior laughed at Marcus. "Let's hit this road."

"Fuck you, man," Marcus joked with his friend.

Marcus sat in the passenger seat and closed the door.

Junior laughed and drove off.

"Can you believe it?" Marcus spoke after a few moments of listening to the radio.

Junior looked at him.

"Your dad has a chance at becoming the governor of Florida."

"It's unbelievable, huh?" Junior chuckled. "To everyone else, they see a lieutenant running for office who killed a White teenager eighteen or nineteen years ago, but to me, I see the man that taught me how to be a man; a better man," Junior spoke. "I know a lot of Florida may hate him, but looking at the numbers, my dad has almost half of Florida in favor of what he's done and is proposing."

Marcus opened the Sprite bottle and drank a sip.

"You just keep making him proud. Do what you have to do. That's all they really want, man," he replied.

Junior looked at his friend and nodded his head.

"Yo, pour me some of that," he remarked.

Marcus looked around the car for an empty container.

"I don't even see anything to pour it in," Marcus replied.

"There should be a bottle of grape soda in the backseat. It doesn't have the label on it, so it'll just be a plastic bottle."

Marcus continued searching and found the bottle.

"This ghetto shit," Marcus chuckled. "Matter of fact," he smirked and poured the remaining grape soda into the bottle of sprite.

"Always stealing my ideas," Junior laughed as he turned right as the light turned yellow.

When he finished, both bottles were mixed with Sprite and the grape soda.

Marcus passed Junior the smaller bottle and Junior took a sip.
He moaned with pleasure.

"Man, that shit is good," he laughed.

He put the bottle in the cupholder and tapped the debate's audio stream on his phone.

"*Unlike my opponent, I am going to ensure everyone has a fighting chance at opportunities and none are profiled whether it be by employers, store associates, or the police,*" Bernard spoke.

"*You mean like Black people are on a regular,*" Christian couldn't control this outburst.

The audience was split with cheers and jests.

"*This shouldn't be a campaign about race,*" Christian cleared it up, "*but as you all can see, my opponent continues hinting towards race.*"

Junior laughed lightly at his father.

"Good old Pops," he continued.

"Your dad cleans shit up real quick," Marcus uttered. "He has the audience stumped."

"You see what Bernard is trying to do, though?" Junior remarked. "We haven't made it far from slavery."

"It's crazy, but we're *far* from racism being over," Marcus spoke.

The gentlemen's conversation was quickly interrupted as they began to merge onto the expressway.

They saw siren lights in the rearview mirror.

"Some shit never changes," Junior uttered.

Junior pulled the car over.

"Same shit, just a different day," Marcus uttered, and he positioned his hands on the dashboard.

Junior shook his head as he put the car in park.

Junior pulled out his license and spoke to his phone.

"Ellie, I'm getting pulled over," he recited.

The two gentlemen discreetly slid on their seatbelts.

"*GPS location sent. Now recording. Calls, S-M-S messages, and notifications will be silenced until the wake word is spoken,*" his phone spoke.

"It's only one this time," Junior whispered to Marcus.

Marcus turned his head slightly but couldn't make out who the officer was due to the bright lights.

Junior looked in his side mirror and noticed it was the same officer that pulled them over before.

"Everything okay, Officer Whitley?" Junior asked as he approached the window.

Brian raised an eyebrow. "Excuse me?" he asked and continued immediately. "I'll be asking the questions. Show me your license and registration," he spoke with attitude.

Junior nodded his head slowly and passed Brian his license.

"Yes sir," Junior spoke. "I can get my registration card for you, but I will have to reach into my glove compartment to retrieve it."

Brian shined the flashlight into the car and nodded him on.

He shined the light in Marcus' face.

"Come on, man. Gon' with that shit," Marcus uttered calmly.

Brian smirked and saw the bottles of soda in the cupholders. He noticed one of the bottles read 'Sprite' on the label.

Marcus adjusted his legs so Junior could open the glove compartment.

"What you guys drinkin', there?" he asked as Junior retrieved the registration card. "A little bit of lean?"

Junior chuckled.

"Nah, man, nothing like that. A little sprite and grape soda mixed. Just left school, actually," Junior tried to keep everything calm as he passed his registration card to Brian.

Brian scoffed.

"We're not friends," he stated, "don't talk to me like we are." Brian inspected the registration card. "Wait here," Brian stepped back to his police vehicle.

"You see how this muthafucka' is acting?" Marcus whispered.

"Yeah, but fuck him," Junior replied. "Let's just do what we need to do to get away from his ass. I'll let my pops handle this shit."

Marcus looked in his side mirror and turned down the volume to the radio completely.

"Let me run a check on a Christian Tate, Jr.," he heard Brian speak over his radio.

He heard Brian's radio receive a transmission, but he couldn't make out what was uttered.

Brian got out of his car and walked over to Marcus' side.

"You got an ID on you?" he asked.

"It's in my pocket. I have to reach for it," Marcus recited loudly for the phone to hear.

"Yeah, yeah, go on," Brian uttered.

Marcus reached in his coat pocket and slowly pulled out his license.

Brian shined the flashlight on Junior.

"My man, keep your hands where I can see them," he instructed Junior.

"I didn't move them, Officer," Junior replied, confused. "They've been in the same position since you left from over here."

"Are you calling me a liar?" Brian questioned more aggressively.

"I'm not saying that," Junior tried to de-escalate the situation. "Look, I don't want any trouble."

"You already got that, boy," Brian spoke. "Take off your seatbelt for me."

Brian snatched Marcus' ID and put it in his vest pocket. He walked around to the driver's side of the car and he pulled his weapon from his holster.

"Fuck," Marcus spoke aloud. "Yo, why are we getting pulled over?!"

He wanted to reach for his phone, but he didn't want to provoke Brian.

"You keep your hands on the dashboard," Brian shouted to Marcus, ignoring his question.

Brian spoke in his vest's radio.

"I'm going to need backup on Sawgrass and 10th," he reported.

"10-4," the dispatcher spoke.

Junior unbuckled his seatbelt and slowly opened his car door.

Junior stepped out of the vehicle and Brian grabbed his shirt. Brian held Junior and walked him around to the hood of the vehicle.

"Put your hands on the hood," he instructed.

"Shit is hot," Junior remarked.

"I don't give a fuck," he uttered as he pushed Junior on the hood. Junior flinched from the heat.

"Police brutality. I see you," he nodded his head at Brian's behavior.

"Don't you fuckin' move," Brian looked up and shouted to Marcus.

Brian patted Junior down. "You got some shit that will poke or injure me?" he questioned Junior.

"Patting me down kind of rough, aren't you?" he asked.

"Give me a reason," Brian whispered through his teeth. "I don't give a fuck who you are."

"What are you talking about?" Junior questioned.

"Don't play dumb with me, nigga," Brian laughed. "You all accept the 'a', instead of the hard 'er', right? Just because your dad is Lieutenant and is running for governor, that doesn't give you the right to be above the law," he continued to pat Junior down. "Drinking and driving and shit. I know you got some drugs on you, too." Brian forced Junior's face on the hood.

Junior had a bad feeling about where this was headed.

"Marcus, call my pops," Junior shouted to his friend.

"Don't you fuckin' move," Brian threatened Marcus. "Where is my backup?" Brian asked over the radio. "I have two Black males, possible DUI, and they're getting belligerent."

Marcus discreetly pulled his phone out of his pocket and dialed Christian's number.

Brian picked Junior up and turned him around.

Junior's muscles tensed up from being jerked around.

Brian grabbed Junior and body-slammed him to the ground.

"Stop resisting," he shouted as he reached for his holster.

"Shit," Marcus shouted.

He held his phone and opened the door and walked around to the hood of the vehicle.

Marcus promptly ended the call and opened his camera to record.

"Get your bitch ass back in the car," Brian shouted.

Marcus stopped in his tracks but didn't return to the vehicle.

He lowered his phone.

"Officer, we don't want any problems," Marcus projected. "We're just trying to get to our destination."

Brian didn't reply to Marcus as he continued to fight with Junior.

Brian loosened his gun, and it fell from his holster.

Junior saw the gun on the ground and knew what would happen next.

Marcus didn't know what to do, so he quickly ran around to the driver's side of the vehicle. He dropped the phone on the floor of the vehicle and started to go through the center console.

"Officer, I'm not resisting," Junior pleaded.

Junior didn't want to resist but he saw there was no talking Brian down.

He kicked his legs and knocked Brian off him.

Brian noticed the gun was on the ground and crawled for it.

Junior noticed Brian going for the weapon and he lunged for it.

Junior grabbed it and Brian got on top of Junior and started punching him.

"Let the weapon go," Brian shouted so his radio and body camera could hear.

Junior held the weapon tightly and the two continued to tussle for it.

A shot rang out and Brian fell back from Junior.

Marcus stopped going through the console and displayed a shocked look on his face upon hearing the shot. He quickly looked out of the car.

Brian grabbed his shoulder.

"Son of a —," he lunged for Junior again and out of fear, Junior fired another shot into the right side of Brian's chest.

Junior dropped the weapon as Brian fell to the ground.

"Fuck!" Marcus exclaimed as he saw Brian lying on the ground.

Brian had his hand over his chest and breathed heavily.

Marcus ran over to Junior, who was frozen in fear. "Come on, man," he tried to bring Junior to his feet.

"It was an accident," Junior explained as he tried to stand.

His legs felt like noodles. He quickly turned his head and vomited on the side of the road.

Marcus kept his hand on Junior's shoulder.

"We gotta go," Junior panicked and tried to walk to the car.

"We can't," Marcus explained as he held Junior's shoulders. "If we run, we're automatically assumed guilty."

"Shit, shit, shit," tears fell from Junior's eyes.

He knew this would be detrimental to *everything* going on; his scholarship, Marcus' scholarship opportunities, his basketball career, not to mention, his father's gubernatorial run.

Marcus and Junior walked over to Brian.

Junior kneeled and Brian eyed the two down as they got closer to him.

Junior reached his hand over and grabbed the radio on Brian's vest; he pressed the button and spoke.

"10-30," he'd learned the code from studying with his father. "Officer down. Roll an ambulance to Sawgrass expressway and 10th Street," Junior spoke shakily.

Marcus wiped his face and put his hands on his head.

"Fuck, fuck, fuck," he worried.

Brian coughed and shouted as Junior spoke on the radio.

"Hurry!"

Junior shook his head and released the button to the radio and put his hands over Brian's chest wound.

He applied pressure.

"Marcus, call my people!" he shouted once more.

Marcus walked around to the driver's door and looked on the floor for his phone.

As he looked around, he heard a siren quickly approach and heard two police officers unload. Marcus dialed Keisha's number while inside the vehicle.

"Miami P-D, let me see your hands!" they shouted to Junior and Marcus.

Junior continued to apply pressure to Brian's wound and Keisha answered the phone.

***

"That's what I plan to do for this great state," Christian spoke on the debate stage.

The audience applauded and Keisha covered one of her ears so she could speak to Marcus.

"Hello," she greeted.

Marcus didn't reply as he looked out of the side mirror and saw the officers with their weapons aimed.

"I can't," Junior shouted back; Keisha heard her son.

"Marcus, what's going on?" she questioned.

Francesca saw the smile disappear and a look of concern appear across Keisha's face.

Keisha walked to the back of the building towards the washroom and Francesca followed her. They both entered the washroom.

Marcus held the phone in his hand and slowly backed out of the vehicle with his hands up.

As he stood erect, a shot was fired, and it made Keisha jump.

"Marcus?!" she shouted in the phone.

He didn't reply and a tear came to her eye.

"Marcus, answer me!" she shouted.

Francesca noticed that something was going on with Keisha and put her hands on her shoulder.

"Keisha, what's wrong?" Francesca asked.

Keisha had tears on her face.

"Something's going on with Junior and Marcus," she spoke.

Keisha was so frantic that Francesca could hardly understand her words.

"Here Keisha, sit down," she motioned her to the bench.

Keisha cried heavily and Francesca pulled her in for an embrace.

"Take deep breaths, Love," Francesca tried to comfort Keisha. "Talk to me."

Keisha slowed her breathing but continued to cry hard.

"I heard a commotion," she started, "and then I heard what sounded like a gunshot," she wailed again.

Francesca held Keisha tightly.

Keisha held her phone in her hand and it vibrated rapidly, which was Junior's texting vibration.

She pulled away from Francesca and looked at her phone.

She covered her mouth and continued sobbing uncontrollably.

Francesca looked at the message and read it aloud.

"Message sent from SafeZone," she started. "I'm being pulled over. I'm at Sawgrass Expressway. Here's a video of the interaction."

She didn't play the video as she was comforting Keisha, but she knew why she was crying.

"Hold on, Keisha," Francesca instructed as she pulled out her phone.

She opened her police radio application and chimed in.

"This is Sergeant Gaines, checking in on the status of police activity on State Road 869," she awaited a reply and rocked Keisha back and forth.

"Shh," she tried to quiet Keisha.

Keisha quieted her cries.

Minutes later, a reply came through the phone.

"*Officer and suspect injured. Subjects transferred to the Westside Regional Medical Center. One in custody.*"

"Identity of subjects?" Francesca questioned.

"*Officer Brian Whitley, injured. Marcus Farris, injured. Christian Tate, Jr., in custody.*"

Francesca put her phone down.

"Shit," she whispered.

Keisha cried harder as she heard the transmission.

"My baby," she cried silently.

Francesca was disturbed at hearing this occurred but was even more disturbed that Brian was involved when Christian has given explicit instructions for him to leave his son alone.

"He doesn't know when to quit," she uttered as she continued to rock back and forth with Keisha.

6

Christian shook hands with Bernard and walked backstage.

He looked around for Keisha, Francesca, his son, and Marcus, but didn't see a soul. He only saw Raymond.

"You did good, man," he congratulated Christian.

"Thanks, man," he spoke as he wiped his forehead. "Where's my wife, Lieutenant governor, and son?" he questioned as he looked around. "He and Marcus should have been here by now."

Raymond slightly shrugged his shoulders.

"I haven't heard from the children. Last I saw your wife, she was with Sergeant Gaines and they were going to the washroom."

"So, they should be coming out soon?" Christian concluded.

"They went in there about thirty minutes ago," Raymond answered. "Not sure what's going on."

Christian pulled out his phone and saw texts from Junior. He read the summary on the lock screen.

He unlocked the phone and viewed the attached video.

"Everything okay, Officer Whitley?" Christian heard Junior ask.

A frown formed across Christian's face.

The video was angled so that part of Brian's face was in the camera and focused primarily on Junior.

"God, no," Christian spoke aloud as he shook his head.

"What's good, man?" Raymond questioned as he saw the concern on Christian's face.

"A little bit of lean?" Brian asked over the video.

"Nah, man, nothing like that," he heard Junior chuckle. *"Just a little sprite and grape soda mixed. Just left school, actually."*

Raymond watched the video with Christian.

"I have told this cat to leave Junior alone," Christian spoke in disgust. "Some people just don't listen."

"You see how this muthafucka' is acting?" he heard Marcus ask.

"Yeah but fuck him."

Raymond cleared his throat.

"I'll let my pops handle this shit." Junior continued over the video.

One of the stage coordinators walked over to Christian and removed his microphone from his chest.

"Great debate out there, Lieutenant," they congratulated Christian before walking off.

Christian nodded at them.

"Excuse me, can I have a lady run into the washroom and check on Keisha Tate and lieutenant governor-elect, Francesca Gaines?" Christian called out as the video continued.

"Will do, Lieutenant," a female employee spoke aloud and walked to the washroom.

"Marcus, call my pops," he heard Junior shout.

Neither Junior nor Brian were in the frame anymore, but he could hear the interaction.

Raymond raised an eyebrow at the video.

"Shit," he whispered. "Come on, son," Raymond spoke to the phone. "Come back into the frame."

"Officer, we don't want any problems," Marcus pleaded over the video. *"We're just trying to get to our destination."*

Raymond and Christian saw Marcus re-enter the vehicle and search for something.

"Come on," Christian spoke to Raymond as they walked towards the washroom.

Christian knew where this was headed as the video continued to play.

"*Officer, I'm not resisting,*" Junior shouted.

Christian and Raymond both stopped in their tracks when they heard the first gunshot.

Christian returned his phone to his pocket and he walked into the washroom; the worker was taking too long to provide an update.

"Keisha!" Christian shouted as he and Raymond entered the restroom.

Keisha wept in Francesca's arms and looked up when she heard Christian enter.

Keisha rose to her feet and hugged Christian tightly.

"They arrested Junior," she cried.

"What the fuck?!" Christian projected as he held Keisha and looked at Francesca.

"Where's Marcus?" Raymond questioned.

"At Westside Regional Medical Center," Francesca answered as she rose to her feet.

Raymond's stomach sank to the floor.

"Wh-Why is he there?" he stammered.

Francesca sighed.

"He was injured in the incident," she answered.

Francesca assumed they'd seen the video.

"Suffered a bullet to the chest," she concluded.

Raymond stood tall as tears escaped from his eyes.

He wiped his face.

"We gotta go," he spoke to Christian and Keisha.

The four of them exited the washroom and walked to the exit of the building.

Cameramen were taking pictures of Christian and the crew as they exited the building.

"Keep your heads low," Christian instructed them as they walked to the car.

Keisha continued to cry heavily and didn't utter a word.

Christian and Keisha got in his vehicle, Francesca got in hers, and Raymond got in his before they left the lot.

Christian's mind was racing as he drove away.

He drove into a nearby gas station and parked the car. Francesca and Raymond followed.

"Wait here, babe," Christian instructed Keisha.

She didn't reply. Keisha was feeling numb.

Christian, Francesca, and Raymond gathered around outside of his vehicle.

"Frankie, can you drive Keisha home?" he started. "I'm going to drive to the hospital with Raymond and then to the station to figure out what's going on."

Raymond continued to hold his composure.

"I got you, Lieutenant," Francesca replied. "Once I get her settled, I'll call you and figure out the next move."

Christian embraced Francesca. "Thank you," he spoke to her.

"Everything will be okay," she assured him and Raymond.

Christian walked over to the car and opened Keisha's door.

"Frankie is going to drive you home, babe," he informed her. "I'm going to ride to the hospital with Ray and then to the station to figure this shit out," he finished.

Keisha gave a slight head nod.

"Come on, babe," he instructed calmly as he helped her out of the car.

He kissed her on the cheek and passed her hand to Francesca.

"I love you," he spoke.

Christian didn't expect a reply as he could see she was frozen and numb.

A tear fell from her eye as she got in Francesca's vehicle.

Francesca hugged Raymond.

"Let me know what's going on," she spoke softly to him.

"Thanks, Sergeant," Raymond responded as he accepted the embrace.

Francesca nodded her head and walked to her vehicle.

"Lieutenant let me know everything. And if I hear anything, I'll let you know," Francesca got in the driver's seat of her car.

Christian put his hands in his pocket as Francesca drove away.

"Where do they have him again?" Raymond questioned.

"Westside Regional Medical Center," Christian immediately replied. "Come on," he gave Raymond their signature handshake and walked back to his vehicle.

Raymond got in his car and followed Christian out of the gas station.

Christian sped away and Raymond followed.

Christian's mind raced as he drove to the center. *Why was his son initially pulled over? What triggered Brian to have him exit the vehicle? What occurred that led Marcus to the hospital and Junior to be in handcuffs?*

Christian couldn't decipher whether to be upset, hurt, or petrified as they inched closer to the center.

He drove in the lot and brought the car to a slow halt. He and Raymond parked in the emergency room parking area.

Raymond got out of his vehicle and Christian noticed his eyes were bloodshot red. He could tell Raymond had been crying. He put his arm around Raymond's shoulder, and they walked into the facility.

Christian pulled out his badge and showed it to the secretary.

"Marcus Farris," he spoke. "Lieutenant Christian Tate with the Miami-Dade P-D."

The secretary typed Marcus' last name into the system and responded.

"Mr. Farris is in surgery," she spoke softly. "You all will have to wait in the waiting room for updates," she typed notes into the system. "What's your relationship to the patient?" she questioned.

"I'm his father," Raymond intercepted.

The secretary noticed Raymond's build and looked a little concerned. She noticed his eyes were red.

"Mr. Farris, I'm sorry," she responded. "He'll be out soon, and the doctors will provide an update," she handed him a Kleenex.

"What was he brought in for?" Christian asked.

She read the computer screen.

"It says here a gunshot wound to the chest," she answered. "He was brought in along with an Officer Brian Whitley," she disclosed to Christian.

A stern look crossed Christian's face.

"Wow," was the only thing that left Christian's mouth.

Raymond could see the frustration in Christian's body language as the words left his mouth.

He nudged Christian. Christian knew why.

"What was *he* brought in for?" Christian questioned.

"One second, Lieutenant," she replied as she typed Brian's name into the system.

The computer screen populated data.

"A bullet wound to the right side of his chest and a bullet wound to the shoulder. Farris' wound was on the left side of his chest."

Raymond could feel his knees getting weaker as she spoke.

"Thank you," he interjected. "Let's go, Chris," he uttered.

"Thanks," Christian spoke to the secretary.

The two of them walked into the waiting room and Raymond sat down.

Raymond twiddled his thumbs in anticipation.

"I told that asshole a few months ago to leave Junior alone," Christian paced the floor. "Now, we're here."

Raymond didn't look up.

"And judging off the video, he was in the wrong. He was the aggressor in the situation," Christian looked at Raymond.

He took a seat.

"He'll be okay," Christian assured his friend. "Just gotta keep our heads up."

"He's doing so well," Raymond spoke. "He has a scholarship to school in L.A, has a good job, his grades are damn near perfect," he laughed lightly as tears emerged from his eyes.

Christian kept his arm around Raymond's shoulders.

"Good kid. Doesn't go out and cause mischief, never been in trouble with the law. Living the life I wish I'd lived growing up."

"I'm here for you, man," Christian uttered softly as they waited.

***

Christian drove to the police station with Andrew after Marcus came out of surgery.

Raymond had gone to sit at his son's bedside and Christian decided to figure out what was going on.

"Frankie," Christian spoke over his phone, "I'm on my way to the station now. I'm right around the corner."

"10-4," she responded. "How's Marcus?" she questioned.

"Just got out of surgery. He's sedated right now, but Raymond is there with him. Is Junior there?"

"Yes," she answered. "He's in lockup right now. I couldn't get to him," she stated. "The chief is here. He seems pretty disgruntled and wants to talk to you," she spoke in a low tone.

"The fuck does he want to speak to me for?" Christian shook his head. "I'm pulling in now. See you in a bit."

Christian ended the call and parked his vehicle.

"Appreciate you doing this, man," Christian spoke to Andrew.

"You all are family. I got you, man," Andrew did his signature handshake with Christian.

Christian grabbed his badge and weapon from the center console and exited the vehicle.

They walked inside the station slowly and noticed the officers scattering around.

"Lieutenant Tate," the police chief called out once he saw Christian. "Conference room five."

Christian glanced at the chief and continued to look around for Francesca. He pulled out his phone and texted her before returning it to his pocket.

"Wait here, man," he spoke to Andrew.

Christian walked into the conference room and saw the chief sitting.

"Close the door," he gruffly spoke to Christian.

Christian obliged and took a seat across from the chief.

"Chief Jonathan Sanders, how are you?" Christian greeted him.

"Well, I was at home enjoying my Friday night routine with my wife. Watching the debate," he started, "when I get a call about an officer-involved shooting that involves your son, his friend, and Officer Brian Whitley."

"Yeah, I got the same call following the debate," Christian replied. "And video footage of the stop. Officer Whitley seems to be the aggressor," he tried to control the narrative.

Jonathan interjected. "This case is pending an investigation. I've just gotten word that Brian has gotten out of surgery and is being questioned as we speak," he looked at Christian sternly. "I don't have to tell you to stay off this case, right?" he reminded Christian. "Focus on your run for governor," he suggested as he wrote some notes on his notepad.

"Are you kidding me right now?" Christian projected.

Jonathan looked at Christian sternly.

"My son is a suspect in the shooting of a police officer, and you have the audacity to tell me not to worry about it?" Christian was offended.

"You are to stay off this case," Jonathan spoke again.

"Not to mention, the officer who was shot has a vendetta against me and has been harassing my son for the past few years."

Jonathan ignored him.

"You're excused, Lieutenant," Jonathan spoke before rising to his feet.

Jonathan walked to the door and exited the room.

Anger consumed Christian as he walked out of the room, shortly after Jonathan exited.

"Everything good?" Andrew asked.

"Same shit, just a different toilet," Christian shrugged.

The two walked to the front desk and Christian spoke.

"I need to see Christian Tate, Jr.," Christian stated.

"Lieutenant, he's in lockup," the front officer responded.

"I don't give a damn about that," Christian projected. "Let me see my son."

The officer nodded her head and directed Christian to the waiting area.

Christian and Andrew walked to the back. Christian put his weapon in the locker as they waited for Junior to arrive.

A loud buzz emitted, and the door opened.

A guard walked Junior into the room. His hands were cuffed in front of him.

Christian quickly embraced his son.

"No touching," the guard spoke.

Christian glared at the guard and ignored his comment.

"Never mind," the guard responded to the glare.

Junior let a tear fall from his eye as his father hugged him.

"Can we get some privacy?" Christian attempted to utilize his authority.

The guard nodded his head and walked out of the door.

"First thing, have you spoken to any of these officers?"

"No," Junior responded. "I was waiting on either you or counsel."

"Very smart," Andrew spoke.

"Andrew," Junior embraced Andrew.

"Everything is going to be okay," Andrew assured him.

"What happened, Son?" Christian questioned.

"Dad, everything went left so quickly," Junior hurried. "There-there was a cop a-a-and there was slamming and fighting, a-a-a-a-and," Junior stuttered.

"Breathe, son," Christian spoke. "Come on, have a seat," he directed his son to the bench.

Junior, Christian, and Andrew sat and Junior inhaled deeply.

"Tell me everything," Christian spoke softly.

Andrew pulled out his recorder and notepad.

He pressed record and took notes as Junior spoke.

"Officer Whitley pulled me and Marcus over after we dropped the girls off," Junior started. "I asked him for the reason for the stop, and he got this attitude and wouldn't answer the question. So, he looked in the car and saw the bottle of Sprite and grape soda." Junior inhaled deeply, "I gave him my ID or whatever, and then he took it back to the car to run it. Then he came around and asked for Marcus' ID. He started a rant about how I moved my hands while he was getting Marcus' ID, and when I informed him that they were in the same spot as always, things escalated."

Christian shook his head. This didn't sound unbelievable to him as this was behavior that he observed Brian exhibit.

Andrew made sure to take specific notes towards Brian's behavior.

"Keep going, Son," Christian nodded.

"He came around and snatched me out of the car and slammed me on the hood, roughly patting me down. Dad, he f—," Junior caught himself cursing, "he assumed Marcus and I were drinking lean."

"He's stereotyping," Christian interjected.

Andrew adjusted the recorder slightly.

"Then he called me a 'nigga' and he made sure to stress the 'a' instead of the 'er'. Pops, he laughed at it. So, that's when I told Marcus to call you, but I think you were busy on stage with the debate so you couldn't come to the phone. Officer Whitley, then, told Marcus not to move and asked about his backup; he claimed we were D-U-I and getting belligerent with him. Whole time, we were just trying to deescalate the situation. He, then, body slammed me to the ground and told me to stop resisting and next thing I know, he's reaching for his gun."

"What did you do?" Christian questioned his son.

Junior sighed. "As a reflex, my legs kicked him off me. I guess the kick knocked the gun loose," Junior continued, "but, then, I saw him going for it, and I knew if he got hold of it, that would be the end of me. I saw the fury in his eyes," Junior uttered.

Christian spoke again. "Bad move in kicking him," he spoke to his son. "But it was a reflex."

"It's sad that police expect civilians to remain calm while they're doing any and everything to detain them," Andrew intervened.

Junior shook his head. "So, I lunged for the gun."

"Junior—," Christian started as he shook his head.

"It wasn't to do anything with it," Junior assured his father. "It was just to keep control until the backup arrived. Then, I was going to let it go, I swear," he said.

Christian slowly shook his head.

"And," Junior sighed again, "in the process of struggling, the weapon went off and he was shot in the shoulder."

"Mmph," Andrew groaned.

"Shit," Christian spoke.

"He came for me once more and I panicked and the next thing I know, he had a gunshot wound in his chest," Junior teared a bit.

"Come here, son," Christian embraced his son.

"Is he okay, Pops?" Junior questioned.

"He's going to be okay," Christian responded. "What happened after that? How did Marcus get shot?"

Junior inhaled.

"C.J., I know it's hard. Your dad wants me to represent you in this case and for me to do that, I need the full story," Andrew remarked.

Junior nodded his head. "I put my hands over Officer Whitley's wound, the way you showed me to apply pressure, and called in for an ambulance. And, then, the backup arrived, and Marcus was on the phone with Mom. When he backed out of the car as they instructed, they shot him. They claimed they thought he had a weapon," tears left Junior's eyes.

Christian embraced his son tighter.

"How is Marcus?" Junior asked.

Christian sighed deeply. "He's fresh out of surgery, son," he informed Junior.

He saw more pain come across Junior's face.

"But he's going to be okay, right?" his eyes welled with tears.

"He's a soldier, just like his dad," Andrew spoke.

Christian had a flashback of when Raymond was stabbed in jail. However, he knew his son's pain was much greater. He'd known Marcus all his life.

"That's my best friend, Dad," Junior uttered.

"The best thing we can do is fight for Marcus," Christian uttered. "Hold it together and I'll bring your Mom by tomorrow."

Junior sniffled.

The guard entered the room. "Time's up!" he projected.

Junior, Christian, and Andrew rose to their feet.

Andrew stopped the recording and put the notepad on the inside of his coat pocket.

"Pop," Junior spoke.

"What's up, Son?"

"Call Bianca for me. Let her know what's going on," he sighed.

"We'll take care of it," Andrew remarked. "Hold your head high," he spoke to Junior.

Junior embraced Andrew and his father before walking to the guard.

"I love you, man," Christian spoke.

"I love you too, Pops."

Junior gave a half-smile to his father and lawyer as the guard escorted him out of the room.

Andrew put a hand on Christian's shoulder.

"Let's get out of here," Andrew remarked as the two left the room.

7

"All rise for the honorable Matthew Zalinski," the bailiff brought the court to a stand.

The judge entered from his chambers and walked behind the bench.

Junior looked around the courtroom in dismay. He couldn't believe he was standing in criminal court.

He looked around until he found his parents. He locked eyes with them.

"I love you," Keisha mouthed out to him.

The courtroom sat, following the judge. "This is case 2908, The State of Florida vs. Christian Tate, Jr. Who's here for the defense?" Matthew questioned.

"Andrew Brownstone," Andrew stood tall next to Junior.

Junior wore the same clothes from two days ago when the events unfolded. There were traces of blood across the shirt.

Matthew looked up from his papers and studied Andrew.

He looked back at the papers and took notes. "And for the prosecution?"

"D.A. Anayi Jiménez," the prosecutor spoke.

Matthew took more notes.

"Mr. Tate, you are charged with one count of attempted murder of a police officer, two counts of aggravated battery with a firearm, and one count of resisting arrest," Matthew looked at Junior.

Christian held Keisha's hand tightly and tears flowed uncontrollably from her eyes. She kept her cries silent.

"How do you wish to plead?" Matthew inquired.

Junior and Andrew exchanged a few whispers before he spoke.

"Not guilty, Your Honor," Junior spoke.

The judge wrote on his pad as he continued. "Where are we with bail?"

"Your Honor, the prosecution is asking that bail be denied for the defendant. His father is currently running in the gubernatorial race, is the lieutenant of his police district, and we feel that ultimately, Christian Tate, Jr. is a flight risk," Anayi remarked.

Junior's heart sunk as he heard Anayi request to deny his opportunity at bail.

"Your Honor, my client is a senior in high school, has received numerous acceptances into many prestigious universities, and has been granted a full-ride scholarship to U.C.L.A. My client and his family want for nothing more than to put this in the past and to continue moving forward," Andrew spoke firmly.

"You just said it," Anayi responded, "he's been granted a scholarship to a school out of the state. And you're saying he's not a flight risk?" she scoffed.

"She's got a point," Matthew remarked.

'So, this is what it's like?' Junior asked himself.

Fear filled his body as he observed the Anayi and Andrew exchange words.

Andrew shook his head and chuckled.

"I'm sorry, maybe you all missed me saying that this is a *high school senior*. He has a 5.0 GPA and is the point guard of his basketball team. He has his whole life ahead of him. You think he's going to willingly do something to throw it all away?" Andrew argued more aggressively.

"If Daddy is there to bail him out, yes," Anayi adjusted her sportscoat.

Andrew hung his head. Matthew continued to write on the notepad before speaking.

"Motion to deny bail is denied," Matthew projected.

A slight smile formed on Junior's face. Christian and Keisha both felt a bit of relief that the judge wasn't remanding their son into prison.

"Bail will be set at $300,000," Matthew continued, "and the defendant will be placed on electronic monitoring pending trial."

"Your Honor, don't you think that's a bit much?" Andrew reasoned. "We're looking at a high-school senior who has never been in any trouble with the law and has a tremendous grade-point-average."

"Don't push your luck, Mr. Brownstone," Matthew warned.

Andrew didn't argue; at least Matthew was awarding Junior bail and wasn't forcing him to sit in prison.

"This court is adjourned," Matthew hit his gavel on the stand, and everyone rose to their feet.

"So, what's next?" Junior whispered to Andrew after the judge left.

"Well," he started, "your parents are going to have to post bail and you'll be out of here. The judge is ordering that you get an ankle monitor strapped to you as we await trial," Andrew finished.

Junior shook his head slightly.

"Don't worry, man, we got this. The judge granting bail is a good thing for you." Andrew patted Junior on the back.

Christian and Keisha leaned over the partition.

"Stay strong, man. We'll have you out of here today," Christian promised his son.

"Thanks, Pops," Junior spoke as he sniffled.

Keisha embraced her son tightly.

"I love you so much," she uttered.

"I love you, too, Ma," Junior remarked.

He felt a sense of warmth overcome him as he was in his mother's arms. He didn't want her to let go.

The court officer walked over to the defense's desk and Andrew tapped Junior on the shoulder.

Junior retreated from the hug.

"I'll see you guys, soon," he remarked before being escorted away by the officer.

Keisha turned and cried into Christian's chest. He held Keisha close to him and spoke to Andrew.

"What do you think?" he asked.

"This will be tough, but I'm certain we got it," Andrew picked up his briefcase and put the strap over his chest. "You know Raymond wants me to take on Marcus' case as well."

"That's because we know you're the best there is," Christian smirked at Andrew.

Andrew smiled at Christian's comment. "Come on, guys," he spoke softly.

Christian turned and held Keisha's sweater. Andrew directed them to the room's exit.

Christian and Keisha walked ahead of Andrew and exited the courthouse. They were greeted by flashes from numerous cameras.

"Lieutenant Tate, over here," one of the reporters called.

"Attorney Brownstone," another reporter called out.

The reporters crowded around Christian, Keisha, and Andrew, forcing them to stop.

"History repeats itself," the reporter shouted. "You represented Christian Tate back in 2019 when he was on trial for the shooting death of Benjamin Smith."

Christian shook his head.

"Will you be representing Christian Tate, Jr. in this trial?" the reporter finished the question.

Christian held Keisha close to him.

"Here we are nearly 20 years since the unfortunate death of Benjamin Smith, and the system hasn't quite improved," Andrew spoke firmly. "I have been speaking with the family and as of this moment, we will not be speaking on the case, but yes, I will be representing Mr. Christian Tate, Jr. in his trial."

There was overlapping chatter coming from the reporters after Andrew answered the question.

"Lieutenant Tate," another reporter called out.

Christian looked up.

"You are currently running to be governor of Florida. Amidst everything that's going on, how does this affect your current run?"

Christian had nearly forgotten about the race. His son was his number one priority and everything else was just an additive.

But perhaps his run is what the state needed to turn things around.

"The State of Florida is a beautiful place," Christian carefully chose his words. "Do there need to be any changes to the system? Yes, which is why I am running for governor. But I am a father and husband first," he looked at Keisha, "and right now, my son and wife need me." He kissed Keisha on the forehead. "No further comments."

"Clear the way, folks," Andrew spoke as the trio progressed forward.

"Lieutenant Tate," a reporter called as they walked.

Christian, Keisha, and Andrew ignored the reporters and entered the garage.

They got inside of their vehicles and drove away.

Andrew drove to the police station while Christian drove with Keisha to the bank for the cashier's check.

Andrew paced the floor as he awaited the two and caught a glimpse of the news.

"*Christian Tate Jr., son of police lieutenant, Christian Tate, made his first appearance in court today for his bail hearing on the attempted murder of Officer Brian Whitley,*" the television showed a side-by-side image of Junior and Brian. "*We don't have many details of the case yet; the Miami P.D. is withholding information, but the shooting occurred late Saturday night and ended with Officer Whitley suffering two bullet wounds and Marcus Farris, Tate's accomplice, suffered a bullet to the chest.*"

Andrew shook his head.

"Accomplice?" he asked aloud.

"*Judge Matthew Zalinski has granted Tate a bail of 300 thousand dollars with electronic monitoring. We will provide information as it arises.*"

"*Thank you for that story*," the news reporter's co-anchor spoke, "*it makes you wonder how this shooting will affect not only the city but the state, as well as his father's gubernatorial run.*"

Andrew paced the floor and observed Christian and Keisha enter the police station moments later.

"I got the check," Christian spoke to Andrew.

Christian approached the desk with Keisha's hand in his. He informed the clerk of his purpose and handed her the cashier's check.

"Have a seat," she instructed, dryly. "He will be out shortly."

The trio walked over to the chairs and sat. A few moments of silence passed before Christian spoke. "Guys, wait here," he instructed.

"Where are you going, babe?" Keisha questioned.

"I need to get more information regarding this case," he informed them.

Keisha and Andrew looked at each other.

"I'm a father first," Christian iterated. "I'm going to do what I can to help my son, especially if I know in my heart that his actions were justified."

Keisha embraced Christian.

"Hurry back," she surrendered.

He walked away from the two and went towards his office.

***

Junior rubbed his ankle as he looked at the car floor.

"Just a minute ago, I was starting point-guard, now I'm a criminal on trial for shooting a cop."

"Babe, everything will work out fine," Keisha spoke as she drove.

"And Pops isn't even supposed to be working the case because it's so close to home," Junior shook his head. "Meanwhile, the media is having a field day with trashing mine and Marcus' name," a tear came to Junior's eye as he thought about Marcus.

Keisha put her hand out, palm up, and Junior interlocked his fingers with hers.

"I can only imagine how Uncle Ray is feeling. His son is laid up in the hospital all because police have a shoot-first mentality."

Keisha didn't utter a word as her son vented.

"If I'd have known it would amount to all of this, I would have aimed for an artery," Junior spoke out of anger.

"You'd have done that; you wouldn't be sitting here with me right now. They would be giving you the needle," Keisha interjected. "You both," she referred to Junior and Marcus, "have one of the best lawyers on your case. And, your father is going to try to do whatever he can to help. We just have to trust the process, babe," she remarked.

Junior nodded his head slightly.

Keisha turned into the hospital's parking garage and parked her vehicle.

Junior and Keisha both exited and walked into the building. With every step he took, Junior felt as though his heart were about to explode. He grabbed his mother's hand and they continued walking. They approached the front desk and Keisha spoke to the receptionist.

"Marcus Farris," she mentioned.

The receptionist entered his name into the computer and wrote his room number on badges. She handed the badges to Junior and Keisha. The two walked to the room and entered. Raymond rose to his feet and embraced Keisha.

"Hey Ray," she spoke softly. "How is he?"

Raymond shook hands with Junior. Natina, Raymond's wife, embraced Keisha.

"He's with us," Raymond spoke softly. "Docs say he's in a coma," Raymond wiped a tear.

Junior walked over and touched put his hand on his friend's chest.

"Bro," he spoke softly. Junior inhaled sharply as he observed his friend laying in the bed. "This isn't him," Junior spoke softly as he looked back at the adults.

Keisha walked over to her son and put both hands on his shoulder. He turned around and wept silently in her arms.

"This isn't fair," Junior added. "The cops can do whatever they want and get a slap on the wrist."

Raymond interjected.

"Last I heard, the officer who fired the shot is on desk duty pending an investigation," he shook his head.

"That's all?" Junior questioned as he shook his head. "My brother had a phone in his hand and was shot, and all the cop gets is desk duty."

Junior was disgusted at the system. He squatted down and scratched around the ankle monitor.

"Meanwhile, I have to walk around with this on my leg."

Raymond wiped his eyes free of the few tears that accumulated.

"This system wasn't designed for us at all," he said. "They get away with too much."

The room felt eerily cold as Junior laid a hand on his friend again. The sound of the machines seemed to be getting fainter with each second that passed.

"I promise," Junior stated to his friend, "we will get justice for this."

Although not responsive, Junior believed his friend's spirit was present and encouraging him to fight.

"Let's see what they're saying," Raymond suggested as he turned on the television.

"*Officer Jake Warren, the officer responsible for firing the shot that has hospitalized 17-year-old Marcus Farris, has been put on paid administrative leave. Warren was previously assigned to desk duty, but the police department tells us that a proper investigation cannot be conducted while he's on active duty.*"

"So, in other words, the community strong-armed them into letting him go," Raymond started.

"Yea, and because of his Whiteness," Junior spoke, "instead of firing him, they put him on paid administrative leave."

Junior shook his head and watched the images go across the television screen.

"Excuse my language in advance," Junior continued, "but this system is a fucking joke."

Raymond nodded his head.

"*This incident occurred unanimously in the shooting of Officer Brian Whitley by Christian Tate, Jr,*" the reporter added. "*Christian Tate,*

Jr., is the son of Lieutenant Christian Tate; the democratic candidate running for governor, who also has an eerily similar past in which he was acquitted for the shooting death of 18-year-old Benjamin Smith, nearly twenty years ago."

"And, here they go bringing up that shit," Keisha remarked. "But, are they going to tell the full story in how Benjamin pulled out a gun on *my* husband?"

Junior kept a hand rested on his friend and looked at his mother.

"Whitley was struck once in the shoulder and once in the chest before backup arrived on the scene. This story is still developing, and we will have more for you as it unfolds."

"I promise, bro," Junior spoke to his friend.

■■

"Control the narrative," Dustin spoke to Christian.

Dustin was Christian's campaign advisor and close to the family. Dustin was preparing Christian for his television interview and he knew they would bring up Junior and his shooting against Brian.

"City is advising me not to discuss it," Christian replied. "It's an ongoing investigation and you know how it is."

"Yeah, but it's not the city's child," Dustin said. "They're not going to feel the same sympathy for your son as you do. You go out there," he adjusted Christian's tie, "and if they talk about C.J., you either sway the conversation to the next topic or you control the narrative." He ensured Christian's microphone was securely clipped onto his tie. "You don't have to discuss the case to defend your son."

"I know that," Christian spoke defensively.

"Then we have to do it," Dustin added.

"You ready, Lieutenant Tate?" the news producer spoke as she peeked from behind the curtain.

"Let's do it," he shook hands with Dustin and followed the producer to the main room.

"And we are back with Lieutenant Christian Tate. We are discussing his current gubernatorial run. Lieutenant, thank you for being here," Ernest talked to the camera.

"Thank you for having me," Christian spoke confidently.

"Lieutenant, you are having a fantastic run," Ernest continued. "Some experts say you have a good chance at winning this race."

"Well," Christian started, "I am speaking from my heart with everything that I say and do, and the people can resonate with that. I speak on the things they feel deeply about and topics that will affect their everyday lives."

"And I think the people are making that abundantly clear in their selection. Now, I want to switch gears a little bit. Your son, Christian Tate, Jr., and his friend, Marcus Farris; they recently had an altercation with officers from your unit," Ernest cleared his throat as he looked at the papers in front of him. "Your son fired two shots at Officer Brian Whitley, which struck Whitley in the shoulder and chest, and Farris was struck in the chest by a bullet fired by Officer Jake Warren. Tate is out on bail and Farris is in serious condition in the hospital."

Christian felt his heart jump as Ernest spoke.

"Lieutenant Tate, can you provide an update as to how this affects your gubernatorial run and what you stand for? How does this align with your plans and policy for building a stronger rapport between law enforcement and the citizens."

Christian picked up the bottle and took a sip of water. He waited a few seconds before answering, but in his silence, the only thing he could think about was the recorded video from Junior's phone.

"It's funny you bring that up," Christian finally spoke. "I am unable to comment or give information on an ongoing investigation, but as far as my run is concerned, what happened with my son and his friend is a tragedy. Our families have been deeply affected by the events that unfolded that night," Christian continued.

Dustin clasped his hands together as he watched the interview on the monitor, behind the production set.

"Come on, man. You got this," he whispered.

"And due to what occurred that night, it has only propelled my campaign and it's showing exactly what I'm fighting for," Christian moved the conversation. "I'll be completely honest, what happened was an injustice; an injustice to Christian, an injustice to Marcus, complete disrespect and disregard for our families," he continued.

"No, no, no," Dustin uttered as he saw where this was headed.

"Not to mention, it showed the judgment of the responding officers and their mental state, and I believe this isn't the directions things should be going. We need to revise our policing strategies and train the police on the new strategies. Too many families across the country have been torn apart by police brutality. Even now, we have a family praying at their son's bedside because he was shot by the police; another unarmed Black male shot down because they assumed they'd seen a weapon." Christian shook his head. "This has got to end and it's going to start one day one when I set foot at 700 North Adams Street in Tallahassee," Christian sanguinely spoke.

Dustin nodded his head in agreement with the way Christian handled the question.

"Lieutenant Tate, all of this happened in your jurisdiction. The initial and responding officers are all from your district. How does this affect operations moving forward and the relationship between you and said officers?" Ernest questioned.

Christian inhaled deeply.

"These officers are from my jurisdiction, you're right," Christian answered, "but I am not one to retaliate or to let something affect my job. I cannot speak too much on the investigation," Christian reminded Ernest, "but I will say that these officers took the steps they felt necessary. They are living through the results of their actions and once the investigation comes full circle, appropriate measures will be taken."

"Even if they are determined to be justified?"

"Even if they are deemed to have been justified, yes," Christian remarked.

"Lieutenant Tate, do you feel these officers were justified in their actions?" Ernest inquired as he raised an eyebrow.

Christian chuckled lightly. "I thought this interview was about my gubernatorial run?"

***

Christian walked towards his office and made eye contact with Brian.

Brian had his arm in a sling and glared at Christian. Christian changed paths and walked towards Brian.

"Officer Whitley, can I speak with you?" he asked aloud.

Brian looked around as if he were looking for an escape.

"Yes, Lieutenant Tate?" Brian spoke timidly.

Christian smirked as Brian spoke like a minor who was guilty, and they knew they'd been caught.

"Let's step into my office," Christian spoke.

He and Brian turned and walked to his office.

"How's your shoulder?" Christian question as he closed the door behind Brian.

Brian walked over to the desk and remained standing. "Doc says I'll be back up and running in a few weeks," Brian spoke. "As for the chest, the vest took most of the impact away from the bullet," he added, "so I'm cleared for that."

"I'm glad," Christian started. "Listen," he walked over to Brian. "What possessed you to defy my orders and pull over my son four nights ago?"

Brian exhaled.

"I was tailing the vehicle that failed to yield at a yellow traffic signal. Wasn't paying attention to who the vehicle belonged to until the stop was in progress."

"What's funny to me," Christian picked up a pen from his desk and clicked it, "is that just a few months ago, you stopped him for a similar incident. Now, I did my research on that stop and found out that you indeed lied about the reason for stopping him," Christian stood tall and paused.

"What are you getting at, Lieutenant? Are you accusing me of lying?"

"I'm certainly not accusing you of being very honest, Officer," Christian continued. "You've lied in the past about this and you and I don't have the best relationship."

Brian laughed lightly. "Lieutenant, I have work to do," he smirked. "Plus, you aren't even supposed to be investigating the case."

Christian glared at Brian and Brian's smile faded.

"My traffic stop was justified. The fact that your son got belligerent and irate with me is beyond me completely," Brian was unaware that there was video beyond his body camera.

Christian didn't bring it to his attention.

"I think you're not being very honest with me," Christian replied. "You are jeopardizing your career, *Brian*," he scolded.

"If you say so," Brian remarked. "Can I go, *Christian*?"

Christian nodded. "Get the fuck out of my office," he remarked.

Brian smirked and left the office slowly. He touched his shoulder and winced slightly with pain.

Christian pressed speaker and dialed Francesca's extension. "Sergeant Gaines, can you come to my office for a minute?" he asked as she answered.

"Be right there," she answered.

Christian ended the call and walked to his system. He knew all his actions would be under a microscope; not only because of his run for governor but by the Chief of police, since his son was being investigated and Christian was advised to stay away from the case.

Christian sat at the computer and pulled out his phone. He put his earphones in and played the video sent to him by Junior's phone on the night of the shooting. He pulled a pen from his pocket and wrote on the notepad.

"*What are you guys drinking there? A little bit of lean?*" he heard Brian ask.

Christian shook his head and jotted down the notes.

"*Nah, man, nothing like that. Just a little sprite and grape soda mixed. Just left school, actually,*" he saw Junior pass the registration card to Brian. He noticed his son's hands atop the steering wheel.

"*We're not friends, so don't talk to me like we are. Wait here,*" he saw Brian walk away from the vehicle.

There was a knock at the door and Christian paused the video.

"Come in," he uttered.

Francesca entered the room. "You wanted to see me, Lieutenant?" she greeted him.

"Close the door, Frankie," he spoke to her.

Francesca closed the door. She could tell by his demeanor and the fact that he called her Frankie, that he wanted to speak to her as a friend and not just as a coworker.

"What's going on?" she asked as she sat down.

"You know I'm under a microscope," he sighed. "I can't do any kind of investigation into Junior's case. Well, on the record," Christian added.

Francesca noticed the notepad. Christian observed her.

"I'm watching the video that was recorded from Junior's phone and Brian's behavior isn't sitting well with me. It's like, he took his vendetta against me out on my son."

Francesca shook her head.

"Tell me what you need from me," she uttered. "I'll help out in whatever way I can," she added. "I've known Junior and Marcus since they were babies. They're good young men."

Christian looked down at his phone.

"Have you seen the body-cam footage from Brian's suit?" he tried to piece together angles that Junior's camera didn't capture.

Francesca shook her head. "I haven't seen it," she admitted. "I think the Chief is keeping a tight rope on everything; mainly because he knows it's your son and the incident involved officers from this unit."

"Do me a favor," Christian started. "Get your hands on that footage for me. Just view it for me." Christian shook his head slightly. "I've seen this video from Junior's phone about a hundred times with Andrew, trying to make sense of it."

"You know as well as I do that Brian has a problem with authority, primarily when it's coming from a Brown or Black authority figure," Francesca spoke. "It's not going to make sense," she continued, "it's your son and he was going to do what he can to make his life a living hell."

Christian shook his head. "He should have been fired long ago," he shrugged. "But the board wouldn't let his ass go."

Francesca concurred.

"I need to see what happened once he took my son out of the car. The cellphone catches him getting out, but after that, it's all audio. And the police department hasn't handed the footage over to the court, so Andrew hasn't even had a chance to review it," Christian rose to his feet. "In order to build a strong case, he needs to see what happened once Brian and Junior were at the hood."

Francesca nodded her head. "I completely understand," she remarked. "I will do whatever I can to help," she finished.

"I got your back on this," Christian protected. "If something goes left, it's on me," he promised her. "Just help me clear my son."

"Governor Tate," Francesca smirked, "everything is going to be just fine. I have your back and will do everything in my power to assist you; I just want you to devote the time and energy into your run; it will help you stay busy and if push comes to shove," she added, "you'll be in a better position to help him when you're in the governor's chair."

Christian smiled. "Thank you, Frankie."

Francesca nodded her head and grinned. "Let me go see what I can find," she walked to the door and opened it.

She exited Christian's office and closed the door behind her.

8

"Your Honor, we have a request to ask of the court," Andrew spoke confidently.

"And what's that, Mr. Brownstone," Matthew questioned.

"I'm requesting that we consolidate the Tate and Farris cases for the sake of time and resources," Andrew answered.

Matthew looked at the papers in front of him, never looking at Andrew nor Junior.

"What benefit do you feel will come from consolidating these cases?"

"Your Honor, these incidents are related all the way around," Andrew answered. "These two gentlemen were together at the time of the incident and both cases feed off one another," Andrew kept his composure although he wondered why the judge was asking a question in which the answer was obvious.

Matthew continued writing down notes as Andrew, Junior, and Anayi stood before his desk. He never looked at Andrew nor Junior.

"Does the prosecution object to this?" Matthew asked.

Junior displayed a smug look on his face and nudged Andrew.

"With all due respect, Your Honor," Andrew started, "this is a matter in which we need your judgment."

"Mr. Brownstone, surely you know that during these trials, the prosecution has the right to object to motions," Matthew looked directly at Andrew.

"Object on what grounds?" Andrew questioned. "This motion to consolidate will save the state time, money, and resources."

"Andrew, we have to play by the rules," Anayi taunted.

Junior glared at her.

"You're new to this," Andrew remarked, "so I'm going to let it slide. Matter of fact, I'll save it for court."

Matthew looked at Andrew sternly. "Have some respect, Mr. Brownstone," he remarked.

"Respect?" Junior intervened. "With all due respect, Your Honor, this is my future; my life and it's screwed up that—."

Andrew put his arm on Junior's shoulder. "I got it, man," Andrew said. "Your Honor, all I'm asking is that we consolidate the cases. They go together like P-B&J. It will save us all time and resources in doing so," he finished.

"Again, I ask, does the prosecution object to this motion?" Matthew looked Andrew in his eyes as he asked Anayi the question.

A few seconds passed before Anayi answered the question.

"No objections, Your Honor. However, the prosecution would like to counter that motion by remanding the defendant into a federal prison during the case," she smirked as she answered the question.

Junior felt his stomach sink as Anayi replied.

"Your Honor," Andrew immediately retaliated, "that request is out of pure retaliation. Surely the court isn't going to go for it."

"I just want to ensure there's no witness or evidence tampering that may occur on the outside."

"Your Honor, my client is a high-school senior. He has a 5.0 GPA and is the point guard of his basketball team. He's recently been granted a full scholarship to UCLA."

"All redundant in a murder trial," Anayi interrupted. "It's cliché, but don't do the crime if you can't do the time."

"What is your problem?" Andrew couldn't handle her remarks.

"Although we are in chambers, I demand order," Matthew said.

Anayi smirked. "I do wonder how Mr. Brownstone will be able to handle and manage both roles as a defense attorney for this case and as a lawyer to represent the Farris vs. State of Florida case.

"It's no issue for me," Andrew rebutted. "Look at my track record; I believe in getting justice and if consolidating these cases does that, then that's what it is," he stared at Anayi.

Anayi chuckled.

"So, you're one of those," Junior spoke under his breath.

Matthew didn't hear Junior and continued writing on his notepad.

"Motion granted," he spoke to Andrew. "With the conditions set forth by the prosecution."

Andrew continued to stand tall and Junior nudged him once more.

"If my client is to be remanded into prison, we request that he be put in maximum security."

"On what grounds, Mr. Brownstone?" Matthew questioned.

"Your Honor, my client is charged with the attempted murder of a police officer. He's a target amongst some of the inmates and officers alike," he answered.

Anayi mumbled something under her breath and Andrew glared at her.

"Motion denied," Matthew spoke to Andrew.

Andrew looked Matthew in his eyes.

Matthew cleared his throat. "I'm sorry, Mr. Brownstone, but as Ms. Jiménez said earlier, don't do the crime if you can't do the time."

"Bro, I was fearing for my life!" Junior blurted.

Matthew looked at Andrew in awe since Junior had just spoken out. Andrew nodded his head.

"I said what I said," Matthew remarked, "and Mr. Brownstone, I advise you to silence your client."

"Just like they did Marcus, huh?" Junior spoke.

Matthew removed his glasses and looked at Andrew. "Mr. Brownstone!" he stressed.

He didn't address Junior directly.

"I got this," Andrew spoke to Junior. "Just remain calm."

"If there's nothing further, we're adjourned until Monday morning at 0900 hours. The jury has already been selected and is ready to move forward. Please enter the courtroom prepared," Matthew instructed, "for both cases. Please generate your witness lists, evidence submissions, as well as have your opening arguments ready to go," Matthew hit his gavel against his desk.

"Thank you, Your Honor," Anayi gathered her things. "See you Monday, Andrew," she winked at him. Anayi left the room before officers entered.

"Bro, I can't do jail," Junior whispered to Andrew.

"Stay strong," Andrew instructed. He glared at Matthew, who was getting prepared to leave the chambers. "Your father and I will figure something out."

Junior nodded his head and the officers escorted him from the room. Once he was escorted out, Andrew gathered his papers and left the room.

■■■

"Did you get it?" Christian asked Andrew.

Andrew was working diligently to get the evidence and witness list prepared.

"I'm trying, man," Andrew expressed. "The judge is clearly going to be an ass. Even when we were in chambers, it seemed like he was siding with the prosecutor."

"Those are the worst judges. I did some digging and I discovered that Matthew is tough, especially when it comes to racial cases like this."

Raymond and Natina held hands and sat on the opposite end of the couch.

"What's the plan for handling Marcus' case?" Raymond questioned as he held Natina tightly.

"These cases go hand-in-hand. We can't have one without the other," Andrew answered, "so I'm going to handle them aggressively in utilizing the evidence and the witnesses."

Christian held Keisha's hand tightly.

"I've filed a motion for the judge to consolidate the cases and that's my first step in merging everything together," Andrew continued. "Even though I'm requesting to consolidate the cases, we will still have two separate verdicts. My job now is to get a verdict of 'not guilty' for Junior's case, and a verdict of 'guilty' for Marcus' case."

Andrew looked at his notes.

"This is really déjà vu," Christian uttered. "It's just flipped around. Guess it's time to see how the state feels about us," he shook his head.

"These are sensitive moments," Raymond spoke. "America has been divided for a while, and with Trump being president almost two decades ago, it divided the country even more. We haven't been the same since."

Keisha looked at Natina and saw the tears in her eyes. She knew she was extremely concerned about her son.

"Girl, come on," Keisha spoke softly. "Let's let these men do their thing and go get pampered. We can go see Marcus afterward."

Natina nodded her head. "Yeah, girl. I gotta clear my head somehow," she and Keisha rose to their feet.

"I'll see you in a bit, babe," Keisha walked over and kissed Christian.

"Okay, Babe. If you get a moment to go see C.J., let him know what's going on with the case," Christian began. "And, there's a package for you in the center console."

Natina walked over and embraced Raymond tightly. "I love you so much," she whispered, and they connected.

A tear fell down Raymond's face. "I love you too, babe. Kiss our boy for me," he reached in his pocket and handed Natina two hundred dollars.

"Andrew," Keisha spoke as she stepped to him. She embraced him. "Thank you, again," she remarked.

"No need to thank me," he smiled. "Christian is like a brother to me and I'm going to do what I can to help him. Same with Ray; although our relationship hasn't been existent for nearly as long as mine and Christian's, he's shown me that he's real and believes in doing what's right."

Natina shook Andrew's hand.

"Mrs. Farris, thank you for trusting me with your son's case. He's in good hands, trust me," Andrew remarked.

Natina nodded her head. She and Keisha walked out of the home.

"So, this is how I'm going to handle these cases," Andrew began.

"Ladies and gentlemen of the jury, it seems like an open-and-shut case," Anayi spoke and looked directly at the jurors. "On Friday, July 20th, at approximately 8:47 pm, Officer Brian Whitley of the Miami-Dade police department pulled over a black Mustang for a traffic violation."

"Here we go," Andrew whispered to Junior.

"Upon stopping the vehicle, Officer Whitley approached the vehicle and tapped three times on the window. At this moment, he realized the driver and the passenger of the vehicle were African-American males between the ages of eighteen and twenty."

"This is a jury of my peers?" Junior whispered as he observed the makeup of the jury.

The jury was comprised of twelve members; eight women and four men. Of the women, two were African American, five were Caucasian, and one was Hispanic. Three of the men were Caucasian and one was Asian.

Andrew shook his head.

"Your father was in the same predicament," he advised. "All we can do is remain strong."

Junior nodded in agreement. He swallowed air as he listened to Anayi speak. He had never been in any kind of trouble with the law; not even a parking ticket, and now he was on trial for the attempted murder of a police officer. He bit his lip as he watched Anayi pace the floor.

"Officer Whitley ran the defendant's license through the system and saw he had a clean record. He collected the passenger's identification card and put it in his vest. Now," Anayi reported, "the reason he put the card in his vest instead of running it through the system is that he didn't have the chance due to a sudden move by the defendant."

Andrew took notes in his notepad as Anayi spoke. He had to have his opening statement hit hard to counter hers.

"The lies start," Andrew mumbled.

"Officer Whitley instructed the defendant to keep his hands visible; this is when things began to escalate and fairly quickly, might I add."

Anayi walked over to a projector and pressed the button. She held the remote in her hand and changed the slide. An image of Junior's hand clenched together displayed. The image was from Brian's body camera.

"Officer Whitley called in for backup to report to his location of Sawgrass and 10th. After he called in for backup, he walked around to the driver's side of the vehicle," Anayi replicated his motions with her body. "Officer Whitley walked the defendant around to the hood of the vehicle and instructed him to put his hands on the hood of the vehicle. This is where things took a turn for the worse."

Andrew put his hand on Junior's shoulder to ensure he remained calm. Anayi pressed a button on the remote and the slideshow advanced.

"Officer Whitley patted down the defendant where he questioned the defendant about any weapons, alcohol, or drugs; he denied all three."

The image on the screen showed Brian's hands on Junior's torso.

"It's hard to make out right here," Anayi uttered, "but later in the trial, we will present evidence to validate the claims set forth by the prosecution." She advanced the image. "After the pat-down, the defendant begins to resist, and Officer Whitley has to use force to get him to the ground. He, then, shouts for the defendant to stop resisting. The defendant kicks Officer Whitley," she advanced the image to show the space between Brian and Junior, and to show the proximity of Junior to the gun, "and the defendant lunges for the weapon. Officer Whitley climbs atop the defendant and begins to wrestle with him for the weapon."

Andrew watched the expressions of the jurors for any signs of emotion as Anayi told her story. He didn't see any signs of emotion and he knew this wasn't a good sign.

"The first shot rang out. *Pow*, right through Officer Whitley's shoulder."

Junior inhaled sharply.

"Still, Officer Whitley persists in attempting to disarm the suspect. As Officer Whitley lunged for the weapon, the defendant fires another shot into the right side of his chest."

Anayi advanced the image and showed an image of Brian's gunshot wound. Andrew saw a few looks of shock across the jurors' faces.

"Moments pass before the defendant and his passenger approach Officer Whitley and upon approaching, the defendant kneels down. He immediately retrieves Whitley's radio, reports a 10-30, and requests an ambulance. Officer Whitley shouts '10-33' over the radio and the defendant releases the button on the radio. He then puts his hand over Whitley's wound and applied pressure."

Junior couldn't stop his foot from tapping or from fidgeting and Andrew noticed this.

"Breathe slowly," Andrew whispered as he poured Junior a cup of water.

Christian, Keisha, Raymond, and Bianca sat in the front row of the audience and they noticed Junior was uneasy. Andrew looked and give Christian an assuring look.

Christian slightly nodded his head and held Keisha's hand tightly.

"A few seconds later, a backup unit arrives with two police officers," Anayi continued. "They announce their presence as Miami P.D. and instruct the defendant and his partner to show their hands." She pressed the button and advanced the image.

The image was from the dash camera of the second police car that arrived.

"Now, I will warn you that these next few images can be pretty disturbing to see," she advanced the photo. "Officer Jake Warren instructs Marcus Farris to show his hands."

Junior inhaled sharply and hung his head. The jurors all watched meticulously.

"Farris was bent over in the vehicle and looked back. Once he saw the officers and heard the command" she advanced the photo, "he backed out of the vehicle with something in his hand."

"Yeah, a phone," Junior muttered.

"Fearful that Farris had a weapon," she advanced to a photo where it showed Marcus getting shot, "Warren fires a single shot into Farris' chest."

A tear formed in Raymond's eye and fell down his face as Anayi showed the image and spoke.

"Once Farris hits the ground, dropping the item in his hand, Warren runs over to him and kicks the item away, which he now realizes was a cellular device. Warren puts his finger on Farris' neck and feels for a pulse. Simultaneously," she raised her voice and walked towards the judge's desk. "The defendant rises to his feet and walks over to Marcus Farris. Officer

Warren and his partner, Officer Amira Rutledge, keep their weapons aimed at the defendant, and as he kneels to his friend, Officer Rutledge walks over with her weapon aimed and arrests the defendant."

Anayi paced the floor and walked over to the jury box.

"Approximately forty-five minutes passed from the start of the traffic stop to the arrest of Tate. Of those forty-five minutes, Whitley was on the ground with a gunshot wound for ten."

Junior observed the jurors as they watched Anayi.

"Your Honor," she addressed Matthew, "with the court's permission, can we take a short moment of silence."

Andrew chuckled as she asked the question.

"For how long, Ms. Jiménez?" Matthew asked.

"Ten minutes — the length of time Whitley was on the ground suffering from his wounds."

"Your Honor, I object to that motion," Andrew projected. "This is a court of law where there are not only one, but two cases occurring," he continued. "To what benefit would a ten-minute moment of silence be to the court?"

"To emphasize how long a respected officer of the law laid on the ground alone; bleeding from his wounds."

"Let's not get beside ourselves," Andrew cut her off, "he wasn't alone. My client was at his side applying pressure to his chest wound to stop the bleeding."

Matthew hit his gavel on the desk.

"Save it for your opening argument, Mr. Brownstone," Matthew spoke. "As far as the objection to the motion, I'll have to agree with Mr. Brownstone. This is a courtroom and we're not talking about a few seconds worth of silence, you're requesting a full ten minutes," Matthew concluded.

"But Your Honor," Anayi started.

"Motion denied," he spoke authoritatively.

Anayi nodded her head and continued with her opening argument. She paced the floor and walked towards the jury box.

"Two outstanding officers of the law were affected that night and now it's time for you to be the jury and make the right call." Anayi looked directly at the jurors and stopped at the jury box. "Ask yourself the following two questions during the trial: was Christian Tate legitimized in shooting Officer Brian Whitley out of fear for his life; and two, was Officer Jake Warren justified in shooting Marcus Farris out of fear for *his* life?"

The jurors looked at her blankly and she nodded her head.

"Thank you," she walked away from the jury and to her desk.

She glanced at Andrew and Christian before sitting.

Andrew emerged from behind his desk and walked to the front. Junior kept his elbows on the table and looked back at his parents and Raymond.

"Ladies and gentlemen of this courtroom; ladies and gentlemen of the jury; Your Honor, let me start by saying 'good morning'," Andrew enunciated.

"Come on, man," Christian uttered under his breath. "You got this."

"We've done the screening and selection process, but let me be real for a second: as I look around this courtroom; at the congregation, the jury, and even the judge, I say the majority of us have been on this earth for close to half-a-century, if not more," Andrew walked to the jury box slowly. "Everyone has heard of the 'Andrew Brownstone & Christian Tate' team, so I'm not going to even be surprised by the thoughts flowing through your minds right now. I'm not here to boost my credentials; I'm not here to make noise in the media," Andrew glanced at the cameras and back to the jury. "I'm here to prove that both of my clients are innocent."

Andrew walked away from the jury box and continued.

"Put aside what you may know about me from previous cases and trials, although I know this is a huge case of déjà vu to many of you. I'm not supporting Christian Tate and Marcus Farris because of the similarities in this trial to previous ones; I want justice and for this injustice to end."

Andrew looked at Junior and Junior smiled slightly. He then scanned the congregation. He looked briefly at Christian, Keisha, and Raymond, but didn't allow his eyes to rest on them, as he knew the cameras would be watching him.

"On the evening of July 20th, Christian and Marcus," Andrew didn't want to only refer to the gentlemen as his clients. He needed to connect with the jurors in some way, and at the end of the day, these were adolescents with a bright path ahead of them. "Were leaving school and on their way to see the gubernatorial debate. After leaving school, they dropped their girlfriends off before continuing the commute," Andrew gave a rough timeline. "After driving, eh, let's say about 20 minutes, they observed lights and sirens in the rearview mirror, and the driver, Christian Tate, pulled over to the right side of the road. I would like to show you video footage, as opposed to still images," he jabbed at Anayi, "obtained from SafeZone's server, of the incident in question."

Andrew walked over to the projector and started to load the video but continued to talk while it loaded.

"SafeZone is an online platform, designed by a group of African-American males to monitor, track, and store data obtained from cellular phone footage or a computer. The free application can be downloaded from your device's app store and with a few setting adjustments, you can set a wake word, the actions you would like for the application to take upon hearing the wake word, such as record a video using either the front camera, the rear-facing camera, or both, log your device's location, send a text message to specified recipients, et cetera, et cetera. A highly useful tool," Andrew added.

Anayi slightly rolled her eyes.

"Here's a disclaimer," Andrew spoke as the video loaded from SafeZone's website, "this is front-facing video footage from Mr. Tate's cellphone and contains strong language from Mr. Tate, Mr. Farris, as well as Officer Whitley."

Andrew pressed play on the video.

"It's only one this time," Junior spoke over the video.

The siren lights flashed brightly on the video and rustling could be heard.

The jury saw Officer Whitley approach and tap on the window. They observed Junior let the window down.

"Everything okay, Officer Whitley?" Junior questioned.

Andrew stood by the projector and watched the video along with the jury and the rest of the court's congregation.

Junior turned slightly and made eye contact with Bianca. He saw the tears in her eyes. She wanted to jump out of her seat and pull him close to her.

Junior blew a kiss to Bianca. He closed his eyes and faced the video.

"Yeah, but fuck him," he heard himself say over the video. *"I'll let my pops handle this shit."* He watched on as the camera recorded him tapping his fingers on the steering wheel.

Keisha rocked back and forth; she was jittery and couldn't manage to sit still.

Christian kept his arm around his wife and held her hand tightly.

"I have to reach for it," Marcus recited over the video.

Junior figured that at the hospital, Natina and Sierra were both tearing as they watched the case unfold. Hearing Marcus' voice almost broke Junior, but he remained strong for his friend.

"My man, keep your hands where I can see them," Brian spoke.

The recording showed Junior's hands go from fully extended to balled into a fist.

"They've been in the same position since you left from over here," Junior uttered.

"Are you calling me a liar?" Brian couldn't be seen on the video since he was on the passenger's side of the video, but his voice could be heard.

"Here we go," Junior muttered under his breath. He inhaled deeply.

"You already got that, boy," Brian spoke.

Junior scanned the room and saw Brian. Brian shook his head at Junior.

"Yo! Why are we getting pulled over?" Marcus shouted.

The video showed Junior getting out of the vehicle and the door shutting closed.

"Shit is hot," Junior could be heard over the video.

"I don't give a fuck," Brian spoke faintly over the video.

"This audio is as-is," Andrew spoke over the video. "No enhancements or anything. As you can see, I've logged into Christian Tate's account with SafeZone to view the video directly on their servers."

The camera viewed Marcus reaching in his pocket and exiting the vehicle.

"Shit," Marcus spoke as he got out of the vehicle.

"Get your bitch ass back in the car!" Brian could be heard.

Slight gasps came from the jury.

"*We're just trying to get to our destination,*" Marcus pleaded.

The video shook as Marcus opened the driver's door seconds later.

"*Let the weapon go,*" Brian projected.

The gunshot went off. Seconds later, the second shot rang out. Some of the jury members jumped at this.

The only visual on the video was of the driver's seat and the siren lights.

"*We gotta go,*" the courtroom heard over the recording.

"*We can't,*" Marcus spoke.

Junior kept his hands on his head.

"At this moment," Andrew spoke while the video played, Christian Tate's cellular phone was still in the holster in the vehicle, that's why you're not seeing any activity."

"*10-30,*" could be heard faintly over the video, followed by "*Hurry!*"

The camera shook as Marcus opened the car door and Jake projected over the video.

"*Miami P.D., let me see your hands.*"

Marcus could be seen on the edge of the camera and he slowly rose to his feet.

"*Gun, gun!*" Jake shouted.

Another gunshot rang out and Marcus could be seen falling.

A tear fell down Junior's face as he saw this. Andrew stopped the video and continued with the opening statement.

"That should be the case, right?" Andrew questioned the jury. "No," he chuckled facetiously, "that would be too simple. Ladies and gentlemen, you will see this video and clips of it numerous times throughout this case. I will walk you through the facts of this case, during this case, and at the end, you will have no choice but to render two verdicts: one for not guilty on Christian Tate's behalf, and a verdict of guilty against Officer Jake Warren, on Marcus Farris' behalf."

Andrew bowed his head and walked away from the jury box.

"Thank you."

9

Junior entered his cell and laid on the bench. The cell was damp and cold, but Junior was used to extreme conditions from his basketball practices. He looked around and observed as the water dripped from the faucet into the sink bowl.

A tear fell from his eye as many thoughts crossed his mind. He thought about his family, Marcus' family, Bianca, and Sierra. Prison was the last place he wanted to be, and he thought about how detrimental of an effect it would have on everything he had going for himself.

He reflected on the trial and how the first day went; he felt that Andrew had done a terrific job in presenting the facts and setting the tone of the cases. He entered the witness list for both cases and submitted the evidence. Jail wasn't for him, but he was glad his lawyer was on his side and had his best interest at heart.

His thoughts were interrupted by a clang against the bars of his cell.

"Yo, Tate," the inmate spoke.

Junior tucked his chin into his chest to look at the entrance of his cell. It was one of the first inmates he encountered, Kanaan. Junior hadn't interacted too much with his cellmates, as this wasn't the life he'd envisioned for himself, but he also knew that if he were to make it through, he couldn't entirely keep to himself.

"What's up?" Junior kicked his legs over and sat up. He rose from the bench and walked over to the bars.

"I got a question for you," Kanaan uttered calmly.

Junior walked over and put his hands on the bars.

Kanaan eyed Junior before continuing.

"How'd it feel shooting and almost killing that cop?" he chuckled.

Junior shook his head. He knew he could either give Kanaan the truth or fabricate a story to give him street credentials in jail. He decided to go with the first option.

"Bro, it was completely out of impulse," Junior chuckled. "Honestly, it wasn't intentional," he admitted.

Kanaan looked around him.

"Yeah, but you know people are hailing you for doing it. These racist pigs do the shit all day, every day, and get a slap on the wrist for doing it," Kanaan paused.

Junior nodded in agreement.

"I mean, look at the pig Warren and his punishment for shooting ya' boy and leaving him in a coma."

Thinking of Marcus' situation boiled Junior and Kanaan could see the frustration in Junior's face.

"Yo, you did it, so own that shit," Kanaan suggested to Junior, "and if they try to make you, don't feel bad about doing the shit," Kanaan leaned against the bars. "Shit, if I were you, I would have aimed for his goddamn head," Kanaan looked around to see if any officers were coming. He pulled a blunt of out his pocket and held it. He reached into his pocket and pulled out a lighter.

He put the blunt in his mouth and put the flame to the end of the blunt. Kanaan inhaled deeply and exhaled through his nose. "This was much needed," he fanned the blunt. "You want a hit?"

"Nah man, I'm good," Junior chuckled. "Just don't let these guards catch you with that."

Kanaan inhaled on the blunt and released a small cloud of smoke before continuing.

"Your daddy's a cop, isn't he? Running for governor?" he inquired.

Junior nodded his head.

"How does he feel about what happened?" Kanaan looked at Junior.

"He saw the video footage. Both from my phone and from the body-cam," Junior began, "he feels what I did was justified and Officer Whitley abused his power."

"Everyone in this prison has seen the footage from your phone," Kanaan replied. "Got the prison divided though. Some of us, shit," Kanaan inhaled on the blunt, "primarily the minorities. That shit you did, *Whitely* had that shit coming to him," Kanaan purposefully mispronounced his name.

Junior looked at Kanaan.

"But then, in the same breath, you got the whites and racist bitches in here that feel like you didn't have to fire the shots at that pig."

Junior shook his head.

"I'll be real. My primary concern is my father's campaign and the effect all of this will have on it."

"I hear you, man. Well, if it counts for anything, you and your pops have my support. 1000 percent of the way," Kanaan spoke. He tapped the blunt and the ashes fell on the floor. "But look, my man, I gotta meet up with a man about a dog," he joked as he looked at the clock on the wall.

Junior chuckled. "Okay, man. We'll get up later, and thank you," Junior thanked Kanaan.

"I'ma fuck with you," Kanaan replied.

Junior returned to the bed once Kanaan left and stared at the ceiling.

***

The inmates were gathered at the round table of the lounge area. The television was on a news channel and Christian was interviewing with the host. He had Francesca at his side.

"C.J., that's your old man, isn't it?" an inmate asked Junior.

"Hell yeah," Junior uttered, "turn that up."

The inmate increased the volume of the television.

"Your lawyer, Andrew Brownstone, is representing your son and Marcus Farris in a trial that has the nation talking. With your current status in law enforcement and the fact that this case involves officers from your district, what effect do you believe this will have on your gubernatorial run?"

Christian raised an eyebrow and chuckled.

"It's funny. Every interview I come on, the media is either trying to compare my trial with my son's or you're trying to draw a response out of me considering officers from my department were involved, but you're not going to draw that reaction out of me," Christian chuckled. *"Now, I and my lieutenant governor are here to answer questions that you may have about the run or about the district, but that's about it."*

Francesca nodded and smiled.

"You all have to understand my running mate's frustration," Francesca spoke. *"We know that you all have a job to do but let's focus on the positives and what we have to bring to this great state, such as police reform and bringing more jobs and internships to the youth,"* Francesca smiled. *"That's where your focus is, isn't it?"*

The host blushed.

"Well, let's shift our focus then," the reported sifted through papers. *"You have been pretty much owning this race. You're doing quite well in the numbers and many of the younger and first-time voters are in your corner. Tell us, what sets you apart from your opponent and his running mate."*

Christian ensured that he stayed away from the topic of race.

"Experience, for one thing," he started, *"I've been in law enforcement all of my life, and that has taught me many things, including how to be a better man and numerous life lessons,"* he firmly added. *"And, regardless of my age,"* Christian chuckled with Francesca and the host, *"that's why I think I can resonate with the youth."*

"Do you think your son is one of the reasons you feel like you can resonate with them? I'm pretty sure you all have daily conversations about what's going on and how it affects him."

Junior shook his head as he saw the reporter divert the focus back to him and the case.

Christian smiled. *"Tyler, I am not here to discuss my son, as I've told you before. Yes, we have conversations and it shapes my views, but overall, the resonation has to come from within."*

Tyler spoke immediately. *"Drawing up a comparison between you and your opponent is something you can naturally expect the voters to do,"* Tyler spoke hurriedly. *"And we can try to ignore it, but there is one major thing that's a direct comparison, and that's the trial. His son was killed, ironically by his opponent."*

Junior saw a smile on his father's face but could sense the frustration.

"And your son is on trial for the attempted murder of a police officer. Your son's friend is in a coma because of an officer from your unit," Tyler persisted.

Christian chuckled.

"Since you want to talk about it so much, let's do that," Christian spoke with a tone that Junior knew wasn't pleasant. *"What do you want to discuss?"*

Francesca smiled and slightly shook her head.

"Do you want to talk about the trial of Benjamin Smith or Christian Tate Jr.?" he questioned; not allowing Tyler to speak. *"Mr. Smith pulled a weapon on law enforcement and prepared to discharge the weapon. The shot was taken on my end, yes, out of self-defense."*

Tyler was silent.

"Legally speaking, I can't give information about the trial of Christian Tate Jr., but I can speak my opinion. So, as the youth say, what's poppin'?" Christian laughed.

Tyler was speechless.

"The comparisons you all are placing is because our children were in similar predicaments but had two different outcomes." Christian adjusted his tie. *"Not to mention that one is Black, one is White. Here's my response: the way our children handled themselves was very different."*

Tyler raised an eyebrow. *"Care to elaborate on that, Lieutenant?"*

Christian smirked. *"It's open to interpretation."*

Junior chuckled and shook his head at his father.

"That your old man?" Kanaan questioned as he sat next to Junior.

"Yeah. He cuttin' up," Junior joked. "The reporters want to play games and question him on things he has already said he wouldn't comment on, so he's toying with them."

Kanaan chuckled. "Shit, y'all are alright with me," Kanaan spoke.

Junior laughed silently.

Another inmate sat next to Junior; he attempted to look intimidating to Junior. The inmate was an older Caucasian male who had a muscular physique. Junior perceived him to be in his mid-to-late 50s.

"So, you're Christian Tate," the inmate spoke gruffly. "The wanna-be cop killer."

Junior glared at the man. "Excuse me?" Junior sat erect.

"Nah, you can kill that shit," the man deepened his voice. "You don't want no smoke," he looked Junior in the eye and three inmates walked towards the table with their fists balled; all older Caucasian males.

"Tim, your first mistake is thinking my homie is alone," Kanaan spoke with confidence and put his hand on Junior's shoulder.

"Shit, one man? Damn near the same size as him. You niggers are cute," the men got closer to the table. "Your dad killed one of us in cold blood and now I'm close to his son. I wonder what he would say if something were to happen to you," Tim laughed.

"Alone?" Kanaan chuckled. "My man, that's not the way I roll, and you know that." Several men that were seated rose to their feet; the group was made of both African American and Hispanic men. All the men had muscular builds.

Tim looked around.

"You sure you wanna do this shit, Timmy?" Kanaan raised an eyebrow and demasculinized him.

Tim looked at Kanaan, then to Junior; he directed his attention to the men that rose and looked back at Kanaan.

"Another day, nigger," he spoke to Junior while looking at Kanaan.

"Come by yourself, I'll knock that damn smirk off your face," Junior replied.

Tim laughed.

He nodded his head before brushing past Kanaan. His crew followed behind him.

"Man, this shit is just getting started," Kanaan spoke. "Keep watch, bro," Kanaan and Junior sat; the men also sat.

Junior felt his heart pounding as he sat. He didn't wish for things to escalate the way they did, and he worried about them getting worse. He looked at the muted television and saw his father's lips moving.

"Please, get me out of here," he spoke silently.

10

Junior stood next to Andrew. Junior wore a white shirt that was tucked into his gray dress pants. Andrew wore a light blue button-down shirt and left the top three buttons undone. His shirt was tucked neatly into his black dress pants and he wore a sportscoat. Andrew looked at Junior and nodded his head.

Junior looked behind him and smiled at Bianca and his parents, as well as Raymond. He turned around and faced the front of the court before releasing a small sigh of relief.

"Your Honor," Anayi said, "we would like to call John Lisle to the stand."

A Caucasian man in his thirties rose to his feet and slowly walked to the front. Christian didn't take his eyes off him.

"Who's he?" Raymond whispered to Christian.

"School security guard," Christian shook his head slightly. "Junior and Marcus don't have the greatest relationship with him. He's always looking to get them caught up in some trouble or something," Christian cleared his throat.

"Raise your right hand," the bailiff approached the witness stand. John raised his hand.

"Do you swear to tell the truth, the whole truth, and nothing but the truth, so help you, God?"

John spoke gruffly, "I do."

The bailiff walked away from the stand and Anayi approached the front.

"Here we go," Andrew whispered to Junior.

"Mr. Lisle, thank you for taking time out of your schedule to be here with us."

"Always a pleasure to help get justice," John spoke while looking at Junior.

Junior looked John in the eye.

"Mr. Lisle, can you please state your occupation for the court?"

John cleared his throat.

"Yes, I work as one of the security guards for Sol College Prep," he spoke. "Been there for 25 years."

"That's a long time of service," Anayi remarked. "What is it that keeps you going to the job daily?"

"The kids," John immediately replied with a grin.

"Fake ass smile," Junior heard Andrew mumble under his breath.

"I must admit, I love working with all of the students at the school. While some give me a harder time than others, all of them make the job worthwhile."

"Mr. Lisle, is security the only job you have at Sol College Prep?" Anayi paced the floor.

"I mean, that's my job title, but I know my duties span far beyond working security. I'm like a mentor to many of the students; a friend, someone they can come and talk to."

Anayi nodded her head and smirked.

"Mr. Lisle, are you familiar with the defendant?" she questioned.

John glanced at Junior.

"Mr. Tate," he projected.

"Objection, Your Honor," Andrew spoke. "Please ask the witness to answer the questions posed to him and not to address my client," Andrew continued to write notes.

"Please stick to the questions, Mr. Lisle," Matthew uttered.

John nodded his head. "Yes, I know the defendant," he reworded his answer. "That's Christian Tate; he's a senior at the school."

"And what would you say your relationship is like with the defendant?" Anayi questioned as she rested an arm on the witness stand.

"Mr. Tate and I have a complicated relationship," John began.

"How so?" Anayi walked to the jury box.

"There's not really much conversation that occurs between us," John answered. "He hangs around with that Marcus fellow; seems to keep to himself."

Andrew scoffed silently and kept writing.

"I see," Anayi walked to the prosecution's desk. "Mr. Lisle, in your interactions that you've had with Mr. Tate, how would you characterize them?" She shuffled through papers.

John chuckled. "A few were hostile," he uttered.

There were a few gasps from the jury box.

"Hostility was projected from who? Mr. Tate or Mr. Farris?"

"Both," he spoke.

Junior shook his head at John.

"Now, why would he sit up there and lie like that?" Junior whispered to Andrew as he tried to recall his run-ins with John.

"This isn't to say that the overall vibe was hostile," John spoke, "but there have been a few bad incidents."

"Any fights, Mr. Lisle?" Anayi questioned.

"Objection. Leading the witness," Andrew interrupted.

"Withdrawn," Anayi rebutted. "Please, Mr. Lisle, provide an example of an interaction between yourself and the defendant."

John scanned the courtroom and made eye contact with Christian. He saw the frustration in Christian's eyes. He quickly looked away

"A few months back," John spoke slowly, "I was doing my daily rounds and I saw Mr. Tate and another student in a verbal dispute, which was rapidly becoming physical."

"How so?" Anayi asked.

"I couldn't tell what they were arguing about," John continued, "but whatever it was had the two gentlemen getting rowdy. It was quickly turning into a shoving match between the two."

"Mr. Lisle, do you remember any of the conversation between the gentlemen?"

John thought for a moment. "It was shortly after Christian Tate announced his run for governor," John looked over to Christian.

The courtroom seemed to look in Christian's direction.

"And I guess the other gentleman that was in the mix didn't agree with him running and I heard something about Benjamin Smith; I'm assuming the argument had something to do with that."

"What was your involvement?" Anayi questioned.

"I'm the security guard," John laughed. "Well, one of them anyway. I see something unfolding, I intervene. Simple as that." John took a swallow of water from the cup in front of him. "I know class is in session and if I see two students in the halls and almost screaming and pushing and shoving each other, it's my duty to intervene."

Anayi nodded her head.

"No further questions, Your Honor," Anayi stepped away and returned to her desk.

Andrew rose to his feet and approached John.

"John Lisle," Andrew held papers in his hand. "You said you're currently a security guard for Sol College Prep, yes?" He inquired.

"That is correct. I've been at the school for so long, it's about the only thing I know how to do."

Andrew blinked his eyes. "What's that? Be security, a mentor, or a counselor?"

John was silent.

Andrew waited a few moments before continuing.

"John, you were able to identity Christian as one of the students involved in the incident you witnessed and you're saying it was probably about his father's case, roughly 20 years back."

The jurors looked at one another.

"John, are you able to identify the second student?"

John thought silently for a second.

"Robert Eikman," he answered. "I think they're in the same grade."

"I see," Andrew replied, "and from your eyes, what's the relationship like between Mr. Tate and Mr. Eikman?"

"I haven't seen much," John responded. "As I said, I've only interacted with Mr. Tate on a few occasions."

"That's interesting," Andrew remarked and walked back to the defense's desk. He retrieved a piece of paper and continued. "School records show that you have had to intervene between Mr. Tate and Mr. Eikman quite a few times; seven to be exact."

John's cheeks turned pink. He remained silent.

"Yeah, and it says here that for five of the interactions, you logged the cause of the incident as an argument involving political and racial topics and that tensions were running high."

"So, what do you want me to say?" John questioned.

"My question is, why'd you feel the need to lie about that? You're here, in the court of law, under oath."

John looked at Anayi for an escape.

"You said you hadn't interacted with my client much, thus not knowing what the relationship was like between him and the other student. But records show, you've intervened numerous times and know the nature of their altercations."

The jurors looked at John with concern.

"Why should we trust anything you've just said to us when you just perjured yourself?"

John opened his mouth, but no words came out.

"Your Honor, let the record show that this witness has ruined his credibility and has perjured himself in this court."

Andrew looked directly at Christian and then to Junior.

Anayi hung her head slightly but didn't show defeat.

"Objection, Your Honor," Anayi spoke. "My witness had a memory lapse; he wouldn't intentionally perjure himself in the court."

"Of course he wouldn't," Andrew remarked. "No further questions, Your Honor," Andrew returned next to Junior.

"You may step down, Mr. Lisle," Matthew remarked.

John stepped down from the stand and walked back to the audience.

Junior looked at his lawyer in awe.

"I see why my dad picked you," Junior whispered.

"Let's not lose our focus," Andrew responded. "We have to keep on knocking these witnesses out."

Anayi ruffled through her papers and looked at the judge.

"Your next witness, Ms. Jiménez," the judge spoke.

"Your Honor, we would like to call Mr. Louis Stanton to the stand," she continued to shuffle through the papers.

Christian turned slightly and saw a male in his mid-to-late 40s rise to his feet. He adjusted his tie and slowly walked to the witness stand.

Louis was sworn in by the court officer and Anayi approached.

"Mr. Stanton, please state your occupation for the court."

"Counselor Louis Stanton. I counsel the juniors and seniors at Sol College Prep," Louis made eye contact with Junior and then looked over to Christian, then to Raymond.

"Mr. Stanton," Anayi dove straight into the questioning, "on the week of July 20th, did you notice anything off with the defendant, Christian Tate?"

"Off like how?"

"Did he seem more," Anayi searched for the word, "how do I put it? Rebellious or anxious?"

"Objection, Your Honor," Andrew projected from his seat.

"Withdrawn," Anayi remarked.

The jurors looked at one another and Louis coughed into his arm.

"How often did you interact with Mr. Tate?" Anayi questioned.

"We spoke a fair amount of times," Louis answered. "Working with Christian has been quite the experience," his voice shifted an octave higher.

"How do you mean?" Anayi stood in front of the judge's desk; roughly six feet away.

"Christian is one of the brightest, most athletic, and outspoken students that I interact with. But," Louis paused, "he has a bit of a temper on him."

"Care to elaborate?" Anayi proceeded.

Junior shook his head slightly and Andrew looked at him.

"Junior has never been one to bite his tongue, especially when it's come to social issues. He's never been kicked out or suspended, to my knowledge, but I have heard about him getting numerous technical fouls over the course of his basketball career and a few altercations he nearly got into outside of school."

Anayi smirked and looked at Junior. She mouthed a phrase to him before losing her smirk. She turned to the jury box and faced the jury but continued to speak to Louis.

"I know all of this happened some months back, but do you remember Mr. Tate speaking to you about an incident at a convenience store?"

"I do!" Louis exclaimed. "I spoke with Christian and Marcus regarding this. Assumedly, this was hours before the championship game, and they were racially profiled by the clerk."

"Do you remember them telling you how it turned out?" Anayi questioned.

"Yeah, I believe Mr. Farris informed me they left the store without incident, but I guess Lieutenant Christian Tate was on the television and it triggered the altercation."

"I'm glad everyone was able to walk away unharmed. Especially if Mr. Tate has a reputation for being a hothead, as you say," Anayi spoke.

"Objection, Your Honor!" Andrew shouted.

"Sustained. Ms. Jiménez, mind yourself," the judge warned.

"My apologies, Your Honor," Anayi uttered. "No further questions."

Andrew rose to his feet and approached Louis with the remote in his hand.

"Your Honor, since the prosecution has discussed the convenience store incident, we would like to present video footage to the court of said event in question. Exhibit 189-C," Andrew pressed a button on the remote.

"Present the evidence," Matthew looked at the screen.

"Thank you, Your Honor," Andrew responded. "Mr. Stanton, I would like for you to take a look at this video obtained from the convenience store regarding the evening in question and tell the members of the court what you take from it."

"Okay," Louis spoke hesitantly.

Andrew pressed play on the remote and audio and video projected from the screen.

The first thing heard was the door chime to the store to indicate the entrance of the patrons. The jurors observed as Marcus and Christian walked down two separate aisles of the store. They saw Junior retrieve the drinks from the cooler and Marcus retrieved a few snacks.

"Is something wrong, my man?" Junior questioned the clerk over the video.

"You look very familiar," the clerk replied.

"Maybe you know him as the next big thing in ball. The Lebron James protégé," Marcus put his hands around Junior's shoulder.

A few of the jurors smiled as they watched the bromance between the two. They saw the clerk shake his head as he continued to ring up the items.

"Nah, that's not it," the clerk responded.

"I'm not going to talk too much," Andrew interjected, "but keep an eye on everything in the video. Including the television screen."

The jurors saw Bernard's image on the television screen and saw him in the suit. They noticed he was being interviewed.

They, then, noticed the television showed a familiar video amongst the country: it was the body camera footage of the shooting of Benjamin. The television then showed Christian's mugshot.

"So, out of all the images they could have chosen, they choose to display him in his darkest moment."

"You already know they're going to do whatever they can to keep the Black man down," Marcus responded over the video.

Andrew noticed the jurors raising their eyebrows at this remark.

"It's a shame he killed that boy. He had such a bright future ahead of him," the clerk responded.

Andrew anticipated an objection from Anayi, but to his surprise, there was none.

"Nah, man, no need to push that button. Just because you see an upset Black man doesn't mean you need to be petrified," Junior smirked as he put his hand in his pocket.

The jurors saw Junior lay the money on the counter, as they could tell he refused to touch the clerk.

They saw Marcus put his hand on Junior's shoulder. *"Not the place,"* he reminded his friend.

The video ended and Andrew continued.

"Mr. Stanton, what do you take from the video?" he questioned.

"In terms of what?" Louis questioned.

"Well, in your words, you called my client a hothead," Andrew tested.

"Objection, Your Honor," Anayi spoke.

"Mr. Brownstone, you objected to the prosecution referring to your client as such, and now you're turning around and doing the same thing?" Matthew looked at Andrew.

"I'll reword," Andrew emitted. He looked at the jurors. "You were saying my client has a short fuse." Andrew stopped in front of the juror box and looked at Louis. "Tell me, what did you take from that video?"

Louis looked at Andrew sternly and smirked.

"When the clerk made a comment regarding Lieutenant Tate, Mr. Tate then displayed aggression in defending his father."

"What aggression did he display?" Andrew challenged. "From the looks of the video, my client remained calm and level-headed throughout the entire encounter."

Louis was silent.

Anayi rose to her feet and opened her mouth to speak.

Andrew saw her in his peripheral vision and posed another question before she could make out her words.

"Mr. Stanton, you have a pretty good grasp on the students' attendance record, behavior, and all those good things, correct?"

"That's right," Louis proudly confirmed.

Andrew chuckled lightly.

"So, Mr. Stanton, can you give us a little background on the individual that Christian got into an altercation with?"

"Robert Eikman," Louis spoke clearly. "B-average student with a bright future ahead of him."

"What makes you say that?" Andrew inquired.

"I can just see it. His passion is what drives him and what will take him far."

Andrew paced towards the witness stand.

"Where would you say he wants to be ten years from now?"

"Objection, Your Honor," Anayi interjected. "Relevance?"

"Your Honor, everything I'm posing will verify whether or not my client has a short temper, as Mr. Stanton has suggested, or if he merely has a passion and replies to things that trigger him."

"How?" Anayi questioned. "Your line of questioning is about the student he got into an altercation with; not him," she nodded towards Junior.

"What's your problem?" Andrew questioned. "Mama always said if you can't take the heat, get out of the kitchen," he took a jab at her.

Matthew raised his eyebrows at the two attorneys.

"My chambers, *now!*" he stressed. "Court is in a fifteen-minute recess," he announced to the crowd.

Matthew raised from his chair and the courtroom officer brought the congregation to their feet.

The officer stood near Junior as the two attorneys disappeared into the chambers. He escorted Junior to the judge's room.

Christian glared at Louis and Raymond observed this. He could tell there was history and bad blood between the two.

"Lay it out for me," Matthew spoke. "What's the issue?"

"Your Honor, I am simply trying to clear Christian's name of being a short-tempered Black man, as the prosecution and their witnesses have painted."

"Your Honor, that is far from the truth," Anayi explained. "I am not trying to paint any image of the defendants," she referenced Junior and Marcus. "I am merely asking my witnesses questions and they are basing their answers on their facts and personal experiences."

"Tell me something," Andrew slightly turned. "What race and ethnicities are the students that the defendants got into altercations with?"

"Mr. Brownstone!" Matthew interjected.

"This has nothing to do with race," Anayi proposed offense.

"Mr. Brownstone, we are not turning this into a case based on race," Matthew spoke.

"With all due respect, Your Honor, that's bullshit. I've tried numerous cases like this before. You can't have a case like this where you have contenders of two different ethnicities, on a topic such as this one, and *not* discuss race."

Matthew raised his eyebrows at Andrew.

"Mr. Brownstone, I will not have my courtroom or rulings questioned."

"I respect that, Your Honor," Andrew responded, "but can Miss Jiménez answer the question?

Junior saw how passionately Andrew was fighting for him and gained a new level of respect for him.

Matthew wrote on the notepad and waved Anayi on.

She reluctantly answered. "He's White."

"My point exactly," Andrew responded.

Junior observed Matthew shake his head slightly.

"How does all of this fall in line with your questioning?" Matthew questioned.

"It plays a role. May we continue the case with questioning Mr. Stanton?" Andrew wanted to hurry back to the courtroom so the jurors could see what was going on. He didn't want them to miss a single detail.

"Mr. Brownstone, you're on a thread right now," Matthew warned.

Andrew nodded his head.

Matthew rose to his feet and the attorneys walked to the door.

They left the judge's chambers, the officer escorted Junior back to the courtroom, and Matthew took his position behind the desk.

"Pardon the delay, Mr. Stanton," Andrew approached the witness stand as court continued. "Where would you say Robert wants to be ten years from now?"

Louis looked over at Anayi once more. Anayi stared at Andrew during the questioning.

"It's allowed," Matthew responded.

"Are you asking me based on my opinion or from what he's told me?" Louis asked for clarification.

"Either or," Andrew remarked. "We just want to know where his future lies."

Louis inhaled sharply. "Well, I can see Mr. Eikman pursuing a law degree. He's a debater," Louis finished.

"And, Mr. Stanton, where do you see my client in ten years?"

"Your Honor, I object!" Anayi spoke.

The jurors looked confused.

"I have warned you in chambers, Mr. Brownstone—" Matthew started.

Andrew immediately replied to Matthew and didn't pause.

"Your Honor, I would like to enter into evidence a screenshot of the witness' social media page where he explicitly states, and I quote, 'Hashtag, I stand with Nanos. Sterling Wallace had no business in that neighborhood at that time of night; he was only doing what he was trained to do. *S-word,*'" Andrew didn't speak the curse word in court, "'"Wallace was asking for it. If you ask me, Nanos did this world a favor. Their kind is always up to no good and they have no future,' end quote." Andrew looked at the jurors whose faces were all full of shock.

Junior shook his head at his school's counselor. Louis' face was red.

"And that's not all," Andrew continued. "Shortly after Lieutenant Tate shot and killed Benjamin Tate, Stanton posted, quote, 'W-T-F! This is an outrage. How does the officer of the law shoot and kill an innocent young man with such a promising future? His life had just begun,' end quote."

Andrew looked directly at Louis and his face seemed as though it was about to explode. Anger filled Christian's face as he whispered to Raymond.

"See, this muthafucka' has been fuckin' with Junior for a while. I *knew* he had an agenda."

"There's no way the jury can overlook this," Raymond chuckled.

"If they do, they're just as clueless as the jury I had during my trial." They directed their attention back to the front.

"So, again I ask, what do you see in Christian Tate's future?"

Louis was silent, as was Anayi and the rest of the courtroom.

"No further questions, Your Honor," Andrew returned next to Junior.

Anayi rose to her feet.

"Your Honor, we ask that the court recesses for the rest of the day."

Matthew looked at the clock before speaking.

"Agreed. Court is adjourned for the day. We will resume these proceedings tomorrow at 9 AM sharp."

Matthew hit the gavel on the desk and the courtroom rose to their feet.

"So, what's next?" Junior questioned.

"They're taking it case by case," Andrew responded. "They're going to settle yours and then move on to trying to prosecute Marcus and exonerate Jake."

"Your Honor, the prosecution would like to call Officer Brian Whitley to the stand," Anayi spoke with confidence.

Brian rose to his feet and did a slight stretch.

There were slight murmurs among the jurors and Christian didn't take his eyes from Brian.

Brian was sworn in before Anayi approached the bench.

"Officer Brian Whitley. I've been looking at your records; you've been with the force for over six years, huh?"

"I have been," he boasted to his accomplishment. "Served the city of Miami well."

"Appreciate your service to the city," Anayi remarked.

Brian nodded his head. He did his best to avoid eye contact with Christian.

"Officer Whitley, can you describe to us, in detail, the events surrounding the stop with the defendant on July 20th?"

Brian scratched his chin.

"Around roughly 8:45 pm, I was on patrol. I was in the area of Sawgrass and 10th when I saw a vehicle swerving as it exited the expressway. I turned on my high beams before turning on my siren," Brian spoke slowly.

Andrew documented pieces of Brian's story.

"The car immediately pulled to the right of the road and upon exiting, I discovered the defendant sitting in the driver's seat and Marcus Farris sitting in the passenger's side."

"Were either the driver or the passenger acting suspiciously?" Anayi questioned.

"Objection," Andrew spoke. "Leading the witness."

"Sustained," Matthew replied dryly.

"After I got the defendant's license, I walked around to the passenger's door and retrieved Mr. Farris' identification. While obtaining Farris' identification, the defendant became belligerent and moved his hands in a motion that didn't sit well with me."

"How so?" Anayi questioned.

"So," he put his hands in front of him as if he were holding a steering wheel, "when I approached the vehicle, the defendant's hands were at 9 and 2. But," Brian shifted his hands, "when I walked over to the passenger's side, the defendant moved his right hand closer to six in a sudden jerking motion," Brian demonstrated how he saw Junior move his hand. "Not to mention, there was an unknown substance in the cupholder; it was purple, and I saw a Sprite bottle next to it."

"What did you think that substance was?" Anayi questioned.

"I figured it was lean."

Some of the jurors displayed a puzzled expression.

"It's a recreational drug," Brian explained. "What people do is they combine cough syrup with a soft drink, such as Sprite, and a hard candy."

Anayi nodded her head. "So, you figured they were drinking and driving?"

"Yes," Brian answered. "Once he moved his hand, I told him to keep his hands in the same position. I walked around to his side and got him out of the car."

"What was the nature of the interaction when he exited the vehicle?" Anayi questioned.

"Quite belligerent," Brian replied. "I walked him around to the hood, and he began to resist the search, so I brought him to the ground."

"The lies," Junior murmured.

"Next thing I know," Brian began. "We were fighting for control of my weapon."

The jurors displayed looks of concern and Junior slightly hung his head.

"After the first shot rang out, I continued to lunge forward to gain control of the weapon. My first thought was that I needed to keep everyone safe and I had no idea what may have happened if the defendant kept control." Brian forced a tear. "I don't remember much after that."

"Thank you for your service," Anayi spoke to Brian. Anayi looked at Andrew. "Your witness," she spoke to Andrew.

Andrew had a folder of documents in his hand. Junior didn't take his eyes off Brian; at one moment, he felt that Brian was smirking at him. Christian didn't display a single smile as Brian took the stand.

"Officer Brian Whitley," Andrew chuckled. "See this folder?"

"I think everyone in the courtroom and the cameras can see it," Brian laughed lightly. "You wanna tell me what's in it?"

"We'll get to that shortly," Andrew held the folder tightly in his hand. "But first, I want you to tell me how many interactions you've had with Christian Tate, Jr., in your tenure."

"Objection, Your Honor," Anayi spoke. "The witness surely handles numerous cases and has handled many more during the span of his entire career. You can't expect him to remember such a number," she explained.

"Really?" Andrew questioned. "Your Honor, I ask that the court asks the witness to take an educated guess to answer the question."

Matthew kept his head down as he wrote but still spoke aloud. "Answer the question, Mr. Whitley," he instructed him.

"I can't remember throughout my tenure," he slightly rolled his eyes.

Andrew nodded his head.

"But over the past year, I would say we've crossed paths a few times; maybe twice?"

"Maybe twice?" Andrew chuckled. "Let's try five times in the past year," he passed Brian two sheets from the folder. "The most recent was the stop that brought us here today, and there was one a few months prior."

"Relevance?" Brian questioned.

"It's ironic that with both traffic stops, Mr. Tate and Mr. Farris were in the vehicle together and they coincidentally both occurred at night."

Brian didn't look to Anayi for an objection. He was an officer and he knew how to handle the situation, but at the same time, he knew there were some things he couldn't speak on based on his position.

"What are you asking me?" Brian questioned.

"I just find it odd that you're saying you didn't know who was driving the vehicle, when Mr. Tate has been driving the same vehicle for the past two years."

The jurors looked at one another.

"Tell me, what was the reason for the traffic stop prior to the stop that resulted in you getting shot?"

"Objection, Your Honor," Anayi spoke.

"No," Brian spoke. "I want to answer this."

Matthew and the jurors looked at him in awe.

"My partner, Officer Hubert Montrose, and I witnessed a vehicle doing about fifteen miles over the speed limit."

Junior kept his eyes on Brian and listened to the story he was presenting. Andrew stood erect in front of the jury box as Brian spoke.

"So, I drove behind the vehicle. No lights, no sirens. Just trailed the car for about a mile. Once I got behind the vehicle, the driver reduced his speed and came to a rolling stop at a traffic signal on 107th and Flager. Once the driver turned right, I turned on my siren and the driver immediately pulled over." Brian accidentally made eye contact with Christian and stuttered a bit. He cleared his throat. "As Officer Montrose and I approached, I couldn't identify the number of passengers, as the windows were tinted. I shined my flashlight into the driver's window and tapped on it. Mr. Tate, there, gave me his license, registration, and proof of insurance," he nodded his head towards Junior.

Junior didn't allow his frown to leave his face.

"He asked me the reason for the stop, and I provided him with an explanation that he didn't come to a complete stop at the red traffic signal. We asked routine questions, including why they were out so late. He told us something about a game and they were heading out for a celebratory dinner; I'd assumed they'd won," Brian chuckled.

A smile didn't cross Andrew's face.

"Well, my partner and I got ID from the two gentlemen and ran their information in the system. Once we saw everything was clean, we sent them on their way. Didn't want to ruin his night with a ticket or a citation, so we let him go with a warning."

Andrew spoke. "Let me interrupt for a moment. We have evidence that you and your partner antagonized and belittled my clients, by making it known that you knew their parents and what they stood for. You're on record saying, 'wasn't your daddy the one who shot and killed Benjamin Smith almost twenty years ago', as if his father wasn't acquitted and as if he wasn't your boss?"

Brian couldn't help but make eye contact with Christian, although he tried his hardest not to.

"And then, Officer Montrose, who is present in this courtroom, went on to say, 'son of ex-convict Raymond Farris', when referring to Marcus." Andrew shook his head at the jurors and saw the looks of shock on their faces.

Raymond raised his eyebrows at this. He hadn't heard this commentary before.

"Your Honor, I object to this line of questioning," Anayi interrupted.

"Not even referring to Mr. Farris as a citizen who served his time to society, but as an ex-convict."

Matthew looked at Brian sternly and then to Andrew.

Andrew didn't show any signs of defeat, regardless of the stare that Matthew was giving him.

"But," Andrew started speaking again, "I must say that your memory of your very first altercation is pretty amazing for someone who couldn't recall the number of encounters he's had with the defendant."

Brian didn't like being challenged and Andrew could see he was pushing his buttons. He decided to hit harder.

"What happened as a result of you pulling my client over that evening?"

"Elaborate."

Andrew could hear the attitude in his response and continued to poke at him. "The next day, what happened?"

"I was reprimanded by Lieutenant Christian Tate for my actions," he admitted.

The jurors gasped slightly and looked at Christian. Some shook their heads.

"Why?" Andrew questioned.

"Let's be real; it was for pulling his son over."

"I want to know: how did that make you feel?" Andrew walked closer to the witness stand.

"Objection, Your Honor," Anayi called.

"I hear you have a problem with authority, Officer Whitley. Primarily when the authority figures are Black or Brown."

Andrew could see Brian was boiling.

"Your Honor!" Anayi shouted.

"How did that make you feel that a Black man was able to chastise you for your actions and behavior in front of your coworkers, and you weren't able to do a thing about it but listen and deal with the repercussions of your actions?"

"Mr. Brownstone," Matthew projected.

Andrew could see Brian was infuriated.

"That was bullshit and Tate knows it!" Brian exploded. "I put in extra hours at the job to keep the streets of Miami clean and I pull over a black Mustang with black tints for a traffic violation with a driver who was operating the vehicle erratically, who may or may not have been under the influence at the time, and that sorry-ass Lieutenant wants to punish me?"

Brian abruptly stopped and the jurors all displayed looks of concern at this outburst. Matthew

"I mean..." Brian spoke.

"Quite choice words there, Officer. We're almost through here," Andrew continued. "Let's fast forward to the incident in question," Andrew walked back to the desk and retrieved the notepad. He saw a note that Junior had written; it was a question for Brian. Andrew nodded his head.

Brian loosened his tie and poured himself a glass of water.

"It is kind of hot in here, huh Officer?"

"Objection!" Anayi spoke.

"Withdrawn," Andrew responded.

He walked back to the witness stand.

"No one seems to want to talk about my other client, Marcus Farris; I wonder why that is," Andrew spoke. He knew this was cross-examination, but he had to get it all out. "Marcus Farris: a straight-A student on his way to college with a full scholarship to Stetson's University College of Law. Why am I bringing up Marcus, you may ask," he spoke to the jury, "because he's an intricate part of this case. Ladies and gentlemen, bear with me." Andrew walked over and picked up the remote. He pressed a button and Marcus' graduation picture appeared on the screen. "Marcus Farris, ladies and gentlemen, although when you saw him last, it was probably like this," he pressed another button and the body-camera footage from the shooting began playing. "Now, I'm not going to dive into my case just yet," Andrew continued as the video played, "but I wanted to put this image in your minds," he looked at the jury. "Ultimately, Mr. Farris was shot and put in a coma following this," he pressed the button on the remote and a video clip of Brian's body camera footage loaded.

"Relevance, Your Honor?" Anayi interjected.

"Mr. Brownstone, this has been a hell-of-a cross-examination. Where are you going with this?" Matthew questioned.

Andrew nodded his head.

"Officer Whitley, can you describe what happened once you saw Christian Tate move his hand?"

Brian knew Andrew had the unaltered body camera footage, so he was careful with his explanation.

"Once Mr. Tate moved his hand from 2 to 6, I alerted him that I had seen his movement. The driver became defensive and stated that he didn't move his hands, and I instructed him to remove his seatbelt. I walked around to the driver's side. As an officer, fearing for my life, I removed my weapon from my holster as I approached the driver's door."

Several jurors nodded as they listened to his story. Andrew displayed no signs of satisfaction as Brian spoke.

Christian and Raymond both glared at Brian as he spoke; Brian could feel Christian's glare, so he did his best not to look in his direction.

"That's when I heard the passenger, Mr. Farris, shout an obscenity beginning with the letter 'f' and he asked why they were getting pulled over, in a very hostile tone."

Junior wanted to defend himself and his friend; he didn't like what Brian was saying about them, but after having plenty of conversations with Andrew and his father, he knew it was in his best interest to let Andrew do the talking.

"I saw the passenger through the rear windshield as he attempted to move his hands as I approached the driver's side, and I instructed him to keep his hands on the dashboard. I, then, radioed for backup. Mr. Tate exited the vehicle and we both walked around to the front of the vehicle. I instructed him to put his hands on the hood and he responded that it was hot. I asserted my authority and ensured he put his hands on the hood of the vehicle."

Andrew interrupted. "As an officer of the law, why is it that you didn't take Mr. Tate to the rear of the vehicle, where you knew the temperature of the hood would be excruciating?"

"It was in the heat of the moment, no pun intended," Brian awkwardly chuckled. The courtroom was silent. "I didn't quite have a long moment to think. So, we walked around to the front."

"But my client told you that the hood of the vehicle was hot, did he not?" Andrew paced the floor.

"He may have mentioned that," Brian started.

"May have?" Andrew asked. "You just informed the court that, and I quote, 'he responded that it was hot. I asserted my authority and ensured he put his hands on the hood of the vehicle,' end quote."

Brian was embarrassed that Andrew remembered what he had previously said verbatim.

"So, what happened after he put his hands on the hood of the vehicle?" Andrew questioned. "Were any words exchanged?"

"I can't recall," Brian spoke. He was aware of what the video captured, but he was hoping it missed the small details. "I patted the defendant down for weapons or drugs, due to his behavior. I shouted for his partner not to move." Brian omitted much of the conversation. "I called for my backup and informed them that I had a possible DUI. The defendant, then, began to resist and that's when the scuffle ensued. I told him to stop resisting and we wrestled on the pavement. I saw his partner standing outside of the vehicle and I instructed him to get back in the car. The defendant then kicked me, and the kick caught me off guard, so I went backward. My gun fell from my holster and the defendant lunged for it."

Andrew continued to study the juror's faces. He saw many disapproving looks and he knew he had to control the narrative, but he wanted to let Brian tell his side of things before he showed the video and displayed everything that was omitted.

"The defendant held my weapon and I threw my weight onto him. I instructed him to let the weapon go, and I stated this into the radio so the responding officers would understand the situation. Somewhere, during our struggle, the weapon fired and hit me in the shoulder. Once the bullet hit me, the blast blew me back from the defendant," Brian touched his shoulder. "Being a protector, I lunged for the defendant to try to get my weapon, and he fired another shot and it struck me in the right side of my chest."

Many of the jurors simultaneously looked at Junior with disgust. Andrew was silent during the ordeal.

"I saw Mr. Farris exit the vehicle and I heard Mr. Tate suggest that they run; Mr. Farris advised him that they shouldn't do that. Mr. Tate did apply pressure to my chest wound after alerting the responding officers that I was down, I will give him credit where it's due. But that's about all I can give to you," Brian finished. "Everything else is kind of a blur."

Andrew nodded his head. "So, you did what you felt had to be done in terms of getting Mr. Tate out of the vehicle and handling him the way you did?"

Brian didn't verbally respond.

"Your Honor, I would like to play Officer Brian Whitley's body camera footage of the incident for the court. I would like for the jury to visualize what happened that evening."

"Go on," Matthew spoke.

"Thank you," Andrew remarked. "Now, I'm going to request that no objections be made, and any comments be held until the video is over," Andrew continued.

He pressed play on the video and the footage started from the beginning of the stop.

The footage captured Brian's hand touching the trunk of the vehicle and walking slowly to the driver's side. The jurors saw him shine a flashlight and tap on the driver's window.

"Everything okay, Officer Whitley?" Junior spoke over the video.

"Excuse me? I'll be asking the questions, show me your license and registration." The jurors could hear the attitude in Brian's voice.

The jurors saw Junior nod his head and slowly hand over his license.

"I can get my registration card for you, but I will have to reach into my glove compartment to retrieve it."

The jurors saw the light shine on Marcus' face. Raymond kept a straight face as he saw the footage.

"What you guys drinking there? Huh? A little bit of lean?" Brian chuckled over the video.

"Nothing like that," Junior replied over the video. *"Just a little bit of Sprite,"* Junior looked at the bottle of Sprite before looking at Brian once more, *"and grape soda mixed. Just left school."*

"We aren't friends. Don't talk to me like we are." The body camera showed the registration card to his car. *"Wait here."*

The jurors saw Brian approach his car and saw him enter information into the computer.

"Yeah, I'm behind a black Mustang with gold trim. I initiated a traffic stop for reckless driving. Got two black males in the vehicle, I want to run a check on Christian Tate, Jr. D-O-B, 7-14-2019. I'm getting out to retrieve the passenger's information."

Brian opened the driver's door to the police car, and they saw him approach the passenger's side of the Mustang. He tapped on the window and Marcus lowered the window.

"You got I.D. on you?" Brian asked gruffly.

Andrew shook his head as he watched the video with the rest of the courtroom. He looked at Christian and saw his fury growing in his eyes.

They saw the spotlight shine on Junior's face.

"My man, keep your hands where I can see them," Brian instructed.

The jurors noticed Junior didn't move his hands in the video, as Brian previously reported to the courtroom. A sense of accomplishment crossed Andrew, but he didn't show it; he could tell the jurors' image of Brian had been tainted.

"I didn't move them, Officer. They've been in the same position since you left from over here."

"Are you calling me a liar?" the aggression could be heard in Brian's voice.

"I'm not saying that. Look, we don't want any trouble, we're just trying to get to the debate."

"You already got that, boy. Take off your seatbelt for me," Brian walked around to the driver's side and the camera shook as he loosened his holster.

Andrew watched the jurors' expressions as well as Matthew's, Anayi's, Christian's, Raymond's, and the rest of the congregation in the room.

"Fuck! Why are we getting pulled over?" Marcus could be heard off-camera.

Although all the jurors had a negative reaction to Brian's behavior, the only ones who seemed to truly be affected were the younger jurors and the African American women.

"You keep your hands on the dashboard!" Brian shouted. *"I'm going to need backup on 10th and Sawgrass."*

The jurors saw Junior put his hands up and exit the vehicle. They saw Brian's hand extend and grab Junior's shirt. They both walked around to the front of the vehicle.

Andrew looked at Brian's face and Brian hung his head.

"Shit is hot," Junior remarked.

"I don't give a fuck!" Brian aggressed as the jurors saw his hand push Junior on the hood of the car.

"Police brutality. Cool. I see you."

The camera moved and Marcus could be seen.

"Don't you fuckin' move," the jurors heard Brian shout.

There were several gasps and murmurs around the room as they witnessed Brian as the aggressor and the way he was speaking to the teenagers.

"Give me a reason, I don't give a fuck who you are."

"What are you talking about?"

Brian chuckled over the video. *"Don't play dumb with me nigga. You all accept the 'a' instead of the 'er', right?"*

Anayi had seen enough as she saw the new direction of her case.

"Your Honor, I object to this video!" she blurted.

Andrew was silent for a second. He knew exactly why she was objecting but seeing as though Matthew had previously agreed to no objections during the video, he knew he couldn't go back on his word; regardless of how he felt.

"Overruled, Miss Jiménez," he spoke.

Andrew blinked his eyes slowly.

The jurors saw Junior being slammed to the ground.

"Stop resisting!" they heard Brian shout. *"Get your bitch ass back in the car!"* they could tell he was talking to Marcus.

"Officer, we don't want any problems. We're just trying to get to our destination," they heard Marcus plead.

The jurors saw the gun land on the ground and heard Junior.

"Officer, I'm not resisting. You don't have to handle me like this."

Brian grunted over the video as space had been created from the kick.

The body camera showed Junior get possession of the gun and the camera shook rapidly as Brian lunged on top of him.

"Let the weapon go!" Brian wrestled with Junior and the video continued to shake.

The first gunshot rang out; it startled the courtroom and Brian fell backward.

"Son of a bitch-ass," Brian started and lunged for Junior once more.

Fear could be seen in Junior's face as he held the gun. As the camera jumped at Junior, the second shot was fired, and the camera fell.

The gun could be heard falling to the ground and Junior could be heard panicking.

Andrew studied the jurors and saw some reactions he was looking for. He smiled on the inside.

"We can't. If we run, we're automatically assumed guilty," Marcus explained.

"Shit, shit, shit!" the jurors could hear Junior's voice cracking.

Junior entered the view of the camera and kneeled.

"10-30, officer down. Roll an ambulance to Sawgrass expressway and 10ᵗʰ street," his voice was trembling over the video.

Andrew looked at Junior and saw his eyes were welled with tears.

"Marcus, call my people!"

A few of the jurors felt sorry for Junior while it was hard for Andrew to read the others.

"Miami P-D, let me see your hands!" they heard Jake shout.

Andrew paused the video and allowed silence in the courtroom for a few moments.

"Officer Whitley, you used some pretty choice and derogatory language in the video," Andrew spoke. "And, ladies and gentlemen, understand this is coming from a sworn officer of the law; he's supposed to serve and protect, but I didn't see much of either going on."

The jurors looked at one another and Andrew pressed a button on the remote. Brian was silent.

"Before playing the video, Officer Whitley attested to the fact that he saw the passenger in the rear windshield making movements in the vehicle, but as you all can clearly see: the back windshield is tinted."

The jurors acknowledged this.

"How did he see Mr. Farris making any movements when there's a deep tint?"

"Objection, Your Honor. Please ask the defense to either direct questions towards the witness or to have him step down."

"Sustained. Mr. Brownstone, please speak directly to the witness unless there's something you're specifically presenting to the court."

Andrew nodded his head. He pressed the button on the remote once more.

"Officer Whitley, you said Mr. Tate moved his hand from 2 to 6, correct?"

"I reported what I believe to have seen—."

"Officer Whitley, did you or did you not tell this courtroom that you saw my client move his hands while you were speaking to Mr. Farris?" Andrew decided to attack.

Brian was silent for a moment. "Yes, I said that."

"Uh-huh," Andrew paced the floor. "But, the video from your camera demonstrates that he didn't move his hand." Andrew walked towards the defense's desk. "In fact, when you walked around and forcefully made Mr. Tate leave his vehicle, you demeaned and ridiculed him."

Brian opened his mouth, but the words wouldn't leave.

"You said, and I quote, 'I don't give a 'f' who you are' and went on to speak racial slurs and then said 'just because your dad is the lieutenant and is running for governor, doesn't make you above the law'."

"That's taken out of context," Brian tried to explain.

"And then you call my client, Mr. Farris, all kind of, excuse my language, Your Honor, 'bitches' and told him to 'get back in the 'f'ing car'. And we're supposed to believe you uphold the law?" Andrew shook his head.

A smirk appeared across Christian and Raymond's face.

Brian hung his head.

"Objection, Your Honor," Anayi spoke.

"Withdrawn," Andrew immediately replied as he glared at Brian. He was genuinely happy he was getting his point across, but at the same time, he was upset that these kinds of police officers were roaming the street and protecting the country. "A few more questions," Andrew looked at the notepad. "Do you believe Mr. Tate intended to shoot you?"

Brian held his head up and spoke. "The first shot, no. The second shot, yes."

"Did my client tend to you and administer aid until your backup arrived?" Andrew questioned.

"Your Honor, where is this going?" Anayi questioned.

"Overruled," Matthew responded. "Answer the question, Officer Whitley," he finished.

"Yes."

"Yet, you still say he intended to fire the second shot. After all the racial slurs and derogatory terms and idioms you used towards both of my clients, they were still willing to aid you in your time of need. Regardless of the harassment from you over the past year, they still rose above the childish behavior," Andrew shook his head slightly. "And you dare to come into this courtroom and lie under oath on this upstanding citizen?" he looked at Junior.

Brian was silent again.

"How many more Christian Tates are there that you've done this to, Officer Whitley? How many more Marcus Farrises are there that you've ridiculed and demeaned? How many Trayvon Martin's have you followed just because they were L-W-B: living while black?" Andrew's voice cracked but he quickly recomposed himself.

"Objection, Your Honor," Anayi shouted. She could see Brian was defeated.

"Withdrawn," Andrew spoke. He knew the jurors would resonate with what he was saying and although he withdrew the comment, he couldn't take it out of their minds. "Ladies and gentlemen, these are the types of officers you have here in America," Andrew walked to his desk. "I'm done with this witness, Your Honor," Andrew stood tall next to Junior.

11

"You go in here and you win this," Francesca spoke to Christian.

"I have to be there for my son," Christian explained. "You know I can't miss a moment of his trial."

"Listen," Francesca continued. "You're doing this *for* Junior. I saw it on the news yesterday when Andrew was speaking in court about the law enforcement and how we have these crooked cops patrolling the streets," Francesca drank from the coffee cup in front of her. "You make it to Tallahassee; you have the power. More power than you had before," she continued, "because now you will really be the man in charge. And," she sighed, "*if* something were to happen, you would be in a better position to help Junior."

Christian knew what she was hinting at. Although he didn't like it, he knew the reality of the situation and understood what she was saying. "To hell with this race," Christian chuckled.

Keisha walked into the kitchen and put on her earrings.

"Babe, when is court?" she questioned Christian.

"The judge delayed it until 10," he answered and looked at his wife. "Babe, what do you think about me doing this press conference and final standoff before the election?"

Francesca sipped her coffee and sat erect at the table.

"Frankie is saying that it would put all of us in a better position. I would be in charge and control. And, if the jury doesn't rule in Junior's favor, I'd be in a better position to help him."

"Babe, look," Keisha put her hands on his chest and straightened his tie. "I know you want nothing more than to be there for Junior today, but if you do this press conference and everything goes in our favor, you are officially at the top of the leaderboard. *You* will have the power and clout."

Christian looked at his wife admiringly. He kissed her on the forehead and embraced her tightly.

"I'll be sure that Junior knows what's going on," Francesca remarked from the chair. "And I will be there today with Keisha and Raymond. Don't worry about it, Chris," she uttered.

Christian smiled.

"Yeah, I guess I have to stop people like Bernard from getting into office and further corrupting us."

Keisha kissed her husband on the lips.

"Bring us back the keys to Tallahassee," she smirked.
∎∎∎

Junior sat in his cell and awaited court. He was confident that they were winning the trial; at least one of them was, in his opinion.

They hadn't touched much on Marcus' case, but it was evident that Andrew was heading in that direction based on how he closed out the previous day.

Junior was eager to see what other tricks Andrew had up his sleeves. He'd heard stories about the wonders Andrew could work, and now he was witnessing it for himself.

Kanaan walked in the doorway of Junior's cell.

"C.J., what's good my boy? I've been seeing you on TV."

Junior walked to the entrance and greeted Kanaan with their handshake.

"And you know I don't even watch the news," he laughed. "But you got me invested in the shit."

Junior laughed.

"Well, I do have one hell-of-a-lawyer. He's putting a hurting on these cops right now and has them shaking."

Kanaan pulled out a blunt and lit the end of it before inhaling.

Junior laughed. "Man, you better watch out. You know these guards are on bullshit with us," Junior looked on both sides for oncoming guards.

"You know who you're talking to?" Kanaan chuckled. "Come, take a walk with me."

Junior looked at the clock. "Yeah, I got like fifteen minutes to spare," he chuckled. "Going to court soon."

"We'll have you back in time," Kanaan laughed.

The two of them walked into the main foyer and Kanaan spoke.

"Listen up!" he called to the surrounding inmates.

Many heads swiveled and the conversations seemed to cease.

"This is my boy C.J. I'm certain most of you know him, but he's rocking with me. I don't want to hear about any of you fuckin' with him."

"K, what are you doing," Junior chuckled awkwardly.

"Nah man, I got this. Because I've been hearing shit going around this jail about how he feels like he's better than everyone else and blasé blasé," Kanaan stuck out his chest. "I'm just letting you niggas know that if I hear about any of y'all fucking with him, it's gonna be a problem and you'll have to deal with me and my crew."

Junior hadn't heard the talk around the jail, but he didn't doubt what Kanaan was saying.

"There is such a thing as keeping to yourself. And that's what my mans is doing," Kanaan announced. "So, if he don't fuck with you, it's as simple as that. He don't have no beef. He don't feel superior or whatever the fuck else y'all thinking; take that shit for what it is and keep it moving."

Junior was glad he had Kanaan's support while he was there. He knew some people probably had it in for him, considering who his father was and his rank.

"K, you didn't have to do that, man," Junior thanked Kanaan.

"I didn't have to, but I got you, bro," Kanaan responded.

"Respect, man," they did their handshake and Junior looked at the television.

*"And we have just gotten word that Lieutenant Christian Tate has arrived and is getting set up for the press conference. Everyone knows the elections are right around the corner, and this press conference is one of the final moments the candidates will have to answer any outstanding questions and to address the public, "*the news reporter spoke over the television.

Junior's stomach sunk a little. He didn't realize that the press conference was today, and he didn't realize his father wouldn't be there in the courtroom to support him.

"What the fuck?" Junior spoke aloud.

"What's wrong, bro?" Kanaan questioned as he flicked the blunt onto the floor.

"My pops. He's not going to be in court with me today," Junior spoke in shock.

"Damn," Kanaan uttered.

No further words were spoken. Instead, Junior walked back to his cell.

When he arrived, he was greeted by a guard.

"There you are, Tate. You have a phone call and we have to get you out of here for court."

Junior nodded his head reluctantly and the guard walked him to the phone.

"We normally don't do this," the guard admitted, "but I made an exception for you. You got two minutes before you have to be in the paddy-wagon."

Junior picked up the receiver and put it to his ear. "Hello?" he spoke.

"Son," Christian spoke.

"Really, Pops?" Junior spoke out of disgust. "You're not going to be there today?"

"That's not fair," Christian spoke. "I'm your number one supporter and everything I'm doing, I'm honestly doing for us," Christian explained.

"Junior," Keisha spoke on the other end. "I told your dad to go to the press conference. He really didn't want to, but in the long run, when he wins, this will be better for all of us."

Junior didn't reply.

"I'll be there, Uncle Ray, Sergeant Gaines, and Bianca will be there. Sierra's at the hospital with Natina but *everyone* is in your corner," Keisha stressed.

Junior didn't reply but he understood what his mom was saying. He knew that everyone wanted the best for him, but part of his frustration stemmed from him being in jail.

"Guys, I gotta go," Junior spoke solemnly.

"Son, I love you," Christian spoke. "Keep your head up and I will be there immediately following the press conference. I promise."

"Love you, Dad. Love you, Mom."

Junior hung up the phone and followed the guard to the van. Junior climbed inside and the van drove to the courthouse.

***

Junior stood beside Andrew as Anayi called her next witness.

"Your Honor, the prosecution would like to call Officer Jake Warren to the stand."

Eyebrows were raised, including Matthew's.

"Officer Warren's involvement sits with the Marcus Farris trial," Matthew spoke.

"Correct, Your Honor. But in this case, since we're combining the cases, it fits," Anayi explained.

"Granted, we are trying both trials at once," Matthew spoke, "but we also have to consider the overall structure of things."

Andrew didn't mind Jake taking the stand. He wanted Jake to take the stand. The cross-examination he had prepared would be excellent and he felt it would have Jake stripped of his badge.

"Your Honor, the defense has no objection to Officer Warren taking the stand at this time," Andrew spoke.

Junior slightly turned his head and could see the tears forming in Raymond's eyes.

"I appreciate that Mr. Brownstone," Matthew spoke as he jotted down a few notes. "Well, come on to the stand, Officer Warren," Matthew put his pen down and looked at the crowd.

Jake approached the stand slowly. Junior could tell that Jake wasn't too much older than he and Marcus. He figured he was new to the force. Jake sat and the court officer swore him in.

Anayi approached slowly, knowing this was the witness, practically the only witness she had, that could beat the case against Marcus.

"Officer Warren," she began, "how long have you been on the force?"

"It's my third year," he admitted.

"Did you come into the force straight from the academy?" she questioned.

"Yes. Officer Whitley recruited me," he added.

Several murmurs were heard around the room.

Francesca held Raymond's hand, as she could see the fire in his eyes. He was staring at the man who put his son in the hospital; one of the same people who were supposed to serve and protect.

"Officer Warren, can you walk us through that night, from your perspective?" she questioned.

Jake nodded his head.

"I was on patrol that night on Sawgrass expressway alongside Priscilla Lawrence when we got a call over the radio for backup regarding a 10-30."

"Can you explain to the court what that call represents?"

"Yes, a 10-30 is a shooting."

"Go on," Anayi remarked.

"Once we got the call, I responded and turned on my siren. I was about 3 miles away, so I accelerated and rushed to the scene. Upon arriving," Jake swallowed air, "I saw Officer Whitley on the ground and the defendant was over him. I couldn't make out what he was doing, but myself and Officer Lawrence exited the vehicle with our guns drawn."

"What happened when you all exited the vehicle?"

"Officer Lawrence and I witnessed someone with their head inside of the vehicle, so I told the individual to show me their hands. The defendant was over Officer Whitley and shouted that he couldn't show us his hands, which I found odd."

"What about the individual in the car?"

"He backed out of the vehicle with an object in his hand. I honestly feared that it was a weapon, so I fired a shot into his chest," Jake admitted.

"Being a newcomer to the force, I know that has to be difficult on you."

Jake nodded his head.

Anayi nodded and looked at Matthew.

"Your Honor, I would like to show the court Officer Warren's body camera footage of that night," she walked over and obtained the remote.

"Proceed," Matthew recited.

"I can't sit in here for this," Raymond remarked as he rose to his feet and exited the aisle. He left the courtroom.

"I'll go make sure he's okay," Francesca responded before following him out of the room.

Anayi pressed a button on the remote and the video appeared on the screen.

The jurors saw the steering wheel to the police car turning and heard radio chatter and the siren.

"Officer Warren, badge 3920, about a mile out," the jurors heard Jake announce over the radio.

The car came to a halt moments later and the courtroom heard the seatbelts unbuckle. The lights in the cab of the car turned on and the camera moved as Jake exited the vehicle.

"Miami P-D, let me see your hands!" he shouted.

"I can't!" Junior replied. *"If I move them, he'll bleed out!"*

The camera saw Marcus as he backed out of the vehicle while raising his hands.

"Gun, gun, gun!" Jake shouted and fired a shot into Marcus' chest.

Raymond flinched as he heard the gunshot outside of the courtroom.

"If I go in there now, I'm not responsible for my actions," he told Francesca as tears flowed down his face.

"I completely understand, Raymond," she began, "but I can't let you do anything that could jeopardize yourself, your family, or this courtroom."

"That man shot my son and I don't even know if he's going to make it another day," Raymond cried silently.

"I know," she uttered. "But as an officer, I'm letting you know that if you do something, I will have no choice but to arrest you."

"We all have choices in life," Raymond spoke. "He made one the moment he decided to shoot an unarmed Black man."

"Come here," Francesca embraced Raymond. "You have one of the greatest lawyers fighting for your son. Let's let him work his magic."

Francesca led Raymond back into the courtroom.

Francesca entered the row they were sitting in, followed by Raymond. Bianca held Keisha's hand tightly as she looked at Junior.

Andrew approached the stand with his hands interlocked.

"Officer Jake Warren," he spoke.

Jake swallowed air.

"Three years on the force, but this isn't your first time firing your weapon, is it?" Andrew questioned as he laid a sheet of paper in front of Jake.

"No," he answered.

"Officer Warren, how many times in your brief tenure have you fired your weapon?"

Jake was silent.

"If you can't recall, it's on the sheet of paper," Andrew remarked.

"Objection, Your Honor," Anayi spoke.

"On what grounds?" Matthew questioned.

"What is the relevance of this line of questioning?"

"Why don't we allow Officer Warren to answer the question and then you'll see the relevance," Andrew replied with a smirk.

Matthew nodded for Jake to answer the question.

He mumbled something that Andrew nor the courtroom could understand.

"I'm sorry, can you speak louder for the courtroom?" Andrew asked.

"Sixteen," Jake whispered.

"Sixteen," Andrew projected for the courtroom.

There were several gasps around the courtroom, and everyone widened their eyes, including Anayi. She wasn't aware of this information.

"Now, I'm not a math whiz, but that's an average of 5.3 times a year," Andrew reported. "Lieutenant Tate has only fired his weapon a total of twelve times during his entire tenure with force."

Raymond glared at Jake during his line of questioning.

"If Lieutenant Tate has been on the force for over twenty years and has only had to fire his weapon twelve times, what justifies you to fire your weapon sixteen times over a 3-year span?"

"Your Honor, I object," Anayi interjected. "What relevance does a comparison to Lieutenant Tate play?"

"Based on the statistics, many would say Officer Warren is trigger happy. You know, the same thing they tried to say about Lieutenant Tate during his trial against Benjamin Smith," Andrew uttered.

"Objection!" Anayi spoke.

"The jury will disregard the last statement about Lieutenant Tate," Matthew looked at the jury. "Mr. Brownstone, you are really trying your luck in my courtroom, aren't you?"

Andrew walked back to the defense desk. Andrew turned and faced the courtroom, opposite of Jake, and held his phone in his hand.

"Officer Warren, I'm going to turn to face you, and I want you to answer my questions, okay?"

"Okay," Jake responded confusedly.

Andrew turned around slowly as he held the phone in his hand. He spoke as he turned around. "Officer Jake, I want you to tell me what you see in my left hand." Andrew ensured he was about the same distance that Marcus was from Jake that night.

"It's a phone," Jake replied with a slight attitude.

"So, you don't think this is a gun?" Andrew questioned.

Anayi, Jake, and the rest of the courtroom understood where Andrew was going with the question.

"In the video, you shouted 'gun, gun, gun' as my client, Marcus Farris, exited the vehicle and turned around slowly. But, for me, you knew it was a phone; almost immediately."

"With all due respect, Mr. Brownstone, it's broad daylight and I don't see you as a threat," Jake talked himself into a corner.

Anayi shook her head.

"So, you took Mr. Farris as a threat?" Andrew questioned. "Even though he turned around slowly and followed all of your instructions, with his hands in the air."

"He had a black object in his hand!" Jake argued.

"Which you just identified as a phone in mine," Andrew passionately spoke. "Mr. Farris and I have the same phone."

Andrew continued to bait Jake in. He knew he would keep replying faster than Anayi had a chance to object.

"What is it that you found threatening about Mr. Farris, Officer Warren?"

"Officer Warren," Anayi called out.

"Was it the atmosphere and the nature of the call you were responding to?" Andrew questioned.

"That could have played a factor," Jake answered.

"Was it the fact that you had a character that you didn't recognize with his head inside of a black Mustang with gold trim?"

"Officer Warren," Anayi called again.

Andrew didn't stop the attack.

"Maybe it was the fact that you saw locs and that petrified you even more," Andrew suggested.

"Objection, Your Honor!" Anayi called.

"Or maybe, just maybe, it was his Blackness that you saw as a threat," Andrew paused and raised an eyebrow.

"Hell, he was probably up to no good!" Jake shouted. "Had his head in the car, coming out of a tinted vehicle with an unknown object in his hand, looking scruffy. I didn't know what was in his hand as he came out of the car and I did what I had to do!" Jake shouted.

Francesca and Keisha had to hold Raymond down as Jake had the outburst. She could tell he wanted to attack Jake.

All the jurors gasped at his reply and the courtroom was divided at his comments. Both sides started arguing, causing Matthew to hit the gavel on the desk.

"Order in this courtroom!" he shouted.

Jake was silent as he'd realized what had just happened.

Andrew shook his head slowly and spoke. "Did what you had to do? He was up to no good? Looking scruffy? Tell me, is this how you characterize African American civilians?"

Jake couldn't say a word. He didn't want to cause any more damage than what was already done.

"Jake," Andrew addressed him by his first name, "just two more things. Take a look at the paper in front of you," he uttered.

Jake looked at the paper.

"What does it show?" Andrew questioned.

Jake stared at Andrew before answering. "It's my police record: traffic stops, citations, the works."

"I'm assuming that paper shows the demographics of your stops, shootings, et cetera. Can you give us the demographics for both your stops and shootings? The top three will do." Andrew spoke.

"Objection. Relevance?" Anayi questioned.

"This will truly demonstrate where this officer's mentality is. As we've already come to know, he's had sixteen shootings over his brief tenure with Miami P-D."

"I'll allow it," Matthew responded.

Jake sighed. "For stops, the top demographic listed is African American, with 55%. The next is Hispanic with 28%, and the third is Asian with 10%. For shootings, the top is African American, 60%; next is Hispanic with 18%, and the third is German with 8%."

The looks towards Jake continued to be harsh.

"Quick question, where do Caucasians fall on that list?"

Jake didn't want to answer, but he knew he had to, or he would be held in contempt of court.

"Last place for both," he whispered. "Zero-point one percent."

Andrew didn't make him repeat his answer as he was truly getting disgusted by Jake. What started as a victory turned out to truly make him irate; similar to the way Brian did.

"That really says a lot," Andrew added as he took the paper from the stand and returned it to the desk. "One more question for you," Andrew turned and faced the witness stand once more.

Jake's face was as red as an apple now. He wanted nothing more than to step down.

"If I had my head in the driver's side of the vehicle that night, would you have taken a shot at me?"

"Objection, Your Honor," Anayi spoke immediately after the question was posed.

"Withdrawn," Andrew looked at Matthew and then back to Jake. "Jake, do you fear me?"

"No," Jake remarked.

Andrew smiled slightly and shook his head. "You said you pretty much feared for your life on the night you shot Mr. Farris, correct?"

"Yes."

"So, tell me. What's so different about me that doesn't bring you fear?"

Jake was silent.

"Take off this shirt, you may find tattoos underneath," Andrew started and rolled up his sleeves, revealing numerous tattoos.

The jurors murmured as Andrew gave his monologue.

"I wake up in the morning, you'll see I'm looking 'scruffy', as you put it. Riding around, I may have my music louder than the average individual. Yeah, when I'm at a cookout with my peers, you may hear explicit language and loud conversation, but that's just who we are. But just because we're black and we may show our satisfaction differently than others, one thing you can't take away from us is our education and professionalism. My blackness is part of me and defines me. And not only me, it defines every African American in this courtroom, everyone in the world, Christian Tate, Jr., as well as Marcus Farris. F-Y-I, he's running on a 4.8 scholarship to Florida's prestigious school of law," Andrew spoke. "That is, considering the gunshot you administered doesn't take it all away from him," Andrew's voice cracked, and he returned to the desk. "No further questions, Your Honor," he spoke after clearing his voice.

12

Christian entered the courthouse and walked through the metal detectors. As he was cleared for entry, he made a left down the corridor and entered the room on the right. As he entered, he saw Andrew preparing to call his first witness to the stand.

Junior turned his head as he heard the doors open. A smile immediately formed on his face. The rest of the courtroom also seemed to turn their heads. Andrew gave a slight smile and nod as he saw Christian. Matthew looked up from his desk and didn't seem amused to have the proceedings interrupted.

Keisha and Raymond made space for Christian to sit down.

Matthew cleared his throat.

"Your Honor, the defense would like to call Miss Bianca Taylor to the stand," Andrew spoke.

Bianca released Keisha's hand and walked to the stand. Junior couldn't take his eyes off her as she approached the bench. He was amazed that his girlfriend continued to support him and stood by his side amidst everything that was going on.

The court officer swore her in, and Andrew approached her.

She discreetly blew a kiss to Junior and he opened his hand and 'caught' it.

"Miss Taylor, how are you doing today?" Andrew questioned.

"Could be better, Mr. Brownstone," she spoke professionally. "Aside from everything going on, I'm doing okay," she spoke.

Bianca did her best not to pay attention to the jurors, whose stares seemed to give her chills.

"Miss Taylor, do you know the defendant, Christian Tate, Jr.?" Andrew questioned.

"Yes," Bianca answered eloquently. "He's my boyfriend."

"How long have you known him?" Andrew asked.

"I've known him for about five years," she chuckled. "he used to be this scrawny little eighth-grader. But now, he's hit the gym and has become the strong man that I know," Bianca smiled and stared dreamily at Junior.

He returned the smile.

"How long have you all been together?" Andrew walked towards the jurors.

"About three years. We were sophomores when he asked me out."

"That's a pretty long time, especially when you're young," Andrew admitted.

Bianca nodded her head in agreement.

"And, in the time that you've known him, has Christian ever exhibited any aggressive or violent behavior?"

Bianca inhaled slowly. She was nervous and it showed.

"Take your time," Andrew spoke. "I know this is hard," he sympathized.

"He's never displayed any signs of aggression towards me," she spoke.

Andrew turned slightly and saw a smirk on Anayi's face.

"So, you're suggesting he has shown aggressive behavior?" Andrew followed up. He didn't give Anayi the chance to ask the question in cross-examination.

"Christian is a gentle soul," Bianca uttered. "I wouldn't even call it aggressive behavior," she mentioned. "I would say Christian gets very passionate about certain things, and he'll debate you in a hot second if you mention something that he's passionate or sensitive about," she chuckled.

"I've never seen him in an aggressive or antagonizing manner, and I'm with him pretty often," she added.

"You say topics that he's passionate about," Andrew walked closer to the witness stand. "Can you give us any examples?"

"Well," she started, "I know you have seen the video, but an example is when he and Marcus were in the convenience store and the clerk said that Mr. Tate," she referenced Christian, "shot and killed Benjamin Smith for no reason. You all saw how he reacted."

Andrew grunted and nodded his head.

"Or, the incident the counselor was discussing previously with Robert. There was some pushing and shoving, but Junior wasn't the aggressor," she started. "Yeah, he was getting loud, but Robert pushed Junior first because he didn't like that Junior was winning their argument," she shrugged her shoulders. "I was there."

Andrew nodded his head. "We have that video in the evidence and we'll get to it soon. But, Miss Taylor, can you explain to us what happened on the night in question. We know you weren't physically there, but you were with my client that day, correct?" Andrew asked.

"Objection. Leading the witness," Anayi spoke as she wrote notes on her pad.

"I'll rephrase," Andrew remarked. "Did you see the defendant on July 20th?"

"Yes," Bianca answered.

"And when did you see him?"

"Well, me, Sierra, Marcus, and Junior got to the school around 3 to do some studying and get some work done," she responded.

"What were you all studying?" Andrew questioned.

"It was exam week," Bianca answered, "so we were studying a little bit of Physics, Social Justice, African-American history. You know, mainly classes we all shared.

"Ah okay," Andrew replied. "Go on."

"About 7:30, we started wrapping up and at about 7:45 or 8, we headed out of the school. Once we got in Junior's car, we drove and picked up food from the fast-food restaurant around my house."

"Were the four of you still together at this point?" Andrew questioned.

"Yes," Bianca replied. "Me, Sierra, Marcus, and Junior."

Andrew nodded his head.

"We got to the restaurant at about 8:15 and we got to my place at about 8:25. Sierra decided that she was going to spend the evening at my place," Bianca added. "As we said our goodbyes, I told Junior to text me so that I would know when they made it to the debate."

"Did you ever get that text?" Andrew asked.

"I got a text. It was directly from Junior," Bianca looked in the jurors' direction. "It was from his SafeZone app, stating that he'd been pulled over."

"When did you get that text?" Andrew walked towards the jurors.

Bianca shrugged slightly. "Maybe about 8:45. It wasn't long after they'd left us."

"Did you get any other texts from Christian?"

"I got one about thirty minutes later with the video attached. I guess his phone died or was turned off, so the system pushed out the message."

"Bianca," Andrew inhaled, "from what you saw in the video, what was your take?"

"Objection, Your Honor? What impact could the witness' opinion have on the facts?" Anayi pressed.

"Your Honor," Andrew responded, "Officer Whitley has a track record of harassing Mr. Tate and Officer Warren has a proven track record of pulling the trigger on African Americans."

Matthew looked at Andrew.

"The witness' opinion on the events that unfolded means *a lot* to this case."

Matthew looked sternly at Anayi.

"Overruled," he spoke. "You may answer," Matthew instructed Bianca.

"I don't know what to take away from the video," she confessed. "Everything seemed to escalate so quickly."

The jurors looked at one another and murmured.

"But one thing I did notice is that Junior didn't provoke Officer Whitley in any way. I noticed he tried to de-escalate the situation numerous times, but Officer Whitley didn't allow that to happen," Bianca paused.

"And, is this the same video that has been presented to the court?"

"Yes," she answered.

"I know the video didn't capture much with Mr. Farris' interaction, but from what you could see, what did you gather from it?" Andrew tried his luck.

"Well, as you've mentioned, I didn't really have a good angle to see the entire interaction with Officer Warren, but I know Marcus and from the way I saw him exit the vehicle with his hands up, he didn't have to be shot," her voice cracked.

"Objection!" Anayi projected.

"On what grounds?" Andrew immediately replied. "Are you telling me that this young lady doesn't have the right to voice her opinion, but Mr. Stanton and everyone else does?"

Matthew raised his head slowly and tapped his hand on the desk. Andrew could tell he was disturbed at the outburst.

Andrew cleared his throat and continued. "Miss Taylor has every right to voice her opinion, based on what she knows, and if it contributes to the case, why not? Unless there's something to hide," he glared at Anayi.

Anayi didn't reply to Andrew; instead, she looked at Matthew.

"Overruled," he spoke.

It was evident to Andrew that Matthew had listened to his outburst. Even if it was a disruption, what he said was the truth and Matthew knew that if he'd silenced Bianca, Louis' testimony wouldn't stand in the eyes of the public.

"The witness' opinion will be upheld."

Andrew nodded with success.

"You were saying, Bianca?" he spoke. He noticed Anayi slightly roll her eyes.

"Marcus nor Junior have ever been violent souls," she used a tissue to wipe her eyes. "So, when I heard the gunshot and saw him fall to the ground, myself and his girlfriend, Sierra, broke into tears."

"I'm sorry," Andrew stopped his voice from breaking. He cleared his throat. "Is Sierra in court today?" he questioned.

"She's at the hospital with his mom," she answered.

Christian whispered to Raymond and Bianca saw this, although she didn't know what they were whispering about.

"Step out and go call Natina. Let her know that I'm sending a car over to get Sierra. She's needed in court as a key witness to Marcus' trial."

Christian tapped Francesca and she followed Raymond out of the courtroom.

"Your witness," Andrew spoke and walked back to Junior.

Anayi approached Bianca slowly with a folder in her hand.

Bianca clasped her hands together tightly as Anayi pulled a piece of paper from the folder.

"Miss Taylor, what is this?" she showed her the paper.

Bianca sighed.

"It's a picture of Junior and Marcus."

"And what are they doing in the picture?" Anayi questioned.

"They're sitting on the porch of Marcus' home."

"Yes, they are," Anayi responded with sassiness in her tone.

Andrew didn't like it.

"But what are they *doing*? What can you tell us about their behavior?" Anayi questioned.

Bianca sighed heavily.

"Your Honor, we'd like the show exhibit 296.3 B to the court," Anayi spoke. She pressed a button on the remote and displayed the image on the screen.

The jurors murmured as the image appeared.

"Perhaps you couldn't really see the picture," she spoke to Bianca.

"Objection, Your Honor," Andrew objected to her comment.

"Sustained," Matthew remarked. "Keep it professional, Miss Jiménez."

Anayi nodded her head.

"What are they doing in the picture, Miss Taylor?" she questioned again.

Bianca was silent.

"It looks to me like they're sitting on the porch with their middle fingers to the camera," Anayi spoke. "I see some cards in the background and Mr. Tate and Mr. Farris both have on sleeveless t-shirts and durags."

Andrew knew what Anayi was attempting to do. Unfortunately, he knew this was coming and there was nothing he could object to; nothing that would stand, anyway.

"What are you implying?" Bianca asked Anayi.

"Well, you are advocating these young men as outstanding citizens of the community," Anayi looked at the question. "Do these look like gentle giants?"

"Objection: argumentative *and* profiling," Andrew projected and glared at Anayi. "Let's not do that," Andrew added.

Matthew glanced at Andrew and then to Anayi.

"Sustained. The jury will disregard the last statement from the prosecution.

"So, you all dug deep for that photo, huh?" Bianca chuckled.

Anayi stopped in her tracks and looked at Bianca.

"You say something, Miss Taylor?" Matthew questioned.

"That picture," she started, "it was deleted minutes after it was posted online," she remarked. "Marcus and Junior were just messing around that morning when that picture was taken." Bianca inhaled slowly. "I took the picture of them and the four of us were joking when we posted it, which is why it was removed ten minutes after it was posted."

Anayi walked back towards Bianca.

"I have thousands of pictures and posts on my page," she remarked, and over half are of Junior and Marcus doing *positive* things, yet, just like a cop, you all dig deep to find the negative images of the Black man!" she cried lightly.

Anayi chuckled but didn't say anything.

"Miss Taylor," Matthew projected in a warning tone.

"Meanwhile, when Lieutenant Tate legally defended himself against Benjamin Smith, to this day, you all find the most positive images of Benjamin to display," Bianca's face was full of tears.

Christian's eyes widened as Bianca spoke.

"Objection, Your Honor," Anayi stated with a smirk as she looked at Bianca.

"Sustained," Matthew spoke. "The jury will disregard the statement regarding Benjamin Smith." Matthew looked at Andrew. "Mr. Brownstone, you know this trial isn't relative to the shooting death of Benjamin Smith. I advise you to alert your witness and bring her up-to-speed."

"With all due respect," Andrew objected to Anayi's objection, "this case is a reciprocated replica of Benjamin's case. We keep saying that it's not, Your Honor, when in reality, that's the primary comparison. Black versus White, it's the world we live in."

Matthew raised his eyebrows at Andrew.

Anayi continued.

"You said this was uploaded to *your* profile?" Anayi questioned.

"Yes," Bianca responded, "I took the picture and was joking with Marcus and Junior."

"Is there anything that could be considered a joke in this picture?" she questioned.

"We're just teenagers having fun!" Bianca argued.

"No further questions," Anayi mentioned.

"Instead of digging deep into my Facebook page and contacting them regarding deleted pictures, why don't you look into my images that are present?"

"Your Honor," Anayi spoke as she sat.

"Like the ones of Junior helping out at the local community center," she explained. "Or the ones of Marcus volunteering to help the elderly at the nursing facility."

"I'm finished with my questioning, Your Honor," Anayi spoke once more.

The jurors all looked at Bianca. Andrew knew he had to have at least one rebuttal question.

"Miss Taylor," Andrew spoke as he rose from his chair. "Just a few more questions."

All the jurors monitored Andrew as he walked toward Bianca. Andrew knew his next question may be objected to and thrown out, but he was one that would ask the questions that no one would dare to ask.

Bianca nodded her head.

Andrew approached with his hands in his pocket and removed them. He wiped his face with the handkerchief he retrieved from his pocket and proceeded.

"Do you recognize this item?" he showed her a chain with a cross on the end of it.

"Yes," she spoke softly.

"What is it?" Andrew asked.

"Objection, Your Honor. This item hasn't been entered into evidence," Anayi spoke as she saw the chain.

"It wasn't entered, and it still isn't being entered," Andrew immediately bit back. "I'm simply asking my witness if she's ever seen it."

"Relevance?" Anayi questioned.

"How about we let her answer? And then you'll see," Andrew remarked.

Christian chuckled softly. Anayi was silent and waved Bianca on.

"It's a chain the nursing home gave to Marcus for his service and dedication," she spoke. "Junior got one just like it," she added.

Andrew nodded his head and asked his second question.

"When was the last time you saw Mr. Farris?" he asked.

"A few days ago," Bianca spoke as a few tears accumulated in her eyes.

"What did his condition appear to be?" Andrew asked.

"Objection, Your Honor."

Andrew didn't entertain her this time.

"On what grounds?" Matthew questioned.

"Still searching for the relevance," Anayi remarked.

"Well, Miss Jiménez, as Mr. Brownstone mentioned before, let's allow her to answer and we'll determine the relevance. Besides," he adjusted his glasses, "we are also trying the case of Farris versus The State of Florida. It's only right to retrieve relevant information."

Bianca answered the question. "The doctors aren't too sure of his recovery," she admitted.

There were scattered murmurs across the courtroom.

Andrew shook his head and grunted. Tears began to flow down Junior's face.

Junior grabbed a tissue and wiped his eyes.

"A generous, hardworking young man is fighting for his life. And here we are— in court trying to determine whether or not he was truly a threat to an officer who was sworn to serve and protect," Andrew looked at the jurors. "He never had any run-ins with the law; not so much as a parking ticket. Same with Mr. Tate," he added, "and you're telling me that *this* is right?" his voice cracked.

The courtroom was silent. Andrew used his handkerchief once more and wiped his eyes; he cleared his throat.

"I greatly appreciate you taking the time out to come for two reasons. One, to stand by your boyfriend; you're a true soldier," Andrew smiled, "and, two, giving us true, honest testimony about Mr. Tate and Mr. Farris. Just one more question, Miss Taylor," Andrew paced the floor. "If, and this is a big one."

Matthew looked at Andrew sternly; he was truly curious to hear what he was about to say although he didn't have a good feeling about where this was headed.

Anayi stared at Andrew and tapped her fingers lightly on the desk. She wrote notes on her notepad.

"If Marcus doesn't pull through," he addressed Marcus by his first name this time, "and that's a big if; what do you feel would be an appropriate serving of justice?"

Junior raised his eyebrows at the question. He didn't realize that Andrew was this bold, and knowing his girlfriend, he knew she would respond.

"Objection!" Anayi shouted.

"Sustained!" Matthew remarked.

Andrew nodded his head and walked back to the desk.

Bianca was silent for a few moments.

"We will no longer be silenced," she uttered.

"I beg your pardon?" Matthew questioned.

"With all due respect, if Officer Warren were Black and Marcus were White, we wouldn't even be in this courtroom today."

"That's enough, Miss Taylor," Matthew spoke.

"Give Marcus the same judgment you would give if the cop were Black and he was White. The same way you did Lieutenant Tate."

The judge pounded his gavel on the desk.

"Miss Taylor," he warned. "That's enough."

"We will not be silenced," she chanted silently. "We will not be silenced," she grew louder.

Those in favor of Junior and Marcus joined in on the chant.

Andrew and Junior looked around the courtroom and a smile formed across Junior's face.

"Free C. Tate, fry O. Jake," some of the courtroom members chanted.

"Bailiff, hold Miss Taylor in contempt," Matthew removed his glasses and spoke.

"I love you, Junior!" Bianca exclaimed.

"I love you, more," Junior replied with tears running down his face.

Andrew stood erect and the court officer removed her from the stand. As the officer escorted Bianca to the holding cell, Matthew desperately tried to bring the courtroom to order.

"Get her out," Junior whispered to Andrew. "I don't want her serving any time for this shit."

"I got you," Andrew spoke. "She won't spend a minute in jail."

"Order in this courtroom!" Matthew shouted and the chants and cheers seemed to silence. The jeers also seemed to silence.

The door opened and Raymond reentered the courtroom with Francesca.

"I'm glad you all stepped out," Christian spoke as Raymond returned.

"Why?" Raymond questioned.

"Where's Bianca?" Francesca inquired.

"In a holding cell," Christian spoke. "She spoke out against the blatant racism. She stood tall for both Junior and Marcus. I think what set the judge off," Christian adjusted his tie, "was that she called out the fact that if the roles were reversed and Marcus was a white boy and Jake was black, Jake would have been in jail." Christian relived his trial, mentally. "And then you have supporters in the courtroom that chanted with her 'we will not be silenced', whereas some took it as far to chant 'free C. Tate., fry O. Jake'," Christian chuckled. "It was crazy in here, man."

Raymond scoffed. "So, he held her in contempt for the truth."

"Nah, he can't hold her. Not if I have anything to say about it and I know Andrew will not let her stay," Christian whispered. "Did you all get in touch with Natina and Sierra?"

"She's en route, now," Francesca spoke. "The officer that picked her up is about ten minutes out."

Christian nodded his head and leaned forward. He whispered to Andrew and sat back in the chair.

"Mr. Brownstone, do I dare ask you to call another witness?"

Andrew smirked. "Yes, Your Honor," he replied. "The defense calls Sergeant Francesca Gaines to the stand."

Francesca approached the stand slowly and held her head high. She took her seat in the witness box.

Andrew approached her after she was sworn in.

"Hello, Sergeant Gaines," he greeted her.

"Attorney Brownstone," she nodded her head.

"I, for one, am really grateful you took time away from the office and your race to be here to speak with us today."

"It's my moral obligation," she replied. "I've known Mr. Tate and Mr. Farris since they were born. What kind of woman would I be to not be here for two great young men in their time of need?"

Andrew nodded his head.

"Officer Whitley is part of your unit, correct?" Andrew asked.

"Objection. Leading the witness," Anayi spoke.

"I'll rephrase. Is Officer Whitley one of the many officers that reports to you?" Andrew questioned.

Francesca looked in Brian's direction.

"Officer Whitley is one of the officers in my unit, yes," Francesca spoke clearly. "He reports to me, as well as Officer Montrose, Officer Warren, and Officer Lawrence." She shook her head slightly.

Andrew glanced at the jurors and did his best to study their faces to determine the direction the case was headed.

"Sergeant Gaines, do you remember the incident where Mr. Tate and Mr. Farris were involved in a traffic stop with Officer Whitley and Officer Montrose?"

"Yes," Francesca answered.

"What can you tell us about what unfolded the following day? Did the officers bring the stop to your attention, considering the location of the stop and the time?"

"The day following the stop," Francesca spoke sternly, "Neither Officer Whitley nor did Officer Montrose announce the stop to Lieutenant Tate or me."

"So, what happened on the day following the stop?" Andrew inquired. "And how did he know about the stop?"

Andrew wanted to eliminate most of the questions that he knew Anayi would ask at cross.

"Christian informed Lieutenant Tate that he was stopped by an officer on the way to the celebratory dinner. He informed his father of the infraction that he was accused of and gave him the name of the stopping officer," she looked at Junior. "The day following the stop, Lieutenant Tate took a look at the traffic cameras and logs to determine if it was a legal and lawful stop."

Andrew interlocked his fingers as she paused.

"What was discovered upon reviewing the cameras and the logs?" he asked.

"The cameras revealed that there was no infraction made. Officer Whitley stated that Mr. Tate didn't come to a complete stop at an intersection monitored by a red-light camera. If this were the case," Francesca uttered, "the camera would have taken a picture of the violator's license plate and recorded video of the infraction."

"And this wasn't the case," Andrew answered.

"Lieutenant Tate and I took it a step further to also review the camera; perhaps, it didn't capture the violator. Well, we did see Christian's vehicle approach the traffic signal at the time reported, but his vehicle came to a complete stop before proceeding to turn right on red."

"What happened as a result?" Andrew inquired.

Brian did his best to avoid eye contact with Francesca; he kept his head down.

"Lieutenant Tate and I confronted Officer Whitley and Officer Montrose about the infraction and let them know their stop was unlawful and illegal. Not because the stop was against Lieutenant Tate's son, but what if the stop were against someone else and they decided to sue the police department for the stop?" Francesca shook her head. "No citations were issued, and the stop wasn't logged. So, if someone were to try to take the department to court, they would have an easy win."

"Which, in turn, wouldn't look good on your end."

"Correct," Francesca added.

***

"And, Miss Flemming, if you were forced to give your boyfriend a final message," Andrew spoke slowly to Sierra, what would you tell him?"

Sierra cried softly. Andrew could see the female jurors get emotional in seeing this.

"I would just tell him that I love him. You know?" Sierra looked around the courtroom and her eyes landed on Christian and Raymond. Sierra saw the tears in Raymond's eyes. "I know he didn't mean to put himself in this position. All his life, he's been raised to respect the law and to obey what he was told, but he was always told to be careful because he was a Black man in America."

Andrew anxiously awaited an objection for Sierra's remark. However, there was none.

"He wouldn't do anything to jeopardize his life and leave his family and friends behind," Sierra continued. "And the thing with Marcus is that he's one of the kindest souls you will ever get to meet. He wouldn't hurt a fly, and so to think of him complying with orders given by law enforcement and still being gunned down is truly unbelievable," she cried harder.

Andrew passed her a box of Kleenex and she pulled a piece out. She wiped her eyes.

"I'm certain he knows how blessed he is to have you in his corner, as well as friends like Christian, Bianca, and a slew of family and friends."

Andrew looked at Junior and smiled.

"Your witness," he spoke aloud as he returned to the desk.

"Miss Flemming, I don't have much for you," Anayi spoke, "but the court needs to know, outside of school and being romantic towards you, what was your boyfriend really like?"

Sierra took offense to this question. She and Bianca were just alike in their attitude, so she replied with sass.

"You mean what was he like outside of helping others and having a contributing heart?"

Anayi stared at Sierra. Sierra returned the glare.

"Or do you want me to say he was defensive and held his own, huh?" Sierra kept a frown on her face. "Does that fit the image of the Black man that you're looking to portray?"

Anayi smirked at Sierra as she defended Marcus.

"Marcus is indeed a protector and he will defend himself if needed, but one thing I saw in the videos was that he didn't even have a chance to talk the situation down. The officer instructed him to slowly back out of the vehicle with his hands up. Marcus did that, and they still shot him down like a wild animal!" Sierra exclaimed.

Anayi's smirk left her face.

"I have nothing else for this witness," she spoke to Matthew.

Andrew decided to test the waters again.

He rose to his feet and approached Sierra.

"Miss Flemming just answer a question for me," he spoke slowly.

She nodded her head.

"Do you think Christian Tate shooting Officer Whitley was intentional?"

"No," she immediately responded.

"Why do you say that?" Andrew asked.

"If Christian intended to harm Officer Whitley, Officer Whitley wouldn't be here today, and Christian wouldn't have administered aid."

Andrew paced the floor. "I know how you feel about Marcus and the shooting, so it's redundant to ask you about that," he shook his head. "But," he continued, "I want to know what you think should happen as a result of the shooting?"

"Objection, Your Honor," Anayi objected.

"No question: lock him up! Lock him up along with any other officers involved," Sierra remarked. She didn't wait for Matthew to either confirm or deny the objection.

The jurors looked at one another. Andrew could tell they were slightly confused at what to do and how to potentially rule.

Andrew didn't press harder. He had to get Bianca out of the holding cell and didn't want to make it harder.

He motioned his hands in a way to tell Sierra to calm down.

"Miss Flemming," Matthew spoke sternly. "Don't make me throw you in a cell," he warned. He looked at the jury. "The jury will disregard the last question and answer from Attorney Brownstone and Miss Flemming. Mr. Brownstone," he looked at Andrew, "you already tried this once; let's not do it again."

A few seconds later, Andrew proceeded. "Thank you, Sierra," he spoke. "No further questions, Your Honor."

He returned to the desk and sat near Junior.

"Your Honor, we have a few more witnesses," Andrew spoke as Sierra returned to the seat next to Raymond, "but we're requesting that the court recess for the day and we go through the remaining witnesses tomorrow."

Matthew looked at the clock on the wall.

"Motion granted," he uttered. "Court will adjourn for the day and will recommence tomorrow with the defense calling their next witness."

Matthew hit his gavel and the courtroom congregation rose to their feet.

Junior watched Matthew as he left the bench and entered his chambers.

"We're in the home stretch," Andrew spoke to Junior.

"Get my girl out of jail," Junior chuckled. "I know where my focus should be, but she can't be in there."

"The judge probably just wants an apology," Andrew remarked. "This won't stick. But I'm going to get her out, no worries, man."

Christian walked to the gate and spoke to Junior. "Tomorrow, me, you, and your mom will be taking the stand to testify," he spoke softly.

"Add Raymond and Natina to that list," Andrew remarked. "You each are going to be speaking on both cases."

"And don't worry," he laughed. "Bianca isn't going to sit in jail at all. This judge likes to scare people, especially for their first offense; and all she did was speak out. She's not going anywhere," Christian assured Junior.

Junior smiled at his father.

"I love you, Pops," he uttered.

The court officer approached and touched Junior's arm.

"I love you, too. Keep your head up, son."

"I love you, baby" Keisha spoke as tears flowed down her face.

"I love you, Mom," Junior blew her a kiss.

The officer escorted Junior away and Christian looked at Andrew. Christian shook Andrew's hand.

"Thank you, man," he started. "For everything."

"Hey man, we're not out of the woods yet," he reminded him. "Meet me at the prison in about four hours with Keisha. I'm going to head over to the hospital to speak with Natina and Raymond regarding tomorrow; make sure they know the direction of everything."

"You know Natina's not going to leave Marcus' side," Christian spoke.

"Yeah, I'm going to speak with the judge and get her to Skype in," Andrew grabbed the briefcase in one hand.

Raymond, Francesca, and Sierra headed for the exit after Andrew motioned for them to exit. He, Christian, and Keisha followed.

"You know Anayi is going to be crossing hard as hell," Andrew continued as they walked to the exit of the courthouse. "So, we have to be on top of our game. The jury's makeup is horrible in terms of playing in our favor, so we need to jerk at the women's emotions."

Christian looked at him sternly.

"Hey, man," Andrew remarked, "Black, White, Asian, Hispanic — all women have the same emotions and the same triggers." Andrew pulled his keys from his pocket. "Leave it up to me."

Christian and Andrew shook hands.

Andrew looked at Raymond.

"I'm going to trail you to the hospital," he informed him. "Make sure you guys are ready for tomorrow."

"Sounds good," Raymond replied.

■■■

Junior entered the foyer and sat at the table while twiddling his thumbs. He saw how quickly the case was wrapping up, and while he felt they were in a pretty solid position to win the case, he remembered his father was in a similar position.

Kanaan approached Junior and sat across from him.

"How are things going?" he questioned.

"Pretty fair for a square," Junior responded as he looked at the clock on the wall. "I don't know where this shit is headed," Junior admitted.

"Man, in times like this, you have to control the outcome. I've been seeing the case on TV and it seems like your lawyer is doing a hell-of-a job."

Junior smiled. "Yeah, I'll admit, he's witty. But I can't read these jurors and that's where my fate lies: in the hands of 8 women and 4 men. Only two of which are Black." Junior shook his head.

"What is your lawyer saying?" Kanaan pulled a blunt from his pocket.

"He's prepping to question my boy's people and my parents tomorrow in court, but he isn't sure the direction either. Remember, he's working two cases at once."

Kanaan licked the rolling paper. "Shit's gonna work itself out; trust me."

Tim approached the table.

"Look alive," Kanaan spoke as he put the unlit blunt in his mouth.

Junior looked up and saw Tim approaching them. His heart started to beat faster.

Tim smirked as he sat across from the two.

"I've come alone," he said. "The only thing we can truly give someone is information so listen and listen good," he cleared his throat.

Junior didn't remove his disapproving look from his face. He was curious to what Tim had to say but didn't want to just sit around and wait for something to go down.

"I know a number of the inmates who all want to see you go down; I and my crew included."

"Haven't we been through this shit?" Junior questioned. "If you wanna rumble, we can go one-on-one right now."

Tim looked at Junior and then to Kanaan. "Nah, not today youngin'. I don't want to have to teach you some manners today," he chuckled.

"You can try," Junior remarked. "I'm not tripping on you or your weak-ass crew."

Tim glared at Junior and then at Kanaan.

Kanaan shrugged his shoulders.

"He has a mind of his own. I'm not quite sure why you're looking at me."

Kanaan noticed one of Tim's crew members lurking in the background. Junior saw the member and commented.

"I thought you were alone," he chuckled. "You brought backup, huh?"

Tim chuckled and looked Junior in the eyes.

"You know what, nigger?" Tim snarled, "you deserve to be in here with the rest of us and I hope they give your Black ass capital punishment."

Junior knew these remarks would come from many of the inmates. He resisted the urge to attack Tim.

"And your wanna-be governor daddy and that pretty little girlfriend of yours."

A stern look crossed Junior's face.

"And ya' fine ass mama. Ooh wee," Tim taunted. "I got people on the outside that are keeping an eye on all of them." Tim extended his arm towards Junior.

"Don't fucking touch me," Junior warned.

Tim laughed.

"Did I strike a nerve?" Tim flipped Junior's chin with his finger.

As Tim finished his statement, Junior's fist connected with his mouth.

"Son of a bitch!" Junior shouted and lunged at Tim.

Junior unleashed a series of punches across Tim's face. Kanaan ran over to pull Junior off.

Tim's crew ran over to help him, who was getting a beating from Junior.

"Bitch ass cracker," Junior spoke as he continued to punch Tim. Junior didn't allow Tim to even try to defend himself. "Don't threaten a man's family."

Kanaan saw the crew and left Junior to fight Tim.

"Saddle up!" Kanaan shouted as he looked at Tim's crew approaching.

Kanaan's crew members ran over, and they all started brawling on the prison floor.

"Say that shit again," Junior remarked as he hit Tim.

Tim discreetly reached in his pocket and pulled out a shank. He inserted it into Junior's thigh and Junior screamed in pain.

Kanaan looked over and saw Junior in pain and released the chokehold on the member he was fighting.

The alarm in the prison rang out and Kanaan ran over to Junior. He kicked Tim in the face and pulled Junior away from the brawl. Kanaan tied the tourniquet tightly around Junior's leg, leaving the shank intact.

"I got you, man," he uttered.

Prison guards ran in with weapons aimed.

"Get the fuck on the ground, now!" they demanded.

Everyone stopped fighting in what seemed to be an instant and everyone but Tim, Kanaan, and Junior laid on their stomachs with their hands behind their heads.

Junior inhaled sharply as a guard approached the two of them with a weapon aimed.

"Why am I not surprised to see you involved with this shit?" the guard commented.

Junior glared at the guard and shook his head.

"Get a medic over here for Tate," the guard called.

Junior couldn't believe what had unfolded and how quickly things went down. What made it worse, is that he didn't know the impact this would have on his case. Junior wondered how his folks would react once they found out.

Kanaan could see Junior was in deep thought.

"Hey," he spoke to Junior to bring him out of his trance. "No matter what happens, I got you, bro," he uttered.

Junior shook his head slightly.

"I'm sorry, Pops," he uttered softly.

***

"What the hell happened?" Andrew sat across from Junior.

Junior rubbed his leg and sat. "Guy named Tim." Junior winced silently. "I was chatting with my guy Kanaan when he came over to me."

Andrew glanced at Junior's leg as they spoke.

"His verbal threats turned physical and I defended myself. We all got to throwing hands and shit popped off from there," Junior finished.

Andrew sat quietly for a moment before speaking.

"How bad is it?" he referred to the cut.

"Got me limpin'," Junior chuckled. "But it's nothing I can't handle." Junior rubbed his leg. "I'm just wondering the effect this will have on my case."

Andrew looked at his notepad and wrote a few things down.

"You said he threatened you physically, correct?" Andrew carefully questioned while nodding his head.

"Yes," Junior caught on to what he was doing.

"And you felt that you had no choice but to defend yourself?"

"Yes," Junior spoke. "Not only for myself but for my family as well," he added.

"Then, that's our defense," Andrew spoke. "I'll handle the leg work from here," Andrew noticed his poorly timed figure-of-speech. "No pun intended."

Junior slightly rolled his eyes.

"Hey," Andrew instructed, "no more fights, you hear me?"

"I'll do my best," Junior chuckled.

Andrew rose to his feet and the guards approached. The guards escorted Junior back to his cell.

13

"Mrs. Farris, how is Marcus doing?" Andrew asked over Skype.

There was a slight delay due to latency, but the jury could still understand her.

"He's not doing too well," Natina cried softly.

The jurors saw the tears in her eyes and the women all sniffled. Andrew noticed this but didn't divert his attention to it.

"The doctors aren't too sure of his chances at recovery."

"I'm sorry," Andrew truly felt saddened at hearing this. They didn't go over her reporting the doctors' exact prognosis, but hearing it tugged at his emotions. Andrew cleared his throat. "How are you doing?" he added.

"The same as any mother in my position," Natina chuckled awkwardly. "The fact that I may lose my son has me in shambles."

Andrew nodded his head and walked near the jurors.

"Mrs. Farris, we're not going to take too much of your time. But can you describe your son?"

She sniffled and blew her nose. Natina sighed and spoke.

"My son is a remarkable young man," she paused briefly. "Always willing to lend a helping hand; one of the kindest souls you'll ever meet; extremely bright. I could go on-and-on," Natina responded.

Andrew smiled as Natina bragged on Marcus. "Tell us about his schooling. Was he ever in trouble, how were his grades? Things like that."

"Marcus' GPA is nearly a 5.0; similar to Christian's. He's not a bad student," she continued. "Every time I went to the school, there was nothing but praise given by his teachers."

"Any suspensions? Detentions?" he knew Anayi would question this.

"For the typical," Natina began. "A few tardies that landed him in detention a few times. But nothing for anything behavioral."

"And Mrs. Farris, what about extracurriculars? What are those like for Marcus?"

"He's not a baller like Christian," she smiled and chuckled as she saw him on the camera, "but he excels in his studies. He landed a scholarship to Stetson and he has big plans for the future."

"Now, Mrs. Farris, naturally, as his mother, you're going to have positive things to say about your son, especially in a case like this. But tell the court what was going through your mind as you saw the video of Officer Warren shooting your son."

Anayi wanted to object, but she didn't have anything that would stick.

Natina cleared her throat. "When I got the call that Marcus was shot, my heart dropped, and I fell to the floor."

The jurors could hear her voice cracking and they all, especially the female jurors, sympathized with her.

"When my husband called and informed me of what happened, he said he'd arranged for an officer to come and pick me up from the house to bring me to the hospital," Natina sniffled once more. "That was the longest ten minutes of my life. When I got to the hospital, my husband showed me the video from Christian's phone," a few tears fell from Natina's eyes. "My son didn't deserve to be treated like that. He complied with Officer Warren's orders to the tee. He slowly backed out of the vehicle with his hands in the air and the moment Warren saw the chance, he shot my son like a dog!" Natina howled.

"Objection, Your Honor," Anayi remarked.

"Why? It's the truth," Natina bit back.

Matthew hit his gavel on the stand. "Order in the court."

Natina and Anayi ceased their words and he continued.

"On what grounds do you object?"

Anayi didn't have a reply. She was merely stunned at the fact that Natina criticized her client and the judge didn't personally object to it.

Matthew raised his eyebrows at Anayi. "Proceed, Mr. Brownstone."

Andrew nodded his head. "Words directly from a mother," he spoke to the jury. "No mother should ever go through what you're going through," he looked at Natina. "No further questions, Your Honor."

Anayi approached the stand and positioned herself in front of the camera.

"Mrs. Farris," she began, "I don't have much to ask of you," Anayi uttered. "Your son is in the hospital and I'm sure you would rather be with him as opposed to in a separate room answering questions for a case."

"Thank you for your concern and condolences," Natina remarked.

"Mrs. Farris, what was your son involved in outside of school? Any gangs or criminal organizations?"

Although Andrew wished to object, he wanted Anayi to dig herself into a hole.

"What kind of question is that?!" Natina asked. "He's a senior in high school with a 4.8 GPA!" she spoke, offended. "He's got a scholarship to one of Florida's most prestigious law schools."

"All I'm doing is asking a question," Anayi interrupted.

"By profiling my son?" Natina bit.

Anayi raised her eyebrow.

"I've been watching the case," Natina spoke. "And you have been doing whatever it takes to paint Christian and Marcus to be the bad guys," Natina cleared her throat. "Digging up five-year-old deleted pictures and such, but in the same breath—"

"Objection, Your Honor," Anayi spoke. "Please have the witness answer the question."

Natina gave attitude.

"No," she remarked. She didn't wait for Matthew to respond. "My brilliant son was not involved in any criminal activity. He assisted the elderly; cared for the community; provided guidance for the youth," she said.

"Sounds like an angel," Anayi responded.

"Objection, Your Honor," Andrew spoke.

"Sustained," Matthew replied. "Careful, Miss Jiménez," he warned.

"Mrs. Farris," Anayi spoke again after nodding her head to Matthew, "your son was pulled over months earlier by Officer Whitley. Were you aware of this?"

"Yes," Natina spoke. "My son and Christian were stopped by Officer Whitley in a supposed traffic violation. However," Natina added, "no citations were issued, and no infractions were committed."

"How do you know this?" Anayi questioned.

"On the following day, Lieutenant Tate reviewed the logs and cameras and verified this," Natina answered. "This has got to stop," she added.

"What has to stop?" Anayi asked.

"This profiling and injustice across America. It's not right and it isn't fair."

"Your son committed a crime," Anayi bit back. "Officer Warren took the actions he was trained to take in those situations."

"A crime?" Natina questioned. "He was riding alongside his best friend, and they were on their way to Lieutenant Tate's gubernatorial debate! Where's the crime in that?" she shook her head.

"He was given an order by an officer of the law!" Anayi remarked. "The initial officer suspected them of drinking and reckless driving; there may have also been drugs in the vehicle."

"Were drugs found?" Natina questioned. "Hmm? Were my boys given a sobriety test if this was a suspicion? No," she continued. "They were profiled for *DWB* in America."

"DWB?" Anayi questioned.

"Driving while black," Natina finished.

Anayi chuckled softly and walked towards the jury box. "Mrs. Farris, if you were overseeing this case, what would your stance be? What would you do to rectify this?"

Anayi knew this question may have been off the mark, but she wanted to see how far Natina would go before cracking.

"I'll do whatever it takes to bring justice to the man who shot my baby boy," Natina remarked.

Anayi had Natina right where she wanted her and got the reply she was aiming for.

"Body-camera footage shows that your son had an unidentifiable object in his hand, which led to the officer firing his weapon."

"I know," Natina started. "He was 'fearing for his life'," she rolled her eyes.

"Objection, Your Honor," Andrew saw where this was headed and wanted to stop Natina before she said something detrimental.

"You're objecting to your witness' answer?" Matthew questioned.

"I'm objecting to this line of cross," Andrew clarified. "Where is this going?"

"Where is this going?" Anayi questioned with a chuckle. "Your Honor, this witness said she would do anything to bring justice to the man who, and I quote, shot her son like a dog."

Matthew looked at Andrew.

"Would she be willing to perjure herself and or others to do this?" Anayi questioned as she looked at the jury members.

"Objection!" Andrew rebutted.

"Withdrawn," Anayi immediately replied. "No further questions, Your Honor." Anayi returned to her desk.

Andrew looked at the camera and nodded his head at Natina.

"Mrs. Farris, this court greatly appreciates you taking the time to speak with us regarding your son and Mr. Tate," Matthew spoke gruffly. "Our prayers are with you."

"Mmhmm," Natina spoke. "Have a nice day," a few tears welled in her eyes.

Andrew and the jurors noticed this as she closed her computer. Andrew cleared his throat and rose to his feet.

He walked in the direction of the judge's desk before speaking.

"Your Honor, the defense calls Raymond Farris to the stand."

Raymond rose to his feet and approached the stand. He made eye contact with Junior and smiled.

Junior slightly nodded his head and returned the smile as he watched the jurors keep their eyes on Raymond. There were a few looks of panic and shock as he approached the stand. Andrew noticed the looks on the juror's faces.

Andrew walked to the stand once Raymond sat and was sworn in by the bailiff. Andrew rolled his sleeves and inhaled sharply; Raymond followed suit in terms of rolling his sleeves.

"Mr. Farris, I know that your blood has been boiling as you've literally come to this courtroom day in and day out of these trials."

"Objection, Your Honor," Anayi interjected.

"Mr. Brownstone, are you making a mockery out of these trials?"

Andrew glared at Matthew.

***

Christian adjusted his tie as he sat on the witness stand.

"Should I call you Lieutenant Tate?" Andrew questioned. "Governor-elect Tate? Mr. Tate?" he chuckled.

Christian chuckled and Junior smiled. "Lieutenant Tate will do," he answered. "And that's *only* to differentiate between myself and my son."

Andrew paced the floor slowly.

"I'm a father before anything. Ensuring that my son has a fair chance and trial is what matters the most to me."

Christian had to ensure that the jury saw him as a father; not just a political figure or law enforcement personnel.

"Lieutenant Tate, let's take it back to the beginning," Andrew recited. "Your son and Officer Whitley have history, am I correct?"

"Objection, Your Honor," Anayi interjected. She knew she wouldn't be able to do much of this; knowing Christian, he could stand for himself. "Leading the witness."

"I'll rephrase," Andrew replied. "Is it true that your son has a history with the police?"

"Yes," Christian spoke firmly. "And it's not because he's my son," Christian added.

"Can you elaborate on that statement?" Andrew questioned.

Christian nodded his head.

"Christian has had several run-ins with Officer Brian Whitley; this traces back years."

"Earlier in the trial, it has been reported by many witnesses from both the defense and prosecution, that Officer Whitley pulled Christian over for allegedly failing to stop before executing a right turn at a red light."

"This is true. It was immediately following his championship basketball game."

"During this stop, there were words exchanged between Officer Whitley, Officer Montrose, Christian Tate, and Marcus Farris."

"Christian and Marcus spoke to the officers with respect and class," Christian added.

"Objection: speculation," Anayi spewed. "The witness' opinion on the conversation is biased and shouldn't be admissible."

"Your Honor," Christian spoke, "there's bodycam footage that verifies my statements. This footage covers audio and video."

Andrew didn't utter a word. He didn't expect Christian to reply, but he knew this case was personal to him.

"Mr. Brownstone," Matthew disregarded Christian. "Please advise your witness that any potential evidence must be submitted through the defense and prosecution."

"I'm right here," Christian spoke with offense. "With all due respect, Your Honor, you can speak directly to me. After serving over twenty years for my city, I deserve a bit more respect than what you're giving me."

Matthew glared at Christian and Christian returned the stare.

Andrew cleared his throat. "Lieutenant Tate, I'm assuming you've seen this footage. When Officer Whitley engaged with your son after his championship game, what was the conversation like?"

"Immediately after Officer Whitley engaged with my son and Marcus Farris, Christian and Marcus drove to the restaurant for the celebratory dinner," Christian made eye contact with Brian. "The next day, I reviewed the logs and security footage. I can't give you word-for-word," Christian admitted, "but the conversation was more along the lines of 'I don't care whose son you are, you can't do whatever you want,'" Christian adjusted his seating. "The court heard it; rewatch the tapes."

Junior looked at his father with a serious expression. He tried his hardest not to show any expressions; he knew that this deep in the trial, all eyes would be watching him.

"But I can assure you that after reviewing the bodycam footage and the logs, as well as the traffic camera footage, no infraction was committed. No citations were issued, no tickets; nothing."

"In your expertise," Andrew chose his words carefully, "was this an unlawful stop?"

"Yes," Christian replied. "Had this been another offender, the entire department would have been sued and would have lost the case," Christian shook his head.

Andrew stood near the jury box.

"Tell us about the stop that has us all in court today," Andrew switched angles.

Anayi took notes.

Christian cleared his throat; he choked every time he had to mention what happened that evening.

"I was at the gubernatorial debate; my son and Marcus were in school doing some studying for their upcoming finals. I saw the footage once I got off the stage."

"Where did you see the footage?" Andrew questioned.

"It was sent to my phone from SafeZone," Christian answered. "Rather than two officers patrolling, which is the routine way of doing things, particularly at night," Christian slightly rolled his eyes at Brian, "only Officer Whitley was present."

Junior silently cleared his throat as his mind raced.

"The first thing I noticed was the approach that Officer Whitley took in apprehending Christian and Marcus. It was very confrontational. Christian was very mild-mannered and even used terms such as 'yes sir' and 'no sir', which we all saw on the video shown earlier." Anger was building within Christian as he spoke, and he refrained from showing it.

"Officer Whitley then insinuated that Tate and Farris had possession of an illegal substance, but played it off," Christian chuckled. "Do I have to retell this story?" he asked Andrew.

"We've all seen the tape, Lieutenant Tate. I think what I'm looking for is your expertise on what happened," Andrew slightly nodded his head.

"Once Officer Whitley pulled Tate from the vehicle, he was not within his rights to make him put his hands on the heated hood. This isn't taught or practiced in the academy or training. He had no right to get as disruptive as he did," Christian uttered. "Shouting obscenities at these two gentlemen when all they did was comply with every command he gave. He slammed Tate on the ground, for God's sake, when, in no way, did Christian resist." Christian looked around the courtroom and then to the members of the jury.

Andrew stood in front of Christian.

"Tate and Whitley wrestled for the weapon. The same way officers fear for their lives, so do civilians," Christian spoke.

Anayi smirked as Christian spoke but didn't object.

"And this is coming from a lieutenant," Christian continued. "We're trained to de-escalate a situation, not to stimulate it. As Tate and Whitley wrestled and the first shot rang out, that should have been the end of it. Whitley, instead, lunged at Tate. With fear already in his eyes, he fired the weapon again, striking Whitley in the right side of his chest."

Christian teared slightly and cleared his throat.

"Had this been an intentional act, Tate wouldn't have remained on the scene and he wouldn't have administered aid."

Andrew played devil's advocate.

"But the prosecution would argue that because that's your son and his fear of daddy, he wouldn't have run regardless."

"Let's try the fact that he's a well-rounded individual who has morals," Christian spoke.

Andrew smiled slightly but quickly recomposed himself.

"Lieutenant Tate, can you let us know your thoughts on the shooting of Marcus Farris?"

"It was absolutely unwarranted," Christian spoke.

"Objection, Your Honor," Anayi said. "The witness has a close relationship with both Christian Tate, Jr. as well as Marcus Farris. Naturally, he's going to say the shooting was unjustified."

"Miss Jiménez," Andrew responded to her interjection, "why don't we let Lieutenant Tate who has well over twenty years protecting and serving this city, give his opinion on the matter? I think he's earned that right."

Anayi sifted through her notes and Christian continued.

"Once Officer Warren announced his presence police, Farris slowly backed out of the vehicle with both hands raised. As an officer," Christian spoke to the jury, "I wouldn't have fired my weapon. Correction," he rectified, "as a *trained* officer," he looked towards Jake, "I would have taken extra precautions to ensure I wouldn't have had to discharge my weapon."

"The prosecution states that Officer Warren feared for his life," Andrew responded. "Was he not warranted to use his weapon in this case?" he asked Christian.

Christian didn't hesitate. "The officer's job in a case where they fear for their lives is to make the best judgment call," he carefully answered. "I'm not going to debate what Officer Warren stated, but being a part of my unit, I know we aren't trained to shoot first. And if we do shoot, the objective is to disorient the suspect, not kill them unless they prove to be a threat."

Anayi studied Christian's body language as he spoke, and she could see how this was bothering him. She jotted down notes.

"Lieutenant Tate, many people are eyeing you on this case for many reasons," Andrew listed. "One, one of the offenders is your son." Junior held his head high as Andrew listed the reasons. "Two, the responding officers are part of your unit;" Jake and Brian looked at each other and did their best to avoid eye contact with their superior. "Three, you are running for governor alongside Sergeant Francesca Gaines;" Francesca ensured she was sitting erect. "Four, you are running against Bernard Smith. And finally," Andrew adjusted his tie. "This trial is eerily similar to your case roughly twenty years back."

"Objection, Your Honor," Anayi opposed. "Is there a question here?"

"I agree, Mr. Brownstone," Matthew observed. "Get to the point."

Andrew felt the tension from Matthew and Anayi, as well as everyone in the courtroom. Rather than show it, he continued.

"Lieutenant Tate," he spoke again, "one question. Do you feel that the aforementioned reasonings are purely coincidental?"

Christian cleared his throat.

"Can you elaborate?" he asked Andrew.

"Well, there has truly been a lot of talk that this is all a ploy for you to win the gubernatorial race and after the race, you'll use your newfound powers for evil. Conspiracy theories, if you will," Andrew continued.

Christian chuckled.

"My previous trial, the fact that the officers involved are part of my unit, the fact that Christian Tate, Jr. is my son, and the completely coincidental fact that I'm running against the father of the young man I shot, has nothing to do with my run."

"Objection," Anayi interjected.

Christian didn't stop. "I became an officer to enforce the law and bring change, which is literally the same reason I am running for governor. This whole country needs change, to be fair, but since changing the country is out of the question, at least I can begin with this state." Christian shook his head.

"Your Honor," Anayi warned.

"Lieutenant…" Matthew began.

"No, this courtroom needs to hear this," Christian spoke directly to the judge. He glared at Anayi.

Anayi was speechless. She wanted to interject again and wondered why Matthew wasn't taking control.

Andrew knew where Christian was going but didn't interrupt him. This case was bogus and who better to express that than the officer who'd been in a similar situation.

"This may affect my run right now, but I'm talking to you as a father. Not as a cop, not as a candidate," Christian addressed the jury. "During my trial, roughly twenty years back, I was facing a similar jury. None of which looked like me," Christian shook his head. "I shot a White boy who pulled a gun out on me, and I was thrown under the bus; no questions asked. Although a weapon was retrieved from the scene and all the evidence proved my statements, the court found me guilty."

"Objection, Your Honor!" Anayi insisted.

"Lieutenant Tate, that's enough," Matthew asserted. "This case isn't about your trial against Benjamin Smith. Might I add, you were acquitted of those charges."

"Your Honor, you say it's not, but it truly is," Christian continued. "When the spotlight was on me: a Black man for shooting and killing a White teenager, it was considered to be a crime; although I administered aid and evidence proved my statement. Yet, Officer Whitley has a history of harassing my son, and the video shows police brutality, but my son is accused of trying to murder Whitley." Christian shook his head.

The courtroom was silent. Keisha shed a tear and Junior was smiling on the inside that his father was speaking on his behalf.

"Same with Officer Warren: this prosecution is swearing up and down he was justified in shooting Marcus Farris because he thought Marcus had a weapon. Your Honor, no weapon was retrieved from the scene. It was a cell-phone."

"Enough, Lieutenant Tate!" Matthew spoke again.

"American hypocrisy!" he jeered. "But I digress." Christian looked at Andrew. "Are we finished?" He wanted nothing more than to get off the stand and walk over to embrace his son; he knew the latter was out of the question.

Andrew nodded his head. "No further questions, Your Honor."

Andrew returned to the defense's desk and Anayi approached the desk.

"Quite a show you just put on," she commented.

"Ms. Jiménez," Matthew warned.

Anayi smirked.

"Lieutenant Tate, I really don't have much to ask or address; you've said a mouthful," she responded. "But there are a few things I would like for you to elaborate on." Anayi wanted to push Christian's buttons and knew exactly how to corner him.

"I'm prepared to answer whatever you have for me," he replied.

Anayi smirked slightly.

"I would like to ask you about the shooting," she remarked. "You say Officer Jake Warren was unwarranted in shooting Marcus Farris." She knew her next statements could be detrimental, but if her plan was successful, she could taint Christian's reputation and win the case. "It's been reported that Officer Warren is, and I quote, 'trigger happy'. What's your take on this?"

Christian saw what she was doing. He smiled and nodded.

"Officer Warren has made quite a few mistakes during his tenure, and he's been reprimanded per mistake. He was put under my supervision because of his numerous infractions."

"How many of his shootings were under your supervision?" Anayi questioned. She was insisting on applying pressure as she recognized this was a sensitive topic for Christian, based on his body language during Andrew's questioning.

"Two," Christian answered.

"Two," Anayi repeated. She didn't pace the floor or walk towards the jury. She looked at the congregation and continued speaking. "Is that including the Farris shooting?" She also recognized that mentioning Marcus would strike a nerve.

"Was he under my supervision at the time of the shooting?" Christian questioned with attitude.

Anayi chuckled.

"Your Honor, please advise the witness to answer the question," she remarked.

"Lieutenant Tate, answer the question," Matthew remarked.

Christian sighed quietly. "It's two including the Farris shooting," he responded. "Two out of his sixteen shootings were under my watch."

"Thank you," Anayi spoke facetiously with a smirk. "I think that equates to about 13% of the shootings."

"It sounds like a lot," Christian acknowledged, "but it's really nothing."

"Isn't it?" she questioned. She knew this was her moment to apply pressure.

"It's not. That's a very low percentage compared to what it could be."

Anayi raised an eyebrow. "So, what are you saying, Lieutenant?" she smirked.

Christian was silent.

"Are you saying that sixteen is a low number of shootings?"

Christian shook his head. "Over a three-year tenure?" Christian questioned. "That's like me saying a criminal robbing sixteen banks over the course of three years isn't a lot."

"So, you're relating Officer Warren to a criminal?"

Christian didn't hold back any longer. "What Jake did was a criminal act; no questions asked," he spoke. "And he deserves to be prosecuted to the fullest extent of the law. I've seen the tapes; Jake didn't fear for his life. Bodycam footage leading up to his arrival shows that he was already having a rough day and he was excited to be called to the scene."

Matthew hit his gavel. "Order," he called.

Christian continued. "The moment he ordered Marcus to back out of the vehicle, his finger was hugging the trigger and once Marcus was about 97% out of the vehicle, Jake saw an item in his hand and is parading it around as though he felt that Marcus had a weapon."

"Lieutenant Tate," Andrew called.

"It's not fair and it's not right," Christian continued. "Sixteen shots over a three-year tenure? You and I both know that's outrageous and despicable," Christian finished, and Junior felt warmth throughout his body.

Matthew hit his gavel harder against the desk.

The courtroom silenced.

"Lieutenant Tate, I am this close to holding you in contempt of court," Matthew spoke with authority.

Christian was silent and Anayi smirked.

"Some choice words from a Lieutenant," she began. "Ladies and gentlemen, this is the person that wants for you to elect him to run the state?" she looked at the jury sternly.

Christian slightly shook his head. Francesca discreetly pulled out her phone and sent a message.

"Don't bring my father's election into this," Junior blurted.

"Counsel, control your client," Matthew spoke.

"And he's one hell-of-a-cop so don't question his morals or intentions," Junior continued.

The audience began to murmur, and the silent whispers turned into audible conversations.

"Son, it's okay," Christian replied.

"Counsel!" Matthew reiterated.

"What did I tell you?" Christian spoke. "We rise above and prevail. Don't fall to their level."

Andrew turned to Junior and whispered.

Matthew hit his gavel against the desk numerous times.

The courtroom silenced and Matthew continued.

"Both of you will *stop* making a mockery of this case," he looked at Anayi and then to Andrew.

The two looked at each other before Matthew continued.

"And Lieutenant, keep trying it," he spoke. "You're really testing me."

Christian didn't say a word. He didn't want to agitate Matthew anymore nor did he want to make Junior and Marcus' trial any more difficult than it already was.

"Lieutenant, on the day after the shooting, your chief spoke with you, is this correct?" Anayi questioned.

"Yes," Christian replied.

"What did you all speak about?"

Christian slightly rolled his eyes.

"Chief Sanders spoke to me regarding the shooting and reminded me that I couldn't get involved with the case," Christian remarked.

"And what was your reply?" Anayi asked.

Junior stared at his father and Christian made eye contact with his son. He gave a comforting glare.

"I didn't have much of a response," Christian spoke to Anayi. "Chief Sanders informed me to focus on my gubernatorial run and that I was to stay off the case."

Anayi stared at Christian.

"Yet, here we are," Anayi mentioned.

Christian gave her a dirty look. "That's my son," Christian spoke with attitude. "I haven't provided any police work to this case," he remarked.

"Really?" Anayi questioned.

"Yes," Christian replied, "really. Everything I've done for this has been from a father's perspective. I've told you before, this isn't about the run or me being an officer; this is about me being a parent!" he stressed.

The jurors looked at one another and a tear formed on Keisha's face.

Anayi scoffed with a slight, quiet laugh. "No further questions, Your Honor," Anayi remarked.

Matthew nodded his head. "You may step down, Lieutenant."

Christian rose to his feet and stepped down from the stand. Christian returned to his seat in the congregation.

Junior noticed Matthew yawn discreetly and slightly nudged Andrew.

"Your Honor, the defense asks that the court recess and resume on Monday," Andrew took advantage of seeing Matthew yawn.

Matthew noticed that Andrew saw this and spoke. "How many more witnesses will you be calling?" he questioned as he wrote on his notepad.

"There are two remaining witnesses," Andrew projected.

Matthew glanced at the watch on his wrist and spoke to the court.

"Court will resume Monday morning at 0900 hours," he hit the gavel against the desk and rose to his feet.

The court officer brought the congregation to a stand and Matthew exited the court.

Junior looked over to Anayi as she packed her things.

Andrew spoke.

"Don't focus on her," he spoke calmly to Junior. Andrew passed a glare towards Anayi; he, then, refocused on Junior. "We are truly in the home stretch, man. Stay focused," he shook Junior's hand.

"I can't wait for all of this to be over," Junior admitted.

"It will be soon," Andrew spoke as he adjusted Junior's sportscoat.

Christian leaned over the gate. "Stand strong, son," he patted him on the shoulder.

Junior turned and embraced his father.

"I will, Pops."

Keisha kissed Junior on the cheek. "I love you, son," she smiled.

"Love you too, Mom," he reached over and hugged her before the officers came over to escort him away.

Andrew reached over and passed Junior the crutches.

"I'll be there this weekend to finalize everything," Andrew added.

Junior nodded his head and used the crutches to walk away with the officers.

"So," Christian spoke as Andrew held his briefcase and they all exited the courtroom, "how do you think things are looking?" Christian put his arm around Keisha.

"I'll be honest with you, man," Andrew began, "the jury looks hung; that can either be a good thing or a bad thing," he added.

"What do *you* think?" Keisha questioned as they walked to the doors of the courthouse alongside Francesca, Raymond, and Bianca.

Andrew inhaled sharply.

"I think we'd better be ready for anything," he enunciated. "Monday, you and Junior are both taking the stand and the prosecution is going to counter *hard*," he stressed. "So, we need to ensure you all are prepared."

Keisha turned the conversation to focus on Junior's injury. "Did my baby tell you what really happened that he's on crutches?" she questioned Christian and Andrew.

The two looked at each other.

Christian sighed. "Babe, Junior was in a fight," he admitted.

"What?!" she panicked. "He told me there was an accident and he'd cut himself on some glass."

"He didn't want for you to get in a frenzy," Andrew interjected. "He knows we need to keep our heads, especially at this point in the trial."

"He and this prisoner got into it as he was defending us," Christian further explained. "Plus, Junior knows how important all of this is," he added. "I highly doubt that he would do anything to purposefully jeopardize this case."

As the group walked outside, reporters swarmed in.

"Stay close," Andrew spoke in a low tone.

"Mr. Brownstone, do you have any updates with the case that you can provide us with?" the reporter questioned.

"Come on, guys," Andrew spoke to Keisha, Christian, Francesca, and Bianca.

The five of them huddled closer and continued to walk.

"Lieutenant Tate," a male reporter called, "your line of questions and answers in the case could have had an impact on the polls and your ratings. What's your take?"

Christian continued to walk with his family and friends; he did his best to ignore the reporter.

"Lieutenant," the same reporter repeated, pushing the microphone closer to his face.

Christian kept his head down as they all walked to the car.

The same reporter stood directly in front of Christian and he spoke.

"You're a persistent little thing, aren't you?" Christian chose his words carefully.

"Tate, come on," Andrew spoke as the four of them walked. Christian didn't move.

"I'm a father, you understand that?" Christian asked the reporter. "This isn't about the race for governor," he added. "This is about me being there for my son."

"So, your opponent, Bernard Smith, leading in the polls has no effect on you?" a different reporter asked.

"The similarities between your son's case and Bernard's son's case are eerily similar," the initial reporter said. "You're saying it does not affect you?"

"You all have heard my argument," Christian spoke to the reporter; adding more bass to his tone. "I'm here for my son and my son only. Nothing else matters right now," Christian spoke. "Not this race, not Bernard, not Benjamin, not my career."

Andrew interjected. "No further questions," he put his hand on Christian's shoulder and applied slight pressure to pull him in his direction.

Christian kept silent and walked ahead with Andrew.

"Avoid the cameras," he reminded Christian.

"I know, man, I know," Christian uttered. "I'll keep giving my focus to my son. That's the most important thing."

Andrew nodded his head in agreement as they arrived at their vehicles.

14

"Is this who I'm running against?" Bernard spoke over the television screen. *"He's basically telling you all he doesn't care about you. All he cares about is his son's case,"* Junior watched Bernard as he and Kanaan played spades with two other inmates.

"Man, how are you so calm about this?" Kanaan inhaled on the blunt and exhaled the smoke. He tossed a card on the table.

"They've done everything in their power to try to break me," Junior uttered with a chuckle. "And I'm not going to lie, they've partially succeeded a few times, but with the helpful words from you, my lawyer, my pops, and my uncle, I'm keeping my composure," Junior played his next card.

"Man, fuck that," Kanaan's teammate spoke as he played his card. "If you want us to, say the word. We'll send hittas his way."

Junior's teammate slammed his card on the table.

"Give us this shit," he laughed as he collected the cards from the table. He played his next card.

"Keep talkin' shit," Kanaan's teammate laughed and played his card.

"Man," Junior said, "I'm so close to the end of my trial, it's not even worth it. What do I look like fuckin' that up?" Junior slid his card on the table.

"You a better man than me," Kanaan inhaled on the blunt and played his card. "Shit, if he was talking 'bout my old man like that, I'd have taken him out a long time ago."

"Nigga, you gotta be cool with your old man first," Junior's teammate chuckled.

"Fuck you," Kanaan laughed.

"Tate!" a prison guard called as he approached the table.

Junior looked in the guard's direction.

"Your lawyer's here," the guard projected.

Junior's heart illuminated but he didn't show his satisfaction.

"Gotta go, fellas," he rose to his feet.

Kanaan laughed.

"Jermaine," Junior called to another inmate at another table. "Play my hand."

The inmate nodded his hand and walked over to the table. Junior grabbed his crutches and followed the guard to the interview room.

Once inside, Junior leaned his crutches against the wall and sat across from Andrew.

"How's it going, Junior?" Andrew questioned. "You ready for Monday?"

"All we can do is be prepared, right?" Junior answered with a smirk.

Andrew chuckled. "This is what I've come up with," he continued as he showed Junior a piece of paper.

"Believe it or not, you are currently leading in the polls," Dustin spoke. "The voters are seeing you as a family man, and you're touching their hearts," he chuckled.

"I don't think you're even understanding," Christian spoke. "As of this moment, I don't care about this run," he responded. "The only thing I care about is getting my son home."

"I understand what you're saying," Dustin began, "but since we know this information, I say we use it to our advantage," he suggested.

Christian shook his head.

"You just aren't listening," he chuckled and walked away. "Tomorrow can essentially be one of the biggest days of my son's trial, and you are insisting on focusing on this damn run. I'm here because you stressed the importance of me being here today, but please believe my mind isn't here."

"Christian, check it out," Dustin trotted to catch up with Christian, "I'm not saying give your energy to this case, but what I am saying, is let's use this knowledge to our benefit."

"Check it," Christian stopped in his tracks. He faced Dustin; the two were eye-to-eye. "This election doesn't mean a thing to me, not right now. The only thing I care about is getting my son out of jail. Once the trial is over and that happens, we can divert our attention over to this run."

"Okay, well do me a favor," Dustin spoke, "give a little focus just to this convention for today, and tomorrow, you go back to being super dad."

Christian looked at Dustin with disgust and chuckled.

"Yeah, whatever man," he uttered.

"And now, we bring to the stage, Democratic nominee, Christian Tate," the announcer stated.

Christian walked from behind the curtain and shook hands with Bernard to show sportsmanship.

He returned to his podium and looked at the camera.

The blinding bright lights shined brightly in his face as he looked at the audience.

Christian heard several murmurs as he observed the business-casual adults chat amongst each other. He looked over to Dustin.

"You got this," Dustin mouthed out.

Christian inhaled and exhaled slowly.
       ***

"How can the Floridians be safe if their governor has a son who has tried to kill one of the members who are meant to serve and protect?"

Christian facetiously laughed.

"Is something funny, Lieutenant?" Bernard questioned.

Christian didn't bite his tongue. "Actually, something is funny," he spoke for the cameras and crowd.

"Enlighten us," Bernard remarked.

"You don't see the eerie similarity in what you just said?"

Bernard displayed a puzzled look.

"You just described your own son's situation," Christian mentioned.

Christian knew mentioning Benjamin to Bernard could have potentially hit a soft spot, but he was truly tired of everyone bashing what his son did, yet they praised Benjamin and remembered him as a law-abiding citizen.

He saw the anger build in Bernard's eyes at the mentioning of his son.

"My son?" Bernard contained his anger.

It wasn't in Christian's intentions to take Bernard out of his element, so he didn't attack.

"My son wasn't doing anything but trying to get away from you and you shot and killed him."

"Mr. Smith," the host tried to get Bernard back on track.

"You profiled him, you pursued him, and you hunted him down like an animal," Bernard's blood was boiling. "My son was fleeing and rather than disorienting him, you killed him at point-blank range."

"Smith," Christian addressed him by his last name, "what happened with your son is a tragedy," he showed empathy, "but your son had a weapon aimed at law enforcement," Christian addressed the case. "With my son, he had no weapon before the officer unloaded his weapon and was truly fearing for his life; what occurred wasn't intentional; he even administered aid to the officer he shot."

The moderators stared at one another in awe.

There were murmurs in the audience.

"Er, Lieutenant Tate, Mr. Smith, let's get back on topic," the lead moderator spoke.

"How about I come over there and show you what it's like?" Bernard threatened and motioned from behind his podium.

Christian shook his head.

"Seriously?" he questioned. "It doesn't even have to be like that. Not to mention you're threatening a police officer." Christian didn't say the next comment he was thinking as he knew all eyes would be on him.

Although Bernard was the aggressor, because of his skin color, the blame would be placed on Christian and he knew it.

The moderators rose to their feet and security walked to the stage.

"We're going to take a short commercial break," the moderator mentioned.

Bernard walked from behind his podium and Christian remained behind his.

Security guards approached Bernard while one remained in front of Christian.

Christian looked over to Dustin; Dustin shook his head in disgust.

"You killed my son and you dare try to throw his name at me?" Bernard spoke from behind the security guards. "I ought to kick your ass," Bernard spoke aggressively.

The crowd's low murmurs turned into audible conversations and gasps.

"What do you want me to do?" Christian finally replied. "You're sitting here trashing my son's name and you don't want me to say anything? I'm not built like that."

∎∎∎

Junior laid in his cell and looked at the ceiling. He anxiously awaited the prison guard to retrieve him for court. He reached in his pocket and pulled out a picture of Bianca and smiled.

"I hope everyone is in court today," Junior spoke to himself.

He knew this was, perhaps, one of the biggest days of his trial and after Bernard's showing on Sunday, he knew the focus would be on him, not only for his trial but to see the reaction to his father's debate.

Kanaan walked past the cell. "Good luck in court today, man," he spoke. "You're one step closer to walking out of here."

Junior sat up. "Man, we gotta get you out of here next," he insisted.

"Don't worry too much about me," Kanaan spoke. "Worry about your trial and getting out of here." Kanaan touched the bars to Junior's cell. "I'm in this bitch for a while. Shit, by the time I'm free, my children will have children," Kanaan chuckled, and Junior saw a tear fall from his eye.

This was the first time Junior saw emotion from Kanaan.

"I got time, bro. Tell me what happened. Why are you here?" Junior limped over to the entrance.

Kanaan sniffled.

"Been in here for years," Kanaan began. "Came in when I was 28."

"I thought you were about 28," Junior chuckled. "How old are you, man?"

Kanaan laughed and pulled a blunt out of his pocket. "I'm 40, youngin'." Kanaan lit the blunt. "Why you think I took you under my wing? You're like a little brother to me and with my cred in here, I knew that nobody would try to fuck with you."

Junior nodded his head.

"Man, when I was 28, I came home to my sister's boyfriend touching my daughter," he shook his head.

"What?" Junior questioned.

"And, shit nigga, you know me. I'ma beat yo' ass first and ask questions later. So, I whooped that fool's ass. Comforted my daughter and walked in the room with my sister, and noticed she had bruises on her arm, from him," Junior could see Kanaan's anger building. "So, I went in there and finished the job. I beat his ass so bad that the nigga went into a coma and never came out of it. He passed away two months later."

Kanaan inhaled on the blunt and exhaled a cloud of smoke.

"Cats around here are hailing me as a hero, but you know you always got that group of muhfuckas' who feel like you did too much. But me," Kanaan inhaled on the blunt again, "I'ma ride for mines."

"Was he black or Hispanic?" Junior questioned.

Kanaan chuckled. "Nigga was White. Why you think Timmy has it in for me? Old White man is stuck in that 1920's mindset."

"Christian Tate," the prison guard walked towards his cell.

Kanaan exhaled smoke to the side and tapped the ashes from the blunt onto the floor.

"It's time for court," the guard mentioned. "Let's go," he unlocked Junior's cell.

The guard smelled the marijuana but didn't mind. He knew Kanaan's story and agreed with what he did. He wasn't going to give him a hard time over something that eased his mind.

"Bro, keep your cool," Junior spoke as he shook hands with Kanaan. "We'll finish this conversation when I get back."

"Aye, man," Kanaan finished their signature shake, "you keep your head on your case."

Junior smiled and grabbed his crutches. He walked with the guard to the gates of the prison.

An officer walked over and retrieved Junior.

"Big day for you, huh?" the officer spoke as they walked to the bus.

"It's supposed to be," Junior responded. "Going to keep looking up, you know?"

"Stay focused," the guard remarked.

Junior walked onto the prison bus and leaned the crutches against the wall. Junior sat and looked out the window. He decided to close his eyes and rest his mind during the drive.

When Junior opened his eyes, the bus was pulling into the courthouse's parking lot.

Junior exited the bus behind the one other inmate who was entering the courthouse. The clouds seemed to cover the sun and it seemed as though rain was in the forecast.

Junior entered the courthouse and sat in the waiting area for the court officer to retrieve him.

Junior clasped his hands together and said a small prayer. He continued to recite the questions and answers he and Andrew reviewed for the questioning.

A few moments passed by and the court officer came and retrieved Junior. The officer walked Junior over to Andrew.

Junior made eye contact with his parents, Bianca, Francesca, and Raymond before leaning the crutches against the gate. He turned and faced Andrew.

"You ready for this, man?" Andrew questioned.

"About as ready as I'll ever be," Junior replied.

"So, you remember what we went over on Saturday, right? Your mom is going to take the stand and I'm going to get her to open up about your childhood, which will open the door to the prosecution's cross. I will have a chance at a rebuttal if I see fit."

"What about what went down with my pops and Mr. Smith?" Junior whispered.

"I'm not going to bring that up unless it comes to that," Andrew responded. "Right now, my objective is to be aggressive, yet passive. I don't want to go on the attack; I want to defend you and prove that your actions were justifiable, and Jake shot Marcus in cold blood."

Junior nodded his head and faced the front. Andrew patted him on the shoulder.

Matthew entered the courtroom and the court officer brought the rest of the court to a stand. Matthew sat and the rest of the courtroom did, except for two members of the prosecution and Andrew.

"Are we prepared to proceed with the case?" Matthew questioned.

"Yes, Your Honor," he answered.

"Call your next witness," he instructed.

"The defense calls Mrs. Keisha Tate to the stand," Andrew called and adjusted his tie.

Keisha rose to her feet and walked to the witness stand. She made eye contact with Junior and teared slightly.

After she was sworn in, Andrew approached.

"Good morning, Mrs. Tate," he greeted her. "How's your day going?" he questioned.

"Could be better," Keisha uttered.

"I understand," Andrew replied. "Mrs. Tate, are you able to describe Christian's lifestyle?"

Keisha inhaled slowly.

"Junior has always been there when in need. He's the first one to offer help and the last one to complain," she began.

Anayi took notes as Keisha spoke.

"He excels in academics, sports, and being an all-around good person."

"What about his interaction with authority?" Andrew questioned.

"Junior has never been a troublemaker," Keisha began.

"Objection, Your Honor," Anayi intercepted.

"Really?" Andrew questioned aloud. "Can we allow the witness to fully answer the question before objecting?" Andrew addressed Anayi and the court. "For God's sake, she's here at her son's trial; I think she's earned the right to express herself."

Matthew didn't look up and continued to jot down notes.

A few seconds later, he spoke.

"Overruled," he replied.

Keisha continued. "This goes for school, extra-curricular activities, and even the law," she provided the answer she knew Anayi would be listening for.

"So, your son has never been in any trouble?" Andrew questioned.

"What child hasn't?" Keisha chuckled.

A few jurors and members of the audience laughed alongside her.

"But what I'm saying is that Junior has never been a troublemaker," she emphasized. "He's never been one to just go out looking for trouble. He has a heart of gold; he and Marcus both do."

"Objection, Your Honor," Anayi spoke again. "The question was regarding Christian Tate, not Marcus Farris."

"Sustained," Matthew responded. "The jurors will disregard the remark regarding Mr. Farris."

Andrew walked towards the jury box and cleared his throat.

"Let's get back on track," he spoke aloud to Keisha while facing the jury. "What are Christian's grades like in school?"

"All A's," Keisha boasted. "The teachers are consistently calling me to brag on Junior and tell me how much of a joy he is to have in class."

"So, he must enjoy school?" Andrew assumed.

"Well, he knows he has to do well to maintain his scholarship and continue to play ball. I can't speak on if he enjoys school," she laughed, "but I know he's a consistent student and does what he has to do in order to get things done."

Andrew walked over to the defense's desk and retrieved a piece of paper. He walked over to Keisha and passed her the paper.

"Can you take a look at the paper I just laid out in front of you?" Andrew questioned.

Keisha studied the paper.

"These are Christian's grades and snippets of his letters of recommendation from various teachers, managers, and advisors."

"Can you read off his GPA to the court?" Andrew questioned.

He had to ensure the jury knew that Junior wasn't a hostile individual with the purest intentions. Although he knew this was a long shot to try to prove his case, he decided to take the chance.

"5.0," Keisha boasted proudly.

Junior blushed and smiled as his mother teared.

"Can you read off one of his recommendations?" Andrew questioned.

Keisha paused for a moment and smiled again as she began to read.

"Let's see," she started, "'Christian is a joy to be around and to have in my class. He's always the first one in the door and the last one to leave,'" Keisha teared slightly as she read. "'His interesting conversations and joyous spirit makes class more enjoyable and his positive energy reverberates through the room and has the ability to impact and uplift even the worst energy. I highly recommend Christian for the political justice internship overseas.'" Keisha looked at Andrew.

"Ladies and gentlemen of the jury, that recommendation is one of the few that are listed on the paper," he finished.

The jurors looked at one another, to Junior, and back to Andrew.

Andrew let a few seconds of silence pass before speaking again.

"Mrs. Tate," he addressed Keisha, "we've already heard of Christian's accomplishments, but I really need to talk to you about the night of the shooting of Officer Whitley and Marcus Farris," he exhaled slowly. "Are you prepared to discuss this?" he asked her.

The jurors saw tears accumulating in Keisha's eyes and she nodded her head.

"We'll need an audible response for the court," Andrew announced.

"Yes," Keisha answered.

"Thank you," Andrew paced the floor. "On that eventful night, what were you doing?"

"My husband, Lieutenant Christian Tate, had a gubernatorial debate," Keisha began. "We were waiting for Junior and Marcus to arrive."

"They were at school, correct?" Andrew questioned.

"Objection, Your Honor. Leading the witness," Anayi spoke.

"Seriously?" Andrew questioned aloud.

"Mr. Brownstone, it's already been established that the defendant was at school before the shooting. Get on with your questioning," Matthew looked over his glasses.

Andrew didn't pay him any mind and continued.

"Mrs. Tate, we've all seen the tape. I want to ask, when was the last time you spoke to your son before the shooting?"

Keisha thought for a moment. "It was while he was at the school," she answered. "However, Marcus gave me a call during the stop, and I heard a bit of the conversation."

"You're not referring to what was shown on the recording?" Andrew questioned.

"Some of it," Keisha admitted. "I'm not sure where the overlap was."

Andrew walked towards the jurors.

"Can you share with us both conversations that you had with Christian as well as Marcus?"

"Objection, Your Honor. Relevance?" Anayi questioned.

"The witness should be allowed to give her account of what occurred, the same way everyone else was able to give their testimony," Andrew responded to her objection.

"My conversation with Junior was brief. It was more along the lines of 'I'm at school, we'll be there once we finish'. With Marcus, it wasn't really a conversation with him," her voice cracked.

Raymond shed a tear as she spoke.

"Take your time," Andrew remarked.

Keisha inhaled slowly and continued. "When Marcus called me, I heard sirens," she recalled. "I heard the police shout to Christian to raise his hands, in which I heard Christian shout that he was unable to do so."

Andrew glanced at Anayi as Keisha spoke.

"And why was he unable to do so?" Andrew questioned, not taking his eyes off Anayi.

She returned the glare.

"Based on bodycam footage and timing, I saw that Junior was applying aid to Officer Whitley," Keisha answered. "I asked Marcus what was going on and not even ten seconds later, I heard the shot fired by Officer Warren."

"Is this your assumption?" Andrew asked.

"No," Keisha answered. "Officer Warren's body-camera displayed that he fired the shot that I heard."

Andrew shook his head slowly. "And what happened after that?" he questioned.

"I called for Marcus to answer me, but he never responded. Instead, I heard the police shouting instructions to Christian and him crying."

"Mrs. Tate, according to the body-camera, at what point did Christian stop administering aid to Officer Whitley?" Andrew questioned and he tugged on his sportscoat.

"Immediately following the shot to his best friend, he stopped administering aid and attempted to go to Marcus, but he was met with two officers aiming their weapons at him."

"So, due to the weapons, I'm assuming he never reached his best friend," Marcus suggested.

"You would think that, huh?" Keisha chuckled and looked at her son. "No, Junior was very determined. Even with the weapons aimed at him, he walked slowly over to Marcus and kneeled."

Andrew teared slightly but quickly recomposed himself.

"Mrs. Tate, at what point did Officer Warren arrest Christian?"

"As soon as he kneeled to Marcus," the tears flowed down Keisha's face, "Officer Warren approached with his weapon aimed. His partner kept the weapon aimed at Junior as Officer Warren violently put him in handcuffs."

Andrew grabbed the box of tissue from the defense's desk. He walked it over to Keisha and grabbed a piece for himself. He blew his nose and continued speaking.

"Mrs. Tate, just a few more questions," he remarked.

Keisha nodded her head.

"Did Christian get a chance to aid his best friend?"

"No," Keisha spoke softly. "As soon as Christian kneeled, like I said, Officer Warren rushed in, shoved him, face-first into the asphalt, and handcuffed him."

Andrew didn't have any further questions for Keisha. His anger was building, and he didn't want it to show. Instead, he decided to wait for Anayi to finish.

"No further questions, Your Honor," he remarked.

Andrew walked back to the defense's desk and sat next to Junior. He put his hand on Junior's shoulder and patted it.

Anayi approached the stand with a smile.

"I was taking a few notes as Mr. Brownstone questioned you," she began, "and it seems that you care for your son deeply," she finished.

"More than anything, as any parent should love their children."

"And, you would do anything; rather, say anything, to protect him, is that right?"

Keisha looked over to Andrew. He rubbed his nose and Keisha answered.

"To an extent," she remarked.

"Care to elaborate?" Anayi questioned.

"I think I know where you're going with this," Keisha responded, "and to be fair, you're going in the wrong direction."

Anayi raised her eyebrows. "And where am I going?" she asked Keisha.

"You're insinuating that I am just saying whatever I need to say to get my son out of trouble. If my son was guilty in any way, I wouldn't go to bat like I am."

"And we're to believe that from a mother?" Anayi remarked.

"Objection; argumentative," Andrew interfered.

"Sustained," Matthew replied.

"Mrs. Tate, you say your son was shoved face-first down into the asphalt, correct?"

"Yes," she spoke.

"How do you know this?" she questioned. "Did you see any tapes or recordings that the rest of us missed?"

"No, my son told me," Keisha said. "And when we went to go see him, he had scratches on his face and body from the brutality."

"But this court has heard that although he isn't a fighter, your son could have a temper."

Junior slightly frowned as he saw what Anayi was doing.

"So, you're suggesting he got into a fight with someone, and as a result, he ended up scratched?"

Anayi shrugged her shoulders and continued.

"It sounds to me like *you're* suggesting it," Anayi snared. "We look at your son today and notice that he's on crutches. The court knows this is from an altercation he was involved in while incarcerated. We can see he's a fighter."

There were slight murmurs from the jury and Junior slightly lowered his head.

Keisha looked at Anayi with disgust. Andrew noticed this and spoke up.

"Is there a question here?" Andrew posed.

"Is there a possibility of your son's injuries stemmed from an altercation other than his arrest?"

"The injuries my son sustained came from Warren's handling of him," Keisha responded.

"If this were the case, there should be some form of evidence that justifies your story."

Anayi walked back to the prosecution's desk. "No further questions," she spoke from behind the desk.

Andrew rose to his feet and walked to Keisha.

"Mrs. Tate, really quickly, the prosecution wants some form of evidence that confirms that Christian experienced police brutality," he glanced over to the jury. All eyes were on him. "I'm sure the jury remembers this video," he pressed a button on the remote and it loaded the footage from Jake's body camera.

Anayi shuffled through her notes.

"We even let the video play out a few times," Andrew spoke as the video played. "Right here, where the camera is shaky, and you see his hands extending; Christian isn't fighting back." Andrew walked to the screen, pointing. "Christian is on his knees, kneeling in front of his wounded friend. And somehow," Andrew slightly raised his voice, "somehow, he ends up on the ground, handcuffed, and the camera is violently shaking." Andrew walked back towards Keisha.

Junior cleared his throat.

"Security cameras from the school captured Christian that night," he added. "Take a look at this image, which was extracted from this video."

He played a fifteen-second clip of Junior, Marcus, Bianca, and Sierra standing from the library table and exiting.

"There's not a single scratch on Christian's face."

Anayi wanted to object; Andrew was tearing her cross-examination to shreds.

"Now, take a look at the following image," Andrew pressed a button and advanced to Junior's mugshots. "Notice the scarring on his face? The messiness of his locs? The tears in his shirt?"

"Objection. Is there a question?" Anayi asked.

"Mrs. Tate, the prosecution insinuates that these scars and tears came from a potential scuffle with a friend," he started again, "when we can see through multiple videos from various sources, that your son wasn't scarred before Officer Warren arrived on the scene. Do you truly believe that Officer Warren caused these injuries to your son?" Andrew finished.

The jury had their eyes on Keisha.

"Yes, I do," she answered.

"No further questions," Andrew finished with a slight smile. "Mrs. Tate, what you're doing for your son is magnificent. And even from knowing you, I know that if he were guilty, you wouldn't be here day-in and day-out fighting for him."

Andrew walked to the defense's desk.

"You may step down, Mrs. Tate," Matthew instructed.

As Junior watched his mother return to her seat, his heartbeat raced. He knew he was next to take the stand and knew that all eyes would be watching him from the first word he spoke.

As Keisha sat, Andrew rose to his feet.

"Your Honor, the defense calls Christian Tate, Jr. to the stand," he called with confidence.

The court officers approached while there were several murmurs around the courtroom. Junior reached over and grabbed the crutches and was escorted to the bench. He sat down and was sworn in.

Beads of sweat formed across his forehead as he awaited Andrew's line of questioning. It wasn't Andrew's questions that had him worried as much as he was concerned about cross-examination.

He glanced at Anayi and saw a smirk on her face. Junior adjusted his tie and Andrew approached.

"Christian, we're going to get straight into it," Andrew spoke. "I want for you to walk us through the timeline of your championship game until the shooting of Marcus." Andrew stood erect in front of Junior.

Junior looked at his parents. They were smiling and holding hands and made eye contact with him.

"I remember the night vividly," Junior recited. "My team and I'd just won the championship game: 97-72," he boasted and glanced at the jurors as he spoke. "I finished with thirty-four points, ten assists, four rebounds, and seven steals," Junior smiled brightly.

"Is there any reason you played so extravagantly that night?" Andrew questioned Junior.

"I was just feeling it, I guess," Junior answered. He continued with the recap. "After the game, I was driving to the restaurant; Marcus was on the passenger's side." Junior inhaled deeply.

"Take your time," Andrew remarked.

Anayi studied Christian's body language and took notes; she particularly paid close attention to his word choice.

"He and I started rapping and as we turned right, a police car turns on its siren. I immediately pulled over to the right side of the road and I stated the command for my phone to start video and audio recording."

Matthew didn't look away from his notes and Andrew noticed this.

"As the officer got out of the vehicle and approached, Marcus and I kept our hands visible and I rolled the window down. I asked the reason for the stop, and he informed me that I didn't come to a complete stop before turning right," Junior made eye contact with Brian. Junior inhaled and continued. "He asked why we were out so late, and I told him we were heading to celebrate my win. He'd asked if we'd been drinking, although I'd just told him that we came from a game. We'd reached inside of our pockets and retrieved the cards, as the officers asked of us."

Andrew continued to watch the jury for any emotional signs as Junior spoke; he saw none.

"Junior, I hate to interrupt," Andrew intercepted, "but what was the conversation once the officers saw your identification cards?"

Junior ensured he was sitting erect.

"Once Officer Whitley saw my license, he asked if my father was the one--."

"Objection, Your Honor," Anayi called. "Relevance?"

"Your Honor, this will help establish the previous encounters with Christian Tate," Andrew began. "Officer Brian Whitley says there isn't a negative rapport with Mr. Tate, and if that's the case, his story should corroborate that."

Matthew nodded his head.

"Overruled. Continue, Mr. Tate," Matthew focused on his notes.

Junior continued. "He asked if my father was the one who killed Benjamin Smith."

Andrew nodded his head and paced the floor slowly. Junior felt as though someone increased the temperature in the room.

"When they returned to the car," Junior continued, "Officer Montrose addressed Marcus as the son of ex-convict," Junior looked at Raymond. "And, he said he found it peculiar that we were riding around together."

"What do you mean?" Andrew questioned. "What did he say?"

"Well," Junior resumed, "he mentioned that it was coincidental that the two inmates who caused the most-noise were riding around together at night."

"It's interesting that you're telling us this," Andrew uttered, "considering Officer Brian Whitley mentioned in his testimony that you all didn't have history."

"We had history," Junior specified. "He's pulled me over a few times for bogus violations," Junior rolled his eyes before continuing. "Anyway, I asked him to give me my ticket so we could proceed to dinner. With what I could sense was an attitude, he told me he was going to let me off with a warning and to come to a complete stop at the lights."

Andrew approached the stand.

"We've had testimony from many others, and it was attested that this was an unlawful stop, especially since no citations were issued and traffic cameras didn't capture any infractions."

Junior shrugged slightly. He didn't want to say anything that could potentially jeopardize his case or bring any trouble to his father.

"Is there a question, Your Honor?" Anayi asked as Andrew paused.

"Just making an observation," Andrew responded. He wanted to ensure the jurors were aware that there was no need for the stop. "What occurred after the stop?" Andrew asked Junior.

"Once I pulled off, I drove to the restaurant and informed my father of the stop. What actions he took, I couldn't tell you," Junior added.

"Christian, was this your first traffic encounter with Officer Whitley?"

"No, as I've mentioned before," Junior projected while looking at the jurors.

Andrew walked to the defense's desk while speaking.

"The way you say he was speaking, he was talking as though he were pretty comfortable in stopping you; as if it were a routine thing."

"Well, as I mentioned, he knew my father and he has pulled me over for violations I didn't commit in the past. If you look at my record, I don't have any tickets from any of the stops performed by Officer Whitley. He knew what kind of car I drove and when the opportunity presented itself, he pulled me over, yet again."

"Objection: argumentative."

"Sustained," Matthew remarked.

"Let's move on," Andrew spoke. "Can you tell us about the stop that brought us here today?"

A tear came to Junior's eye.

He pulled a tissue from the box, wiped his eye, and inhaled deeply.

"We'd just come from school," Junior cleared his throat. "No, actually, we came from school, got food, and dropped the girls off at home," he smiled at Bianca.

Bianca returned the grin.

"You guys were studying at school, correct?" Andrew asked.

"Objection: leading," Anayi interjected.

"Sustained," Matthew immediately replied.

Andrew was expecting this during questioning, so he didn't make an issue out of it.

"Where were you all coming from?" Andrew asked Junior.

"We had tests coming up," Junior answered. "We were all studying at the school. After dropping the girls off, I merged onto the expressway, and shortly after doing so, there were police sirens in the rearview mirror. So," Junior slowed his words as this was emotional for him to talk about. "I pulled over to the right almost immediately."

Christian kept his eyes on his son as he held hands with Keisha. He glanced over to Brian, who seemed to attempt to avoid eye contact by any means necessary.

"I informed my phone that I was getting pulled over and it started recording the interaction. This is when I noticed it was only one officer this time, as opposed to two."

Andrew studied the courtroom and noticed Anayi jotting down notes extensively. He imagined smoke emitting from her pen as heavily as she was writing.

"I asked if everything was alright and I addressed him by name, and he replied with attitude and told me he would be asking the questions and asked for my license and registration," Junior shook his head lightly. "I told him I would have to reach to retrieve it and he nodded his head for me to do so. As I was reaching for it, Officer Whitley shined his light in Marcus' face." Junior felt his voice crack as he discussed Marcus. Junior chuckled a little. "He told Officer Whitley to get the flashlight out of his face; I remember laughing in my head at that."

Andrew refrained from asking any questions as Junior told the story.

"And then, Officer Whitley kind of profiled us," Junior displayed a shocked look on his face. "He asked if we were drinking lean because he saw a Sprite bottle with a purple liquid. I explained to him that it was Sprite and grape soda mixed and that we'd just left school."

Andrew and Junior noticed a few looks of disapproval across the juror's faces.

"He gave me attitude and told me that we weren't friends and stepped away from the vehicle. When he came back, he asked for Marcus' ID. As Marcus gave it to him, he instructed me to keep my hands where he could see them, but the thing is," Junior looked at Brian, "I didn't move my hands." Junior looked at the jury once more. "When I told him they were in the same position, that's when things escalated."

"How so?" Andrew questioned. "If all you did was tell him that you didn't move your hands, things shouldn't have escalated, correct?"

"Officer Whitley walked over to my side of the car. While he was walking, Marcus asked why he was stopping us; he didn't reply. Instead, he told Marcus to keep his hands on the dashboard. "He requested backup and when he opened my car door, he walked me around to the hood of my vehicle. He shoved me against it"

"A hot engine that had been running for nearly 30 minutes, and an officer of the law leans you against it? What was going through your mind as this happened?"

"I couldn't think straight," Junior admitted. "I was fearful of what would happen next?"

"What do you mean?" Andrew questioned.

"I didn't know if I would be the next *Say Their Names* victim," Junior inhaled. "Look, it's 2039 and this hasn't gotten any better in terms of police brutality against Blacks."

"Objection, Your Honor!" Anayi pressed.

"Sustained," Matthew showed irritation in his words. "Counsel, control your witness."

"Your Honor, my client has had it rough," Andrew defended Junior. "Since the initial stop, to being beaten in prison, I feel as though he's earned the right to speak today."

"He has the right to speak but he will also be respectful of my courtroom," Matthew immediately retaliated.

"What's not respectful?" Andrew questioned. "The fact that he said he didn't want to be another victim?"

"Counselor," Matthew stated with a warning tone.

"No, seriously," Andrew continued. "These major cases where we have Black people being brutalized by those who are supposed to serve and protect. Trayvon Martin, Sandra Bland, Laquan McDonald, Jacob Blake, Eric Garner, George Floyd, Anaiya Jones; need I continue? All these people were victims of police brutality and it's really getting tiring. My client feared for his life once Officer Whitley pulled him out of the car and slammed him against a steaming hood of a car, and if you don't feel that he had a reason to fear for his life, then, to that, I challenge you to turn on a television," It was obvious that Andrew was irate and emotional as he looked to the jurors.

Christian rubbed Keisha's hand and looked around the courtroom. He could see Andrew's mini speech had just made several members in the congregation uncomfortable; yet, he knew this is what Andrew was aiming for.

Matthew hit his gavel against his desk. "The jury will disregard that final statement from Mr. Brownstone," he spoke sternly. "I'm not going to warn you again, Mr. Brownstone," Matthew addressed Andrew.

Andrew knew the jurors couldn't un-hear what he said, and he truly didn't care. He handled all his cases with precision and often took the cases personally.

Andrew looked to Junior. "Mr. Tate, what happened after you were put on the hood but Officer Whitley?" Andrew chose his words carefully as to not do any damage to the case. He wanted to incite just enough chaos to get the jurors thinking but didn't want to get the case thrown out.

"I told him the hood was hot and he blatantly told me, he didn't give a 'f'," Junior didn't swear in court. "I felt that was a little odd coming from someone meant to serve and protect. Anyway, I told him I was onto the brutality and he looked at Marcus and told him not to move."

"Marcus was in the car, correct?"

"Marcus was in the vehicle holding his phone at this point," Junior spoke. "He wanted to capture what was occurring on camera."

"But there's no footage collected from Mr. Farris' phone," Andrew replied.

A tear formed in Junior's eye. "He didn't get a chance to record," Junior mentioned. "Once Officer Whitley told him not to move, he dropped the phone."

"Proceed," Andrew directed.

Junior wiped the tear and proceeded. "Officer Whitley patted me down and when I asked why he was so rough, he told me to give him a reason and that he didn't care who I was." Junior scratched his head. "When I asked what he was referring to, he used a racial slur and said just because my dad is running for governor, it didn't put me above the law. He then accused me of drinking and driving and stated that he knew I had drugs on me."

"And what was the basis of his argument?" Andrew inquired.

"I don't even know," Junior remarked. "It all just happened so quickly and escalated out of nowhere. I shouted to Marcus to call my father, considering that was Officer Whitley's superior and to inform him of what was going on."

"That call was never made, was it?" Andrew asked.

"Yes," Junior immediately answered. "Officer Whitley told Marcus that he'd better not f-ing move, but while Officer Whitley wasn't looking, he picked his phone up and dialed my father's number. Officer Whitley, then, spoke over his radio and asked where his backup was and that he had two Black men getting belligerent and that we may have been intoxicated."

"Mr. Tate, were any sobriety tests performed? Did you breathe into a breathalyzer?"

"No," Junior responded.

"So, his assumptions had no basis?" Andrew walked over to the defense's desk.

"That's correct," Junior said.

Raymond shed a tear but smiled as Junior spoke eloquently on the stand. He knew he would bring justice to both himself and Marcus.

"Well, he turned me around and as he was jerking, you know how your body naturally tenses up?"

Andrew nodded his head.

"My muscles tightened, and Officer Whitley slammed me to the ground and shouted for me to stop resisting. Marcus got out of the vehicle and Officer Whitley told him to get his bi-" Junior cleared his throat, "his b-a back in the car. Marcus didn't comply and told Officer Whitley that we were just trying to get to our destination."

"What happened next?"

"I can't swear by it," Junior continued, "but I thought I saw Officer Whitley reaching for his gun. Or, he loosened it or something."

"Why do you say that?"

"It ended up on the ground. I told him I wasn't resisting but we continued to tussle on the ground and kind of like a reflex, my feet kicked him off of me. I noticed Marcus in my peripheral vision with his head inside of the driver's door," Junior looked at his father and saw a stern expression on his face. "I saw Officer Whitley crawling for the gun, and I lunged for it."

Several jurors gasped and Andrew knew this would be the reaction. He quickly had to control the story.

"Pause right there," he interrupted. "What was your reasoning in lunging for the gun? Did you plan on using it?"

"No," Junior shook his head. "I was going for the gun so that he couldn't go for it. I saw how irate he was, and I knew that if he got ahold of the gun, that would be the end of me."

Andrew saw a slight change in the jurors' expressions.

"As I held the weapon firmly, Officer Whitley began punching me repeatedly and shouting for me to let the weapon go." Andrew shook his head and looked at Brian. "We fought for control, and the next thing I know, a gunshot rang out and Officer Whitley fell back off of me."

"He was shot…" Andrew spoke.

"Yes. He grabbed his shoulder, called me a son of a b and lunged towards me. Without thinking and out of fear, I fired another shot into the right side of Officer Whitley's chest. I immediately dropped the weapon to the ground."

"Christian, what happened after you fired the shot?" Andrew questioned. "What was going through your mind?"

"Not going to lie," Junior answered, "my first thought was to run. But Marcus and I decided it wasn't in our best interest to do that. After vomiting on the side of the road, I kneeled and called over Officer Whitley's radio that we needed an ambulance. I placed both of my hands over Officer Whitley's chest wound and applied pressure; the same way my father has shown me how to care for a wound. And then, I told Marcus to call my parents. He opened the car door to retrieve his phone and I heard a siren approach and car doors open. I heard police announce that they were with Miami P-D and they yelled for me to show my hands."

Andrew paced the floor and looked at the clock on the wall. Junior felt his heart was racing as he spoke about what was going on.

Junior knew all eyes were on him and he could feel the pressure. He kept catching glimpses of Anayi's hands as they quickly jotted down notes. Junior and Andrew knew that her line of questioning would be nothing nice.

"I couldn't show them my hands," Junior uttered. "If I'd have moved them, Officer Whitley may have died."

"What makes you say that?" Andrew questioned.

"He was going into shock," Junior responded. "And I feel that if my hands weren't there to slow the bleeding, the results would have been a lot worse."

Andrew nodded his head for Junior to continue.

"Well, the next thing I know when I looked at them, they had their guns aimed and were shouting directions to Marcus. They asked him to back out of the vehicle slowly with his hands raised." Junior picked up a tissue and wiped the tears from his eyes. "He complied and once he was out of the car, Officer Warren shouted gun and fired one shot."

Andrew softened his tone as the entire courtroom seemed to silence. Christian patted Raymond on his shoulder while holding Keisha's hand. He knew hearing this had to be hard for Raymond.

"And what happened after the shot rang out?" Andrew inquired.

"I heard and saw the shot and I took my hands from Officer Whitley. I immediately rose to my feet," Junior closed his eyes and remembered the incident. "I remember walking over to Marcus while guns were being aimed at me; I didn't care," Junior spoke softly, "nothing else mattered once I saw my best friend hit the ground." Junior wiped his eyes again.

"Come on, son," Christian mouthed to Junior, although he knew Junior wasn't looking at him.

Junior's lip quivered and Andrew noticed the jurors' expressions as this occurred.

"What happened next?" Andrew asked.

"I kneeled in front of Marcus and I saw the blood rushing from his chest near his heart." Junior teared more and Andrew spoke.

"Breathe," he spoke softly.

Junior inhaled deeply and exhaled slowly. He could feel his heart rate increasing as he spoke.

"I extended my hands to touch his and care for his wound, but it seems like as soon as I extended them, the officer pushed me face-first into the asphalt and put me in handcuffs," he sniffled. "I could even touch him to see if he was breathing."

"Junior," Andrew called him by his nickname, "when was the next time you saw Marcus?"

"After my parents bailed me out of prison. The officers put an ankle monitor on me and my mom drove me to the hospital."

"How was he?" Andrew asked.

"Stable, so they say," Junior sighed. "He's in a coma and has been that way for months; basically, a vegetable."

"Objection," Anayi spoke.

"On what grounds?" Andrew questioned. "Your Honor, I asked my client a question and he answered." Andrew glared at Anayi. "Or do you just not want the jury to hear about my other client's current health status?"

Matthew hit his gavel against the desk. "You two have been going at it since the start," he adjusted his glasses. "Ms. Jiménez, your objection is overruled."

Anayi scoffed in disgust.

"Mr. Brownstone and Ms. Jiménez, you all stop acting like children in my courtroom."

The jurors looked at one another as if they were suddenly conflicted. To Andrew, it seemed as though they'd previously made up their minds on the verdicts, but after hearing Junior's testimony, their minds changed.

"Christian," Andrew spoke again, "do you fear law enforcement?"

"What do you mean?" Junior asked.

Andrew paused for a potential objection; there was none, so he proceeded. "When you're driving or walking down the street, and you see a police officer, how do you feel?" Andrew rephrased.

"Objection," Anayi gave the objection Andrew was looking for.

"Withdrawn," Andrew conceded. He walked back to the defense's desk. "Your witness."

Anayi gathered her notebook and walked over to Junior.

"Christian, why is it that you all were pulled over during the stop that resulted in Whitley's injury?"

Junior cleared his throat. "I'm not sure, Officer Whitley never informed us of the reason for the stop."

"So, you're speculating that it was because he knew your vehicle and was on the hunt for you."

"Objection," Andrew intercepted.

"Sustained," Matthew replied.

Junior exhaled slowly.

"I want for you to take a look at the screen, okay?" Anayi walked over to the prosecution's desk and grabbed the small remote.

The court directed their attention to the screen.

"Now, just listen closely," she spoke as she loaded the video from Junior's phone on the night of the stop.

The volume of the radio decreased in the video and Junior was overheard.

"It's only one this time."

"Right there," Anayi spoke. "What was that noise?"

Junior displayed a puzzled look.

"I'm not sure what you're referring to," he replied.

"I'll play it again," she rewound the video to the beginning. She increased the volume and played it again.

This time, the court heard Marcus and Junior fastening the seatbelt.

"Sounds like a seatbelt fastening to me," Anayi spoke.

Junior slightly shrugged his shoulders.

"After dropping the girls off, we'd forgotten to put our seatbelts back on," he spoke slowly after looking to Andrew. "What does this have to do with anything?" Junior questioned.

"Well, you're saying you don't know why Officer Whitley pulled you over. There's a violation right there."

"Objection, Your Honor," Andrew rolled his eyes. Matthew looked over his glasses. "Are you telling me that at night, Officer Whitley could identify that these gentlemen didn't have on their seatbelts, while driving behind them?"

Anayi didn't respond to his question. "Withdrawn," she spoke. "Mr. Tate, one thing you continue to mention is that Officer Whitley knew who you were, and you keep insinuating that he was consistently on the lookout for you. During the first traffic stop you've described to us, he and Officer Montrose pulled you and Marcus over for failing to come to a complete stop before turning right on red."

"That's correct," Junior spoke.

"Yet, there were no tickets issued, no citations, or any of that, correct?" Anayi walked towards the stand.

Andrew saw where her line of questioning was going, and he jotted down some writing on the notepad. He looked behind him and got Christian's attention and passed him the notepad.

Christian read the note and nodded his head. Andrew nodded his head and redirected his attention to the front.

"How were you made aware that there was no footage of you running the light--?"

"Objection, argumentative," Andrew spoke.

"And that this was an unlawful stop," Anayi finished her question.

Junior looked left and then to the right. He made eye contact with his father.

Christian gave Junior a comforting look as though to say, 'it's okay'.

Andrew waited to see how Matthew would respond to his objection; he didn't.

"I know I didn't run a light," Junior defended. "As a matter of fact, I know I came to a complete stop because I was talking to Marcus about the game before I completed my turn."

"You say you didn't, but that's not my question," Anayi reiterated. "How did you know?"

Junior swallowed air. "The next day, Sergeant Gaines informed me that she reviewed the tapes and that there weren't any infractions committed by my vehicle at that intersection on the night in question."

Anayi smirked.

"Christian, who is Sergeant Gaines' superior?" she questioned.

Junior glanced at Francesca and his father.

"Objection, Your Honor," Andrew spoke immediately.

"Your Honor, I find it highly unlikely that Sergeant Gaines took it upon herself to look into the logs of stops the night before. We're trying to prove a case, and this will help establish credibility. The defendant just said Sergeant Gaines informed him that the stop was unlawful. How did *she* know what happened the night before?"

The jurors' eyes seemed to fixate on Junior; he could feel the pressure.

"Christian, you will answer the question," Matthew responded to Andrew's objection. "Objection overruled."

Andrew sat in the chair and waited for Junior to answer the question.

"Lieutenant Christian Tate is Sergeant Gaines' superior," Junior remarked.

All eyes went from Junior to his father and Francesca.

"You mean, the same Lieutenant Tate that isn't supposed to be on cases that he's closely related to?" Anayi taunted.

"Objection, Your Honor!" Andrew spoke.

"Withdrawn," Anayi remarked. She walked towards the jurors. "Mr. Tate, on the night of the stop where Officer Whitley was shot, you have made several claims that things were illegal. Are you taking law in school?"

"Objection, Your Honor," Andrew spoke again.

"No, I want to answer," Junior remarked.

Andrew looked at him sternly and Junior returned the stare.

Matthew looked at Andrew to see what he would do next.

"Objection, withdrawn," Andrew remarked.

"No," Junior answered Anayi. "I'm not studying law, but certain rules of engagement should be common sense," he continued. "For example, if I was an officer and I had to search a suspect and I know he'd been driving around in a vehicle, there's no way I would direct him to the hood of the vehicle to rest on, knowing it was hot."

"You say it's common sense, but the question is, is it *illegal?*" she questioned.

"I've been in prison for a while now," Junior resumed. "I've been speaking with my prestigious lawyer as well as my parents. I'm pretty sure I have an idea of what is and isn't legal."

"Your parents, or your father?" she cunningly asked.

"My parents," Junior bit back.

"You've made mistakes before, correct?" she questioned.

"I think we all have," Junior answered.

"So, using your answer, it's safe to say that Officer Whitley had a lapse in judgment when he said you moved your hands from the steering wheel."

Anayi acknowledged that Junior never moved his hands and she wanted to paint a picture of Brian to be as human as possible.

"No," Junior answered. "Even if it was a bad judgment, once I told him I never moved my hands, it shouldn't have turned into what it turned into," Junior was getting upset.

Andrew noticed this.

"Everything that escalated stemmed from some of the comments," she explained. "When you were pulled from the vehicle, it stemmed from the hand movements. Slammed to the ground, you were resisting arrest and stated, 'police brutality'. Officer Whitley lunging for the gun: you kicked him," Anayi shook her head slightly.

Andrew saw most of the jurors slightly nodding in agreement.

"Your Honor, I object," Andrew rose to his feet. Matthew looked above his glasses. "As an officer of the law, Officer Whitley is trained to de-escalate situations. Every incident Ms. Jiménez just brought to this court's attention would have been de-escalated by a trained officer with the right mindset."

"Sustained," Matthew remarked without hesitation.

"Let's fast forward," she continued, "to the shooting of your best friend." Anayi knew this would be a trigger for Junior and was hoping this would be his breaking point.

Junior inhaled sharply.

'Remain calm,' Andrew mouthed to him.

"You have testified to this court that you provided aid to Officer Whitley and continued to do so up until you were arrested."

Junior nodded his head.

"Yet, you also testified that once you saw Mr. Farris get shot, you stopped aiding Officer Whitley to check on Mr. Farris."

"This is correct," Junior spoke. "I administered aid to Officer Whitley for as long as possible; ensuring I kept applying pressure to his wound to slow the bleeding." Junior sat erect in the chair and Anayi walked towards the witness stand. "However, once I saw Officer Warren shoot my best friend, my focus diverted to him and I had to go check on him." Tears accumulated in Junior's eyes once again.

"So, you lied to the court about your intentions," Anayi asserted.

"No, I didn't lie," Junior started.

"You told this court that you did everything you could to assist Officer Whitley," Anayi attacked.

"And I did," Junior argued. "But—."

Andrew saw that she was on the attack and looked sternly at Junior to see how he would handle himself.

"When in reality, you comforted and handled him while it was convenient for you." Anayi aggressively paced the court. "But the moment you heard the gunshot and saw the body hit the floor, all the 'aiding' stopped."

"Objection!" Andrew shouted to her comment. "Your Honor, she's badgering the witness."

"Ms. Jiménez," Matthew spoke.

Anayi nodded her head to acknowledge Matthew but Junior continued.

"You're damn right," he spoke aggressively. "Officer Whitley has had it out for me since my father became his superior."

"Junior," Andrew spoke sternly.

"Marcus has been my best friend since forever," he continued. "Naturally, I'm going to ensure that he's okay. He's my damn brother."

"Son," Christian rose to his feet from the crowd.

Keisha held Christian's hand tightly.

"And you think that racist pig's life means more to me than my own brother's? Yeah, I wanted to help Whitley, due to my nature, but the moment Officer Warren's trigger-happy ass drove up and shot my best friend as though he were on a hunting spree, all that helping shit went out the window."

"Junior!" Christian firmly shouted from the crowd.

Matthew hit his gavel on the desk and the courtroom erupted in cheers and jeers. Andrew studied the jury and could see the confusion on their faces.

Junior showed a side to them that they weren't familiar with. He'd let all his emotions bottle up during the case and when Anayi touched certain topics and attacked, he let them all out.

Junior kept his head down.

"Lieutenant Tate, I got this," Matthew projected. "Sit down or I'll have you removed from this courtroom."

Christian sat and shook his head.

"It'll be okay," Francesca remarked.

Keisha kissed him on the cheek and continued to hold his hand tightly.

"Mr. Tate," Matthew spoke to Junior. "Keep it up," he warned.

Junior didn't acknowledge Matthew. As he thought about it, he realized this was the first time Matthew looked at and addressed him directly.

Anayi smirked. "Just a few more questions, Christian," she walked towards the witness stand.

Junior glared at her.

"After you fired the first shot towards Officer Whitley, what was running through your mind?"

Junior looked to Andrew; Andrew nodded his head.

"I grabbed the weapon just for the simple fact that I didn't want Officer Whitley to have it. If he'd have gotten it," Junior breathed deeply, "this would probably be an entirely different case right now. After the shot," Junior answered, "I was mortified," he admitted. "I didn't even know he was shot until he fell off of me. It wasn't even intentional; the gun just went off."

"So," Anayi pressured. "If you were mortified, why did you shoot again?"

"Look at him," Junior nodded towards Brian. "He lunged at me and it was a reflex. The gun was in my hand and I fired the weapon."

"Just, one more question," Anayi continued. "Based on your earlier outburst, do you wish the second shot hit Officer Whitley in a different part of his body? A vital organ, perhaps?"

"Objection, Your Honor," Andrew shouted.

"Withdrawn." Anayi nodded slightly. "No further questions." She walked back to the prosecution's desk.

Andrew walked to the witness desk. "Just a few questions for you, Christian. Do you feel in your heart that things would have gone differently that night had you let Officer Whitley take complete control, as he wanted?"

Junior answered. "Without a doubt."

"Had you not been Lieutenant Tate's son, do you feel that there would have been a different result?"

"I don't think I would have been stopped if I wasn't his son," Junior answered.

"What about Marcus?" Andrew questioned softly.

Junior slightly raised his eyebrows.

"If Marcus had come out of the vehicle even slower with his hands more visible, would he have been shot?"

Junior caught onto Andrew's direction.

"Your Honor, where is this going?" Anayi questioned.

Matthew shushed Anayi with his fingers. "Let's see where this goes," he remarked.

"I promise you," Junior began, "and we all saw it. Marcus backed out of the vehicle extremely slowly with his hands towards the top of the vehicle and as he backed out, his hands were to the sky. He couldn't have moved any slower."

"Why do you think Officer Warren fired the shot, if that's the case?" Andrew asked.

Anayi caught on and quickly called an objection.

"Sustained," Matthew remarked.

Andrew chuckled softly. "One more question, Christian."

Andrew paced the floor slowly. He looked at the clock, then to Christian, Keisha, Raymond, Francesca, and Bianca, to Brian, then to the jurors, and back to Junior.

"Do you regret firing the weapon twice that evening?"

Junior inhaled deeply and sighed.

"You know, anything I say will be turned and twisted by the prosecution in an attempt for the jury to see me as a monster, so does it really matter what I say?" a tear fell from Junior's eyes.

"Christian, please," Andrew spoke softly.

All the jurors looked directly at Junior.

Junior felt his heart racing as he could see all eyes were focused on him.

"No," he answered dryly.

"Were those shots taken genuinely out of fear for your life?" Andrew followed.

"Yes," Junior uttered.

Andrew walked back to the desk. "No further questions, Your Honor."

Court officers approached the stand and escorted Junior back to the desk.

Andrew turned and saw tears in Keisha and Bianca's eyes as Junior was escorted to the desk. Bianca turned and embraced Keisha and cried quietly.

Keisha put her hand on Bianca's back and Christian passed her a tissue.

Andrew faced the front and addressed the court as Junior stood next to him. "The defense rests, Your Honor."

Matthew took notes on his notepad before Anayi spoke.

"The prosecution rests, Your Honor," she said.

"Court will resume tomorrow at 0900 hours to begin with closing arguments. Jury, please remember to not discuss the trial with anyone outside of the twelve of you and there should be no communication or interference with anyone outside of the jury pool," Matthew glanced at the clock. "Attorneys, please come prepared to deliver closing arguments tomorrow. Again, we will resume with the prosecution tomorrow at 9 am sharp," he hit his gavel against the desk.

"All rise!" the court officer spoke and brought the congregation to a stand.

Junior exhaled deeply.

"You did great up there," Andrew assured him as Matthew exited the courtroom. "Don't let anyone tell you any differently."

"But I had the outburst. I'm sorry man; I just couldn't hold it in any longer," Junior apologized.

"No need to apologize at all," Andrew responded. "I'm going to use that outburst to our advantage. While the prosecution is going to try to use the outburst to paint you as a monster, I'm going to use it to pull at the jurors' hearts, primarily the women."

The court officers walked over and touched Junior's shoulder.

Christian and his gang walked over to the gate and embraced Junior before the officers began to escort him away.

"I'll be there tonight after your family leaves to go over tomorrow, Junior," Andrew spoke.

Junior nodded his head and walked with the officers.

"What a damn day," Andrew scoffed as he closed the briefcase.

15

Junior awoke early the next morning and sat in the foyer alongside Kanaan. Kanaan rolled up a blunt and pulled his small lighter from his pocket.

"Closing arguments, huh?" he questioned Junior.

"Yep," Junior looked at the television. He watched the news reporter's lips move as the headline read *'Tate Refers To Officer Whitley As A 'Racist Pig' In An Emotional Outburst'*.

"Man, what was all that about?" Kanaan questioned as he inhaled on the blunt.

"I can't even tell you, bro," Junior uttered. "She was pushing buttons that shouldn't have been pushed, and it just came out." Junior sighed. "But I'll be real with you," he lowered his tone, "I don't regret doing that shit. Junior shrugged his shoulders and continued. "My brother was shot, and bleeding and Brian has had it out for me ever since my father was put over him."

"With your father being a lieutenant, I would expect for you to be on the outside already," Kanaan inhaled on the blunt.

"I know, right," Junior remarked, "but legally, he can't be involved in the case. That's why everything he does, he does it as my father. Whether it's for the case, his gubernatorial run, or whatever else."

"I feel you, man," Kanaan spoke. "Well, I'm letting you know, that I'm behind you no matter what happens. You're a good dude, C.J.

And if anyone can sense when someone is bullshitting, it's me," Kanaan exhaled a cloud of smoke. "And I can tell you're not bullshitting me at all."

Junior looked at him with curiosity. "Thanks, man."

Kanaan noticed the look. "What's up?" he chuckled. "You want a hit?"

"Man, I shouldn't. I gotta be on my A-game for court."

"Gotta ease your mind," Kanaan reminded him. "I'm not telling you to do the shit because you know what's best but remember to keep your mind at ease. That's the best way for you to get by with all this pressure."

Junior gave thought to what Kanaan was saying.

Junior walked next to Andrew and stood erect. His shoulders were slumped, and Junior rolled his head around.

Andrew looked at Junior and studied him. "What's up?" he questioned.

"I'm just chilling," Junior spoke.

Andrew could see he wasn't fully there. He studied Junior's eyes and posture.

"Are you high?" he whispered to Junior. He didn't smell any marijuana, but he noticed Junior wasn't acting right.

"High off life," Junior remarked with a chuckle.

"Fuck," Andrew whispered. "Today of all days, really?" he questioned.

Christian was looking at Andrew and Junior's backs, but he could tell something was wrong.

"Straighten up," Andrew whispered sternly as he aggressively adjusted Junior's suit jacket. "We can't afford any fuck-ups today."

"Relax," Junior laughed quietly.

Christian leaned over and tapped Andrew. "What's going on?"

Andrew shook his head and motioned for the court officer to come over to them. When he reached, Andrew spoke again.

"Can you escort Mr. Tate to a quiet room where myself and Lieutenant Tate can speak to him?"

The officer nodded his head and touched Junior's shoulder. He walked him to a room; Christian and Andrew followed.

Keisha looked on to see what was going on but as they disappeared into the back, she held Bianca's hand tightly.

"What's going on?" Christian asked as the court officer left them in privacy.

"Your son is high," Andrew remarked.

Christian glared at Junior; Junior smirked at him.

"C.J., are you stupid?" Christian questioned. "Today is make-or-break for you and you come to court high?"

"Pops, fall back off me," Junior rebutted. "I wouldn't even be in this shit if your punk-ass cop didn't have it in for you."

"Lower your fucking tone and watch how you speak to me," Christian spoke sternly.

"Why should I have to watch my tone?" Junior spoke. "It's true, Pops."

"You and I both know Brian had absolutely no reason to stop you that night, and I'm doing what I can to get you out."

"How?" Junior remarked. "I've been in jail for a year now, Dad!"

"It's hard but that's no excuse for you coming in high," Christian reiterated.

Andrew wiped his face and paced the floor and the two went back-and-forth.

"What difference would it make?" Junior argued. "Either way, tonight, I'm going back to that uncomfortable ass cell."

"The best outcome right now is if we get this case dropped. But we need you to be on your A-game."

"And what if that shit doesn't happen?" Junior uttered. "What's plan B, *Dad?*"

"If that doesn't work, and that's a big if," Christian reminded his son, "when I win this election, I'll be in a better position to get you out."

Junior's eyes accumulated tears. He chuckled. "So, it's all about the election for you, huh?"

"You know that's not the case," Christian explained.

"Be my father!" Junior exclaimed as he raised his tone.

"C.J., that's not what your dad is saying," Andrew interjected.

"If that's all that matters to you, go back and work on your campaign," he cried lightly.

"Son," Christian spoke softly.

"Just go," Junior responded.

Christian wiped his eyes. He was hurt that Junior was hurt and it made him feel worse that there was nothing he could do to get his son out of the situation.

He walked closer and embraced Junior. Junior pulled away.

Andrew walked next to Christian. "I'll handle this," he assured him. "I know how to fix this. Trust me, I got you."

"I hope so, man," Christian spoke as he exited the room. He returned to his seat next to Keisha.

Andrew walked over to Junior and took off his suit jacket. "Sit down," he demanded.

Junior smirked and sat down.

"What's my name?" Andrew questioned.

"Andrew Brownstone," Junior rolled his eyes.

Andrew noticed that Junior's eyes were red.

"Don't do that in court," Andrew instructed. "Here, drink this," he gave Junior the bottle of water that was on the desk.

"What's the problem?" Junior questioned.

"Look," Andrew was getting irate, "straighten up! This is perhaps one of the most important days of the trial and we can't have anything messing it up."

Junior thought about what Andrew was saying and sat erect in the chair. He opened the water bottle and sipped it.

"Why is this happening to me?" Junior spoke softly.

"It's okay, we'll get this handled," Andrew continued to pace the floor. "But from here on out, we have to be on top of things," Andrew lowered his tone. "You are not to speak in court today." Andrew sniffed Junior's clothing. "You don't smell like marijuana, so we don't have to worry about that, but I need you to focus, Junior."

Junior nodded his head.

***

"Ladies and gentlemen of the jury, the court, Your Honor," Anayi began, "we are handling two separate cases: The State of Florida versus Christian Tate and Marcus Farris versus The State of Florida. Today, I'm going to review what has been presented to you throughout these cases."

The jurors all stared at Anayi. Andrew looked over to Junior, who was sitting beside him, fidgeting with his fingers.

"It's a lot of information, so we'll go slowly," she added. "Friday, July 20th, the skies were clear, and the roads were dry when Officer Brian Whitley observed a black Mustang making a traffic violation. On this night in question, he was riding solo. Although the protocol was to have two riders per car in the evening, his partner called off. Whitley was on his way to the station to retrieve his secondary ride along from the station when he was noticed the infraction being committed."

Andrew lightly tapped his fingers on the desk and continuously looked over to Junior; Junior appeared to be nodding off. Andrew nudged him under the table and passed him a glass of water.

"What do we know? Let's see," Anayi continued. "When Officer Whitley pulled the vehicle over, he was able to identify the driver as the defendant, Christian Tate, Jr., and the passenger as the defendant, Marcus Farris. Officer Whitley observed a beverage concoction that he believed to be lean; a beverage that consists of the carbonated beverage Sprite and is mixed with cough syrup." Anayi glanced at Junior and Andrew; she looked back to the jurors. "Whitley was able to make a positive identification due to previous interactions with the defendants. After making the positive ID on the defendants, Tate became irate and was removed from the vehicle."

Andrew kept his hands on the table as Junior sipped the water.

"We know Tate tensed his muscles and resisted arrest from when Whitley tried to detain him. We know that he fought with Whitley on the ground and kicked him; using so much force that the blow knocked Whitley off him."

Andrew looked at Junior once more and noticed he was pouring his third cup of water. He hoped Anayi and the jurors didn't notice his odd behavior.

"We know that as he and Whitley fought for control, the gun went off. The defense may press that the shot was an accident and there isn't evidence to show that it wasn't. So," Anayi laughed lightly, "let's just say it was an accident."

Andrew glared at her as she smirked.

"After the first shot, we know Tate continued to hold the weapon. Had it been an accident as the defense presents, why did he hold on to the weapon?" Anayi took a sip of her water. She returned the cup to the desk. "Once Whitley realized he was shot, he figured the city would be in jeopardy had Tate controlled the weapon. He lunged at Tate for the weapon, and Tate fired a second shot," she demonstrated where the bullet struck Whitley. "Right here," she pointed, "this is where the bullet landed." Anayi walked to the prosecution's desk. "The defense would want for you to believe that Tate was fearing for his life and didn't intend on shooting Whitley, and the proof they provide for this: Tate provided aid to Whitley."

Andrew saw Matthew look at Junior as he'd depleted the water dispenser and was examining the container for more water.

"Ms. Jiménez, one second," Matthew interjected.

Anayi stopped talking and looked in Matthew's direction, and then to Andrew and Junior.

"Mr. Brownstone, is there something wrong?" he questioned.

Andrew cleared his throat. "Nothing, Your Honor. My client is just a little dehydrated. He had an extensive workout last night and this morning, and the breakfast he had dried his mouth out."

Andrew did his best to cover for Junior, but it was proving to be difficult, especially since all eyes were now on them.

"We'll work on getting another pitcher of water for your table," Matthew uttered. "But right now, we are in the middle of the prosecution's closing argument. Please advise your client to tone it down."

Junior whispered in Andrew's ear.

"We will do that, Your Honor," Andrew complied, "but I also have a request that the court grant my client a short bathroom break. He's been drinking water all morning and he really must use the facilities."

Matthew looked at them sternly. Christian looked at Andrew and understood why he was calling for the recess.

Christian kept his hand on top of Keisha's.

"Seriously?" he questioned.

"I'm very serious, Your Honor," Andrew spoke. "It's weird because he's been drinking water all morning, but he's still dehydrated. He'll be okay though; he just needs to use the washroom and to get a little air."

Matthew studied Junior, but the only thing that appeared to be out of the ordinary was his unusual thirst.

Anayi also studied Junior for a weakness in the defense. She examined him closely.

"I'll grant your client the short recess, although we are in the middle of arguments. Your water will be refilled upon return and with a court officer escort, your client will get a five-minute intermission to be outside."

"Thank you, Your Honor," Andrew remarked.

"Court will resume in fifteen minutes," Matthew hit his gavel against the desk.

Matthew was the first to leave the courtroom; the jurors were escorted to the jury room, and then the congregation except for Junior's family, the prosecution team, and Andrew.

The court officers walked over to Andrew and Junior. The officer held Junior's arm.

"We'll be escorting him to the washroom and if you wish to consult with your client, we will be on the first-floor washroom and we'll use the South entrance to go outside."

Andrew nodded his head. "Be right there, Junior."

Anayi walked over to the defense's desk. "I don't know what stunt you're trying to pull," she spoke to Andrew, "but I'm watching you."

"Good luck, Miss Jiménez," Andrew smiled as she walked away.

Andrew turned to Christian, Keisha, Bianca, Raymond, and Francesca.

"I know what's up," Raymond chuckled, nearly immediately.

Andrew shook his head with a scoff.

"What do you mean?" Keisha questioned. Christian didn't inform her of what was going on.

"Keisha, there's something going on with Junior, but your husband and I have it handled," Andrew responded.

"What's going on?" Keisha raised her eyebrows. "Raymond, what's up?"

Keisha knew Andrew wouldn't tell her anything to worry her and since Raymond spoke up, she figured her could tell her what he meant.

Andrew threw his hands up in defeat.

"Keisha," Raymond sighed, "your son is high. I can see it in his behavior."

"Is that boy stupid?" she shook her head. "Why on Earth would he show up high, today?"

Christian interjected. "Babe, let's just be cool. Andrew says he's got it handled," Christian looked at Andrew.

Andrew nodded his head.

"So, let's let him handle it," Christian finished.

"I'm going to go out there with him," Andrew uttered. "Keisha, don't hold this against him," he looked at Keisha.

"He's going through something none of us could imagine," Christian shook his head. "Being in jail, it does something to your mind and you start acting out of character."

"You're right about that," Raymond confirmed. "He's just going through something right now, Keisha," he finished.

Andrew patted her on the shoulder. "Everything will be fine," he concluded before walking away.

Andrew walked outside and waited for the guard to escort Junior from the building. He pulled out his phone and checked the time.

"Where are they?" he questioned aloud.

As he spoke, the officer walked outside with Junior.

"Officer, can I get a moment with my client alone? I understand you all have to be nearby, but I have a matter I would like to discuss in private," Andrew explained. "I will keep my hands visible at all times where you can see them, as will my client."

Junior nodded in agreement.

"We have to have him back in a few moments," the officer explained, but I'll give you two some space."

The officer walked away before Andrew began speaking.

"Okay, I'm covering for you as much as I can, C.J.," Andrew uttered, "but I need your help, now."

"I'm good," Junior responded as he cleared his throat. "This air is what I needed."

"No one's happy about today," Andrew continued. "The stunt you pulled was off-the-wall," he recited.

"I don't know," Junior responded. "It's like, I know I shouldn't, but Andrew, that place is eating me up," he sighed.

"I've spoken to your folks and everyone on our side, but we need to ensure the jury doesn't know what's going on. We need to keep the judge out of it, but most importantly, we need to keep Anayi clueless," Andrew looked at his watch. They had to be back in the courtroom in three minutes.

"I got it," Junior answered again. "I don't know why I decided to even try the blunt before my court appearance," he spoke softly. "But I'm good now."

"Let's go back in here and kill it, then," Andrew adjusted Junior's sportscoat. Andrew looked at the officer and nodded his head.

The officer walked over and touched Junior on the shoulder. Andrew didn't notice, but Anayi was merely inches away and heard the entire conversation.

She smiled devilishly and walked inside the courthouse.

Andrew and Junior took their places at the desk once they arrived back in the courtroom. Anayi trailed and stood behind the prosecution's desk. She grinned in the direction of Andrew and Junior.

"All rise," the bailiff brought the courtroom to a stand.

Matthew entered and sat down. The court officer brought the jury in and they had a seat.

"Are we ready to proceed?" Matthew questioned.

"Yes, Your Honor," Andrew responded.

"Miss Jiménez, the floor is yours."

Anayi nodded her head and walked from behind the desk.

"Before the break, I was explaining to you how the defense would argue that since the defendant, Christian Tate, Jr., provided aid to Officer Whitley, that it was a mistake. Two shots are no mistake," she insisted. "They say it was a reflex," she slowly paced the floor; one foot in front of the other. "My question that I tell you to pose is 'how'," Anayi looked at the jurors.

Andrew glanced at Junior; all seemed normal now.

"Sure, Tate administered aid to Officer Whitley, but look at where the bullets struck him," she pressed a button on the remote and the projector switched screens. "The first was in his shoulder; the second was in his chest. A couple of inches over, and Officer Whitley would be six-feet under," she exaggerated to get a response from the jury. "And all this over what, a traffic stop with weed and alcohol in the vehicle."

"Objection, Your Honor," Andrew spoke. "My client's toxicology report showed no traces of weed or alcohol in his system and police recovered nothing illegal from his vehicle."

"Stick with the facts, Miss Jiménez," Matthew spoke.

Anayi smirked.

"Surely, Officer Whitley had to be a little nervous. He has these two, muscular men who could completely obliterate him if they'd wanted to."

"Objection, Your Honor!" Andrew insisted.

"Miss Jiménez, I'm not warning you again," Matthew warned.

Anayi shook her head slightly and continued.

"The defense says Tate provided aid to my client up until his arrest. She walked in front of Matthew and turned to face the court. "This isn't accurate. He administered aid up until about 9:15 pm. Forensics show the first shot was fired around 9:06 pm. So, he provided roughly nine minutes of 'aid'," she used her fingers to insinuate air-quotes. "Officer Warren and his ride-along arrived around 9:14 pm," she switched cases. "Why am I mentioning the times?" she questioned as she walked towards the jurors. "This information is critical because it will show exactly what went on during this whole ordeal. Tate stopped administering aid at 9:15 pm, which is the moment that Officer Warren's bullet struck his friend."

Andrew shook his head lightly and took notes.

"Tate even said it himself," Anayi recited. "He called Officer Warren a racist pig, called him trigger-happy, and even said 'all that helping 's' went out the window'." Anayi looked in the direction of Junior. "And you're telling me he's remorseful? You're telling me it was an accident when he said himself, and I quote, 'you think that racist pig's life means more to me than my own brother's'?"

The jurors all looked at Junior. Andrew seemed unphased by this as he knew Anayi was going to take this angle.

"Marcus Farris," she looked directly at the jurors. Similarly to Judy, Andrew could tell she'd practiced speaking directly to the jurors. "How did he get tangled in all of this?" she questioned. "Riding around at night with Tate to get to the debate. Which is interesting, because I don't know of a single teenager who's interested that much in politics to rush to see a debate, after a long night of studying."

"Yea, but if your dad is running and you support him 100%, you'll do what you have to do," Junior mumbled.

"But, back to Marcus," she put her focus back on Marcus. "During the entire stop with Whitley, you could hear how uncooperative his tone was." Anayi began to paint the picture. Junior's blood began to boil.

"His very first words to Officer Whitley were 'go on with that s'," Anayi shook her head slowly. "Followed by whispers saying, 'you see how this m-f is acting'. Later, 'f, why are we getting pulled over'." Anayi looked at the jurors again.

Andrew looked at Matthew and then to the jurors for signs of emotion.

"And later, Officer Warren arrives on the scene and shouts for Tate and Farris to show their hands. Tate informs Warren that he's unable to do so and Farris is in the vehicle. Now," she paused, "it's dark. Tints on the windows," she pressed a button and showed Junior's vehicle on the screen, "and a muscular male is inside of a vehicle."

The jurors showed looks of surprise, yet agreement, with what Anayi was saying. Some shook their heads.

"Warren shouts for him to come out of the vehicle with his hands up slowly. Farris complies, but as he backs out, he has something in his hand."

Christian looked at Jake; he kept his eyes forward and avoided eye contact with Christian.

"In the eyes of Officer Warren, he's thinking 'oh no, he's got a weapon. He's going to shoot', and as a result, he fired his weapon one time to disarm the suspect. Unfortunately, that shot was a little too close to the heart and, as a result, has left him in a coma, but Officer Warren truly felt that he and his fellow officer's lives were in danger."

Some of the female jurors had tears in their eyes. One of the male jurors cleared his throat.

"Was there a motive for either of these gentlemen before either of these shootings occurred? Defendant Christian Tate has been known to speak up and get riled up over the smallest of things. You've heard from the security guard, the counselor of the school as well as an encounter at the convenience store in which Tate's behavior took others by surprise; numerous technical fouls throughout his career, many altercations at the school. So, why is it surprising that he has a short temper?" Anayi continued to question. "And we all know the expression you are who you hang around," she continued.

Junior glanced at her but remained silent.

"Every single time Mr. Tate has been in some kind of trouble, Mr. Farris was there as well. Whether it's in the picture of the two the prosecution has presented earlier to their last encounter with the law."

Anayi paced the floor and walked closer to the defense's desk.

"When Officer Whitley pulled the two gentlemen over, it was for a traffic violation but when he pulled them over, he mentioned that he observed what he assumed was an illegal substance in a Sprite bottle and presumed the two were engaging in narcotics before the drive. The defense denies these claims, as the toxicology reports show no evidence of alcohol or narcotics in the system, but when your father is a police officer and one father is an ex-convict, you can get around stuff like that," Anayi spoke.

Andrew worried where she was heading with this, so he shouted for an objection.

"Objection, Your Honor!"

"Including showing up to court intoxicated," Anayi finished; the objection came at the same time she was finishing her statement. Anayi grinned and all eyes turned to Junior.

Andrew stood tall but his stomach sunk as there were murmurs around the courtroom.

All the jurors studied Junior and Matthew displayed a concerned look. He looked at Andrew with disappointment.

Christian held Keisha's hand tightly and shook his head.

"Objection, sustained," Matthew spoke. "Referring to the parents and accusing them of being able to make a charge disappear or beat the system isn't something I'm going to tolerate," he spoke to Anayi. "But, counselors, approach."

Andrew adjusted his tie and rolled up his sleeves. He patted Junior on the back and walked to Matthew's desk; Anayi came from the other end.

"Counselor, you are under oath," he spoke to Andrew. "Is your client intoxicated, as Jiménez has just claimed?"

Andrew wiped his face but didn't show weakness. He looked over his shoulder at Junior.

Andrew chuckled.

"Your Honor, certain things are beyond our control and—."

"Is your client intoxicated or not?" he pressed once more.

Andrew sighed. "He was earlier, Your Honor…"

Matthew groaned lightly.

"But he's good-to-go now," Andrew finished. "He's alert and vigilant."

"Mr. Brownstone, having your client show up intoxicated is beyond disrespectful to me, to this courtroom, to this case, to himself, his family, as well as you and your practice," Matthew cleared his throat. "We are so far along in this case, I will keep this off-the-record and I'm not going to prolong it, but I hope you have one hell-of-a closing argument."

Junior looked on from the defense desk as he noticed Matthew speaking in a whisper and Andrew nodding his head. Junior was upset with himself for putting them in this situation.

Andrew and Anayi turned around and Andrew stood next to Junior.

Matthew took notes. "The prosecution may proceed."

"Ladies and gentlemen," Anayi spoke to the jury again, "with all of the evidence presented to you, you have to see that Officer Jake Warren was justified in firing his weapon against Marcus Farris and that Christian Tate wasn't justified in firing his weapon against Officer Brian Whitley. The first shot, we can say was probably an accident, but when he fired for the second time, the innocence of the first shot was voided."

Anayi looked at Junior with a piercing glare. Andrew returned the glare on behalf of Junior.

"Ladies and gentlemen, what occurred with Officer Whitley and Christian Tate may have not been premeditated, but it wasn't justified. Tate intended to do harm to Whitley. Shot number one may have been an accident, but it leads us to ask: why did Tate lunge for the weapon in the first place." Anayi looked at the jurors. "Have you all ever heard the phrase 'if you pull a gun out, be prepared to use it'?"

The jurors looked at one another and back to Anayi.

"That's precisely what Tate did. He lunged for the weapon with the intent to use it. When he took that second shot, it wasn't a reflex, as the defense claims. It was an intent to murder Whitley."

Anayi ran her fingers through her hair and made eye contact with one juror.

"The intent to murder isn't always deemed as committing the murder," Anayi spoke again. "This has been proven, as Officer Brian Whitley is still here with us today. Christian Tate, Jr., intended to cause great bodily harm to Officer Whitley, or else, he would not have fired two shots into my client. As presented, the first shot may have been an accident, but as the ballistics show, a few inches to the left and Officer Whitley would be six feet under." Anayi looked at Junior again. "The defendant didn't fear for his life," she argued. He and Whitley had a vendetta, as so when the opportunity presented itself, he decided to take advantage." She looked back to the jurors. "Using what you know, the state asks that you return a verdict that not only supports the evidence presented, but is also fair, and that is a verdict of guilty of the crimes of attempted murder of a police officer, two counts of aggravated battery with a firearm, and one count of resisting arrest. The only fair verdict in the Marcus Farris trial is an acquittal, as Officer Warren truly feared for his life in firing the shot that injured Marcus Farris. Thank you," she returned to the prosecution's desk.

Andrew exhaled and looked at the jurors as they awaited his argument. Anayi looked over to Andrew and Junior and put her files away in her briefcase.

Andrew took a deep breath and spoke clearly after rising to his feet.

"Christian Tate, Jr. and Marcus Farris are innocent of said crimes," he began. "At the beginning of the case, Judge Zalinski polled each of you," he looked at the jurors, "on whether you would be truthful, be fair, follow the evidence and hold the prosecutors to their burden of proving these young men guilty of such heinous acts. You were also expected to presume Christian Tate Jr., and Officer Jake Warren innocent throughout the trial; this was explained to you when you were selected to be jurors."

Christian watched Andrew as he spoke and began to relive his own trial.

"Now, it's time for you to own up to the promises you all made." Andrew walked towards the jury box. "Let's take a look at the evidence presented and I'll demonstrate why they have failed to prove Junior's guilt and Officer Warren's innocence. *Safeway*," Andrew cleared his throat. "The video from the application is a key piece of evidence, and without it, it would pretty much be an open-and-shut case." Andrew looked at Christian for a split second before continuing.

"We aren't arguing that Christian didn't shoot Officer Whitley, yet we're arguing the reasoning behind it. We're not arguing that Officer Warren didn't shoot Marcus; we're arguing his motive behind the shooting. Nothing can be done about what happened; it's unfortunate on both ends. There are two questions posed: was Christian Tate, Jr. fearing for his life during his encounter with Officer Brian Whitley, and was Officer Jake Warren fearing for *his life* during his encounter with Marcus Farris?" Andrew looked to Anayi but continued to speak to the jurors. "See the similarity? The answer couldn't possibly be yes to both questions."

Andrew walked over to the defense's desk and picked up a folder. He walked back over to the jurors after reading the piece of paper within.

"Which side of the fence are you on?" Andrew questioned, rhetorically. "I guess it comes down to which story you believe more. Do you believe the testimony of John Lisle, the school security guard, who wasn't able to identify Robert Eikman as the aggressor and has perjured himself in court?" Andrew glanced at John in the audience and back to the jurors. "Perhaps, you're trusting the word of Mr. Stanton, the school counselor who argues that a White adolescent would be successful in ten years, as opposed to a young Black man. The same counselor who has posts on his social media showing his bias towards Nanos in the Wallace-v-Nanos case nearly twenty years back."

Andrew noticed a few looks of curiosity on the jurors' faces.

"Perhaps you're siding with the officers in this case." Andrew glared at Brian and Jake. "After all, they are sworn to serve, protect, and abide by the law at all times."

Junior could see the concern on the jurors' faces, but he kept his head held high; he didn't want to show weakness.

"The same officer who shouted racial slurs to the defendant and demeaned him numerous times throughout the encounter; you've seen and heard it for yourself," Andrew reminded the jury. "During the encounter, Christian feared for his life: imagine being an eighteen-year-old teenager and after the first shot rang out, you have a 290-pound officer lunging for you, shouting, excuse my language, 'son of a bitch-ass'," Andrew swore for the jurors in order to get his point across. "What about Officer Warren, who has fired his weapon sixteen times over his three-year tenure; 60% of the time, the shootings were on African-American men. The same officer who, and I quote, 'did what he had to do'."

Christian looked over to Raymond and nodded his head at Andrew's closing argument.

"Or," Andrew turned around and paced the floor towards the defenses' desk. "Do you believe the words of Bianca Taylor; the person who, aside from his parents, saw Christian Tate Jr., regularly, and has spent the most time with him? Sergeant Gaines?" Andrew raised his tone. "Not only has she known Christian and Marcus since birth, but she's also ranked pretty high in the police department. If we're listening to officers' testimony, she's testified that neither of the stops were lawful and Officer Whitley had no reason to stop Christian. Sierra Flemming," Andrew looked at Junior and then back to the jurors. "Marcus' girlfriend. While she was on the stand, you saw the tears in her eyes and the fear on her lip. She's with Marcus all the time," Andrew emitted. "If anyone knows him, it's her. She referred to him as one of the kindest souls you'd ever get to meet. Christian and Marcus' mothers; what mother wouldn't say what has to be said to help her son?" Andrew acknowledged what the jurors were thinking.

There were a few chuckles of awkwardness around the courtroom and from the jurors.

"But you saw Mrs. Farris crying as she testified under oath, over Skype, right outside of her son's hospital room. "She said the doctors aren't sure of his recovery. Imagine that," Andrew shook his head and saw the women jurors' accumulate tears in their eyes. "A brilliant young man who may have had his future taken away, all because of an officer who thought he saw a weapon." Andrew looked around the courtroom and saw a mixture of emotions. His eyes landed on Jake. "The same officer who said Marcus was probably up to no good and didn't fear me."

Andrew made sure to point out the crucial testimony from each of the witnesses to sway the jurors' decision.

"Lieutenant Tate," Andrew looked at Christian. "He's over his whole department. As I said, if we're taking the testimony of sworn officers, we must listen to the top-ranking officers. Both Lieutenant Tate and Sergeant Gaines have testified that the stops were unlawful yet were made. No tickets were issued during the first stop, no citations were given; if there was an infraction, ladies and gentlemen," Andrew looked at the jurors, "why wasn't anything issued? How about the defendant himself, Christian Tate, Jr. Now," Andrew paced the floor. "I know what you all are thinking, of course the defendant would say what he has to say to get off, but this is an honor student — the star point guard of his team. Why would he go and intentionally get himself tangled up in some mess like this and risk losing everything he's worked for?"

The jurors looked around, but Andrew wasn't sure if he'd convinced them, so he decided to turn up the pressure.

"Ladies and gentlemen, I'm presenting these cases to you, and I can't help but wonder: when did it become illegal to be Black in America?" Andrew questioned.

Several jurors expressed shock in their eyes; Christian's eyes also widened. He knew Andrew was taking a big leap, but he also knew his passion for cases like this.

"Being the professional I am, I get nervous when I'm driving down the street at night. I ensure my volume is turned down so low that I can barely hear it, just to avoid getting pulled over. So, I can only imagine how two 'A' students feel. Picture me this," he cleared his throat, "you've just scored the winning shot for your team and you're so ecstatic that you and your family go and celebrate. While driving along, you see sirens in your rearview and you promptly pull over to the side of the road. Two officers emerge and you feel obligated to keep your hands at ten-and-two on the steering wheel."

Andrew made sure to attempt the establishment of eye contact with the African American jurors.

"You know you have nothing to be nervous about, yet you can't stop your heart from racing as they approach. However, you remember your manners and etiquette and present them flawlessly; saying 'good evening' and 'yes sir, no sir'. But still, it isn't enough for the officers to engage in a professional way."

Anayi wanted to object but remained silent. She knew any objections, unless essential, wouldn't stick.

"After about fifteen-to-twenty minutes later, the officers let you go with a warning," Andrew took a pause. "The real reason for the stop, to establish dominance; not because you've broken any laws. When you meet up with the rest of your family, you inform them of the stop because you can't believe what had just transpired."

Andrew paced the floor slowly and Junior lifted his head.

"Fast forward a few months, you and your friend are driving after leaving school. You're so excited because you know that each of you is going to dominate your exams," he continued.

Bianca smiled slightly as she listened to Andrew. Junior looked behind him and made eye contact with her.

'I love you,' she mouthed to Junior.

Junior nodded and smiled. 'I love you, too.' He turned around in his seat.

"Suddenly, you notice sirens as you merge onto the expressway, so you follow protocol," Andrew uttered. "Hands at ten-and-two, you immediately pull over to the right. You do nothing to make the officer nervous."

Junior swallowed air as Andrew spoke passionately.

"As the officer speaks to you, you can see he's irate. Meanwhile, your friend is trying to calm the officer down with his words; nothing seems to work. Suddenly, the officer shouts obscenities to you and says he saw you move your hands, so he pulls you out of the car; ripping the fabric of the new t-shirt you'd just purchased. Instead of walking you around to the trunk of the vehicle, he walks you around to the hood and demands you lean against it." Andrew shook his head lightly. "Remember, you'd been driving your car for nearly twenty-to-thirty minutes, so the engine's temperature is over two-hundred degrees. You explain to the officer that the hood is hot, and he forcefully slams you down, all while continuing to shout obscenities to you and your friend."

Christian noticed tears on some of the jurors faces. He knew that Andrew noticed this and would take advantage.
"He swings you down to the ground and starts shouting for you to stop resisting. But you notice that as he's fighting, he's loosening his gun-holster with his free hand. This is when you see no other choice but to defend yourself in some way. As the gun falls to the earth, you and the officer both go for it, and while tussling, a shot rings out. *Blaow*," Andrew made the sound effect. "The officer is struck, and you have control of the weapon. You'd never shot a weapon before, so you're mortified as to what's happened. But that shot doesn't stop the officer," Andrew stopped pacing the floor and looked at the jurors. "He lunges at you and out of fear, you fire the weapon again. As he falls to the Earth, your first thought is 'what have I done' and you just want to run, but instead, you provide aid to the officer."

Andrew walked to the desk and took a sip of water.
"The time is now roughly 9:07 p.m. The weather is clear, but the sun has set; it's a crescent moon out, so there's little visibility, considering where you were stopped lacked adequate lighting. You shout to your friend to call your parents and he complies. Roughly five-to-ten minutes later, another police car arrives on the scene." Andrew gently bit his lip. "Your friend is still in the vehicle as the officer shouts for you to show him your hands. You inform him that you're unable to do so, and the same officer shouts for your friend to exit the vehicle with his hands raised. Your friend begins to exit the vehicle; he inches out with his hands raised as high as they will go while he's in the vehicle. But what your friend doesn't know is that a gun is being aimed at him as he exits the vehicle.

First, his tattoos are revealed, and then his dreads. This is enough to startle the officer. Your friend's face is slightly revealed, and the officer sees an object in his hand; he fires one shot. *Blaow,* your friend falls to the Earth."

Several jurors had tears in their eyes; even the men and while he was happy to get this response, telling the story infuriated him.

"The aid you're administering ceases as you immediately rise to your feet to check on your friend. Not even considering the weapons being aimed at you, you walk slowly over to your friend and kneel, and as soon as you get on your knees, you are arrested. You weren't able to confirm if your friend was even alive," Andrew cleared his throat. "My apologies, your best friend. Someone you've known all your life; someone who's been there through thick-and-thin."

Christian nodded his head slowly as Andrew spoke.

"Now, imagine these two young males are White and the officers are Black. Would this country stand for it?" Andrew looked at each of the jurors before continuing. "Do you see the hypocrisy? Not just the hypocrisy, the American hypocrisy?" he corrected. "Any other country wouldn't permit this. Pardon me in advance, Your Honor," he looked at Matthew and back to the jury. "400 years of suffering to build a country that doesn't even want us. Slavery ended roughly 175 years ago, but the mindset hasn't gone anywhere. We follow every order, yet, we're still gunned down in the street. We comply with orders, yet we're still abused. We are the most accepting group, yet the most hated. You love and imitate our culture, our dances, our food, our hairstyles, yet you hate *us.* Something about the pigment of our skin just petrifies America. Even the clerk at the convenience store got scared once Christian began to defend his father. Now," Andrew turned slightly and looked at Junior, "if he didn't defend his father's name, he would be considered a punk, a wuss, maybe even a sellout." Andrew faced the jurors again. "We can't win for losing. What's so bad about being Black?" Andrew paused for roughly ten seconds for effect. He ensured to enunciate every word of his next sentence, for emphasis. "Emmet Till, Anthony Hill, Oscar Grant, Tony Robinson, Walter Scott, Philando Castile, Sandra Bland, George Floyd, Jacob Blake, Damian Clark, Michael Brown, Breonna Taylor, Margaret Mitchell, Alesia Thomas, Ahmaud Arbery, Tamir Rice, Aiyana Jones,

Trayvon Martin —" Andrew wiped his eyes as a few tears had accumulated. "Christian Tate, Jr., Marcus Farris." Andrew sniffled. "When will it end?"

There was an eerie silence in the courtroom as Andrew walked back to the desk. Several jurors used Kleenex to wipe their eyes. Many members of the court had tears in their eyes following Andrew's closing argument, including Anayi.

"The defense rests, Your Honor."

16

Junior sat in the weight room alongside Kanaan as the television played.

"I saw your lawyer on TV during closing arguments, young blood," Kanaan commented. "He's pretty solid." Kanaan curled the weight as he kept one hand on his knee.

"Yeah, he's doing his thing," Junior spoke with a smile. "I have a good feeling about the outcome of everything."

"Man, like I keep telling you," Kanaan put the weight down and rose to his feet, "keep your head high and keep pushing."

Junior nodded and looked at the television.

"We are entering week 2 of jury deliberations in the infamous Christian Tate and Marcus Farris trial. After two powerful arguments from both the prosecution and defense, the jurors were given instructions and left to deliberate on two trials." The news report displayed both Junior and Marcus' image on the screen. *"Marcus Farris is still fighting for his life, following the gunshot administered by Officer Jake Warren. Officer Brian Whitley is on active desk duty following his interaction with Christian Tate."*

Junior shook his head as they spoke. Kanaan noticed this.

"We will be following this trial with up-to-the-minute results, as the jury is expected to return at any moment with a verdict."

"Thanks, Geri," the male anchor spoke as the camera panned to him. *"Talks of this trial are also proving to influence Lieutenant Christian Tate's gubernatorial run. Polls have shown that interest in Lieutenant Tate has gone up nearly 75% since his son's lawyer's closing argument. The last we have heard from Tate, publicly, was roughly a month ago. Sources reveal to us he is diverting the bulk of his attention to keeping the city safe and supporting his son."*

Junior turned the television down and smiled.

"Sounds like you have a hell-of-a-father," Kanaan remarked.

"Yeah, man, he's pretty amazing," Junior admitted. "But on the day of closing arguments, I kind of went off on him."

"Why?" Kanaan lit a blunt.

Junior pointed to the blunt. "Because of that thing right there," Junior chuckled. "I shouldn't have smoked that weed before my case."

Kanaan exhaled smoke. "The thing about this is that it will relax your mind," he chuckled. "What did it do to you?"

"Man," Junior laid on the bench. "Spot me," he instructed.

Kanaan put the blunt between his lips and walked behind Junior.

"I was fried, you feel me?" Junior laughed as he lifted the weight. "My lawyer could tell, my uncle could tell. Shit, we tried to hide it from the prosecutor, but somehow, she found out." Junior continued to lower and raise the weight.

"She use it against you?" Kanaan questioned.

"She tried to," Junior spoke. "But Andrew controlled it. But don't give me that shit before sentencing," he chuckled as he grunted with the weight.

"You a grown-ass man," Kanaan laughed. "I didn't make you smoke it, boss."

Junior laughed. "You're right. But peer pressure is a muthafucka'," he laughed.

"God put this on the Earth for us," Kanaan uttered as Junior lifted.

"Man, if you don't get that cliché ass line the fuck up outta here," Junior remarked as he returned the weight to the rack and sat erect.

Tim and his crew entered the weight room. The last man to enter looped a shirt through the handles of the door to prevent entry or exit.

Junior and Kanaan rose to their feet and Junior's heart started to beat rapidly. Tim looked at Junior and wrapped a shirt around his fist.

"So, this what we're doing now?" Kanaan spoke as he saw they were outnumbered.

"With all due respect," Tim spoke, "this don't got shit to do with you, K. This is between me and the kid."

"With all *disrespect*, if it's between you and my mans here, it's got everything to do with me." Kanaan looked around at Tim's crew. "You've been on his ass ever since he came into this place."

"Tell me he hasn't deserved this shit," Tim replied.

"What the fuck? How?" Junior spoke. "The fuck did I do when I got here?"

"Nigger, your daddy is top cop and killed Smith 20 years back," Tim argued passionately.

Junior groaned. "Man, y'all have got to let that shit go!" Junior spoke. "Benjamin's punk-ass pulled out a gun on my father and even called him a nigga with his dying breath."

Tim's crew walked in front of Kanaan as Tim approached Junior.

Kanaan tried to fight around the men, but there were four of Tim's crew members; he couldn't take them alone.

Tim approached Junior and Junior put up his fists. Two more of Tim's guys came behind Junior and grabbed his arms.

"What the fuck?" Junior questioned as he tried to jerk away.

"This is for Benjamin," Tim landed a punch in Junior's stomach.

Junior grunted and winced with pain as the punch connected.

"And Zimmerman," he punched Junior again. Tim smiled at Junior's pain.

"Come on, Tim, that shit isn't cool. "At least let him defend himself," Kanaan shouted over the men.

"Roof," Tim landed another punch in Junior's ribs.

"Fuck!" Junior exclaimed as he fell to his knees.

Tim's crew members picked Junior up on his feet.

Junior felt helpless as Tim continued to land punches. He saw the men holding Kanaan and shook his head.

Kanaan hated to see this, and he didn't care about the repercussions. He didn't traditionally believe in his next action, but something had to be done before Junior was severely harmed.

Kanaan punched one of the men holding him in the face and as they let him go, he pulled out a shank. He aimed the weapon at the men and began to cut at them.

It all occurred so suddenly that neither of them had a chance to react before they were each cut; all in their sides.

Tim paused from punching Junior and saw this.

"Get that nigger," he instructed the men holding Junior.

They released Junior and he dropped to the floor. He grabbed for his stomach and coughed.

The men went for Kanaan. Kanaan ran over to the door and removed the shirt from the handle to allow entry and exit. He pushed the button on the wall and the alarm sounded; he took his fighting stance as he taunted for the men to come at him. He slid the shank into his pocket.

One man punched at Kanaan and he ducked. Kanaan ran in and tackled the guy to the ground and punched him repeatedly.

"Frank, get this nigger off me," the man shouted.

"I got it, Benny," Frank replied as he grabbed for Kanaan.

Kanaan pulled the shank from his back pocket and aimed it at Frank while keeping his arm pressed into Benny's neck.

"You sure you want to do that?" Kanaan remarked.

Frank paused and Tim noticed this.

"What the fuck are you doing?" he questioned. "Get his ass." Tim turned and faced Junior once more.

Frank attempted to grab Kanaan once more, and in an instant, Kanaan cut Frank before stabbing Benny. Kanaan made sure to avoid major arteries, as he didn't want the officers to pin murders on him.

As the men lied on the floor, Kanaan rose to his feet and took off his shirt.

Tim didn't realize the men were down and continued to speak to Junior.

"All those cops and shooters who did it to your people, they should be fucking praised and let off. They only did the world a favor."

Junior glared at Tim as he held his stomach.

Tim pulled out a shank and kneeled to Junior. Junior felt his heart sink as Tim got closer to his neck. He'd never felt more hopeless.

"And this," Tim paused. "This is for Brian Whitley and Jake Warren. They should have killed you and your friend when they had the chance to do so."

Tim brought the knife closer to Junior's neck and Kanaan grunted loudly as he came from behind Tim and pulled the shirt tightly around his throat.

Tim gagged and dropped the knife and attempted to pull the shirt from his throat.

When Tim mentioned Junior and Marcus should have been killed, it enraged Junior. He gathered the strength and rose to his feet. Junior began to return the punches as Kanaan strangled Tim.

"You punk bitch," he spoke as he struck him repeatedly.

Tim began to cough blood as Kanaan kept a tight grip around his neck and Junior punched him.

Junior could see Tim losing consciousness and his anger slowly subsided.

He stopped punching Tim and looked at Kanaan.

"What's up?" Kanaan questioned as he held the shirt around Tim's neck.

"Let him go, man," Junior shook his head. "Look at us."

Kanaan was slightly confused.

"If we kill his ass and his whole crew right now, we're no better than these pieces of shit," Junior's conscience was kicking in and Kanaan could see this.

Kanaan didn't loosen his grip and Junior continued.

"Look, man, we do this shit, they throw five bodies on us. I'm not trying to spend the rest of my life in this bitch, are you?" he looked at Kanaan sternly.

Kanaan gave thought to what Junior was saying but kept his hold on the shirt.

"Right now, we got a self-defense claim. We haven't killed anyone, and these niggas are just injured. Let's let the shit go. They won't try the shit again."

Kanaan spoke finally over the alarm.

"Man, you got a good head on your shoulders," he released the shirt and Tim fell to the ground and gasped for air. "That shit is going to take you places." Kanaan looked at Tim in disgust and looked at the blood on his shirt. "You know these officers are about to swarm this room. What you want to do?"

"Play it out," Junior remarked. "Revenge is a dish best served cold." Junior used Kanaan's shirt and picked up his shank. "This shit is theirs. We just took it from them to defend ourselves."

Kanaan and Junior performed their signature handshake before numerous officers came into the room.

Kanaan and Junior both locked eyes and lowered to their knees with their hands up.

"We need medics up here in the weight room," one of the officers spoke over his radio.

"*10-4*," the dispatcher responded.

"What the hell happened here?" the guard questioned.

"Me and my homie were lifting weights when these guys ran up on us and attacked us," Junior lied as he and Kanaan kept their hands up. "Right?"

"Yeah," Kanaan nodded his head. "We were just working out when they ran up."

Kanaan agreed with what Junior's angle was regarding Tim and his boys. He appreciated that he had his head on straight and didn't just act on impulse; this was another reason he knew Junior wasn't guilty.

"Tapes will be reviewed for accuracy," the guard remarked. "Let's go," they brought Junior and Kanaan to their feet.

Christian held his head high although he was extremely nervous. He held Keisha's hand as he drove in the direction of the courthouse. The jurors had an update and he didn't want to miss a minute of what was going on.

"Raymond and Frankie are going to meet us at the courthouse," he uttered as he drove.

Keisha rested her head on his arm as they listened to the radio.

"The jury is back with an update regarding the Christian Tate and Marcus Farris trials. We have word that they haven't reached a verdict but have a question for the judge. Folks are lining up to get a seat inside of the courtroom for what has to be two of the biggest trials of the century." The reporter switched stories. *"In other news, the voting for the gubernatorial seat is today. Thousands have already voted and based on current numbers, Smith is beating Tate by roughly 500 votes. But it's still very early in the day and there's a lot of state left to vote; miracles happen every day, let's see if one can happen."*

Normally, hearing about the election would add to Christian's anxiety, but he truly realized he didn't care about winning. Even if he were to lose the election, if his son came home, that would be a win in his eyes.

Christian pulled into the parking lot and managed to find one open spot. He exited the vehicle with Keisha, and they were swarmed with cameras.

"Christian Tate, with the election being today, how are you holding up?" a reporter asked.

"Come on, Keisha," Christian maneuvered around the reporters and held his wife's hand. They approached the door and entered the courthouse.

They proceeded through the metal detectors and walked to the room. Christian looked around and saw Raymond and Francesca. Christian and Keisha walked over to the two and sat.

Christian saw Andrew standing alone at the defense desk and whispered to him. "Yo, where's Junior?" he asked.

"There was an altercation at the prison," Andrew whispered. "He's sitting in the back; just waiting on the court officer to bring him out."

"Fuck," Christian whispered.

Keisha overheard Andrew and shook her head. "That boy isn't going to last much longer in there."

Christian kept his hand on his wife's hand and the bailiff brought the court to a stand for the judge and jury to enter.

The court officer brought Junior into the courtroom and escorted him next to Andrew.

"You good?" Andrew whispered to Junior.

Junior put his hand over his side. "A little bruised, but I'm still standing," he smiled. He looked over his shoulder and saw his parents, Raymond, and Francesca. His smile didn't fade as he faced the front.

"I understand there's a question from the jury," Matthew uttered.

"We have two, Your Honor," the foreman spoke. He passed the card to the bailiff, who walked the card to Matthew.

"The first question reads: these are two separate cases and should be treated as such. How and where are we to draw the line between the two cases?" Matthew read off the card.

"It took them over three weeks to come up with that question?" Junior whispered to Andrew.

"Shh," Andrew whispered in response.

"Jurors, you all have been deliberating for a little over three weeks now," Matthew spoke. "I'm confident that you have done a fine job. These *are* two separate cases, you are correct. You are to draw the line between the cases where the second shot was fired with Officer Whitley and when Officer Warren appeared."

"Thank you," the foreman replied.

Matthew nodded his head.

"The second question reads: since they are being treated as two separate trials, the verdicts don't have to coincide with the other. What happens if there's a hung verdict on one of the trials?" Matthew read.

Junior's heart sunk a little upon hearing the question.

"In the event of a hung jury, we will then poll each of the jurors. The court will also ask you to deliberate further. If a verdict cannot be reached, this court will have no choice but to grant a mistrial. Per the prosecution's request, a new trial will be set forth; which will result in the evidence and case being represented to a new jury," Matthew answered.

"Thank you, Your Honor. That is all."

"Thank you all for your continued service. This court leaves you to continue deliberation and will hear from you all soon." Matthew removed his glasses.

"All rise!" the bailiff brought the court to a stand and the jury exited followed by the judge.

"This isn't a bad thing," Andrew turned to Junior. "Don't worry about anything; I'd rather have a few questions from the jury than to not have questions."

Junior nodded his head. He had faith in what Andrew was telling him, but he was still nervous.
***
Junior twiddled his thumbs and bit his lip. He tapped his foot and watched the television in the foyer.

Kanaan sat next to him and spoke. "A little television to calm the nerves?" he asked.

Junior looked at Kanaan and chuckled. "Yeah, man."

"Why you lookin' so nervous man?" Kanaan laughed. "They cleared us, and Tim and his boys aren't on our asses anymore.

Junior turned up the television.

"Today was election day," Junior spoke. "Last I checked was earlier today and my dad was trailing in the votes."

Kanaan clicked his tongue. "That's what's up. Well, that was a long time ago," he reminded Junior. "What are they saying?"

"They haven't said much," Junior remarked. "Shit's been on commercial since I turned this thing on," he laughed.

The report came on television and Junior locked his eyes on the screen.

"The final polling place closed nearly half an hour ago and the votes are being tallied. So far, Tate is trailing Smith by 200 votes and the polling place has reportedly taken in roughly 900,000 votes, so the election can go either way."

Junior bit his nails and scratched his hair. Kanaan inhaled on a blunt and offered it to Junior.

"Nah man, I'm not fucking with that anymore," he laughed. "Fucked me up last time."

"I'm going to be real, I wanted to thank you for keeping your head on straight during the fight. I was ready to kill those fuckas'," Kanaan spoke. "If it wasn't for you, I'd have had six bodies thrown on me and I wouldn't have any chance at getting out."

"One of us has to be level-headed," Junior chuckled as he shook hands with Kanaan.

"The votes have been counted and we have an update for you all," the reporter spoke. *"After trailing nearly all day in the polls, Lieutenant Christian Tate has been elected as the governor of Florida."*

Junior nearly jumped out of his seat as he heard the news. He was truly proud of his father and the outcome of the election.

"We are awaiting speeches from both Lieutenant Tate as well as Mr. Bernard Smith regarding the outcome."

"Told you, man," Kanaan gave Junior another handshake. "Congrats to your old man."

"Thanks, man," Junior responded.

"One victory down, two more to go," Kanaan said.

17

After hearing of his victory, Christian decided to drive with Keisha over to the hospital to sit with Raymond and Natina.

They walked inside of the hospital building and there was a round of applause as the inhabitants saw Christian.

Christian smiled and put a hand up. "No photos for now," Christian chuckled. "Save it for after the victory speech," he chuckled.

He spoke to the secretary and she directed Christian and Keisha to Marcus' room.

Keisha kept her arm around Christian's and kissed him on the cheek.

"I love you," she mentioned softly as they walked to the room. "Congratulations, Governor," she smiled.

"I love you, too, First Lady," he smiled and knocked twice on the door.

"Come in," Raymond spoke from behind the door.

Christian and Keisha entered the room. Keisha immediately approached Natina and embraced her tightly. Christian shook hands with Raymond and crossed his arms.

"Governor Tate," Raymond chuckled. "Sounds good, huh?"

"It's fitting," Christian replied. "You're my security detail, so don't get too comfortable here in Miami," he joked. "Plus, I still gotta give this speech."

"You got one set?" Raymond questioned.

"Already wrote one; one for if I won, and one for if I lost," Christian laughed as they both looked at Marcus. "How is he?"

"Still the same," Raymond uttered. "We're just waiting."

Christian walked closer to Marcus and hovered over him. Christian touched Marcus' hand and felt his muscles move; he immediately looked at his face.

Christian noticed Marcus' eyes fluttering.

"Ray, Natina, look," Christian whispered.

Natina released Keisha's embrace and walked near her husband. They both stood in front of Marcus.

Marcus opened his eyes slowly and looked around to the best of his abilities.

"Marcus!" Natina exclaimed as she put her hand over her mouth.

Raymond shed tears as his son looked around. "Thank you, God."

Christian pressed the button and called for the nurse to enter the room.

Everyone seemed to be astonished that Marcus had awoken from his coma. The chances of him pulling through seemed to be slim and every doctor made it known.

He tried to talk, and Christian noticed this. He was unable to do so.

"Don't rush into talking, man," Christian spoke softly.

Marcus cleared his throat.

He scanned the room as if he were looking for something — or someone.

"Where's C.J.?" he groaned, raspily.

The adults looked at one another. Marcus had been in a coma ever since he was shot, and he didn't know Junior was in prison.

"He'll be here," Raymond uttered. "You just get some rest, son. You gave us all quite a scare."

Marcus continued to look around.

"What day is it?" he asked slowly.

"November 9th, 2040," Natina answered her son.

Marcus couldn't believe so much time had passed since the shooting. Marcus continued to frantically scan the room for his best friend.

"He'll be here," Raymond repeated as he looked at Christian.

■■

"Has the jury reached a verdict?" Matthew spoke the next day.

Andrew stood next to Junior and they both kept their heads held high.

Bianca, Raymond, Christian, Keisha, and Francesca sat behind the two. Natina and Sierra were muted on a Skype call as they awaited the verdict.

Junior could feel his heartbeat increase and he realized his fate rested in the hands of the jury who looked nothing like him or his friend.

Back at the prison, Kanaan sat at the table, shuffling cards, as he awaited the verdict.

"This just in, the jury has returned with a verdict in the Christian Tate & Marcus Farris trials. This is a disclaimer, we will be showing live footage of the verdict, so there may be explicit or sensitive audio and/or video presented."

"Come on," Kanaan whispered. Members of his crew watched the monitor with him.

"We have, Your Honor," the forewoman spoke. She rose to her feet. "In the case of The State of Florida versus Tate, we, the jury, find the defendant, Christian Tate, Jr. —."

Junior's heart was beating rapidly as he awaited the verdict.

Andrew kept his hands clasped together as he anxiously awaited with his client.

"Not guilty for the count of attempted murder of a police officer."

Junior sighed heavily as the first charge was charged with was officially dropped. There were numerous sighs and outbursts around the courtroom.

Matthew hit his gavel. "Order!"

The court settled and the forewoman continued.

"On the first count of aggravated battery with a firearm, we, the jury, find the defendant, Christian Tate, Jr., not guilty."

Junior took a seat. Keisha shed a few tears as the jury read the verdicts.

"On the second count of aggravated battery with a firearm, we, the jury, find the defendant, Christian Tate, Jr., guilty."

Junior's heart sunk as the jury read a guilty verdict. Andrew remained standing with his head focused on the jury.

"On the count of resisting arrest, we, the jury, find the defendant, Christian Tate, Jr., guilty."

Junior put his head down and his mother had an outburst at the verdict. Christian held her down as Francesca shook her head.

Matthew hit his gavel against the desk numerous times. As the court silenced, Matthew continued.

"Please present your verdict on the second case."

"In the case of Farris versus Jake Warren and the State of Florida, we, the jury, find Jake Warren guilty of negligent discharge of a firearm with intent to murder."

Raymond cried tears of joy as the verdict came against the officer who put his son in the hospital. He looked over to Jake, who seemed anxious as the indictment was brought about.

Christian looked at Jake with disgust; Junior kept his head down as he listened to the verdicts. He was ecstatic that Marcus was getting the justice he deserved. Junior was just upset that it took so long for justice to be brought about.

Andrew spoke as the jurors finished. "Your Honor, the defense would like to poll the jury on the Florida-v-Tate case."

"Ladies and gentlemen, when an indictment has been brought against someone in a jury trial, the indicted individual has the right to poll the jury, to ensure these verdicts were brought about by each member of the jury on their own accord and to validate there have been no coercion, promises, or briberies to sway the verdict," Matthew announced. "Counselors, approach."

Andrew and Anayi walked to the bench and faced the jury. Andrew posed the questions to each of the jurors.

"Were those then, and are these now your verdicts?"

Each juror answered yes.

"Did you come to this verdict on your own accord? That is, you verify that you haven't been threatened in any way, promised anything, and haven't been coerced into making this decision?"

All the jurors confirmed.

Matthew nodded his head.

"Ladies and gentlemen of the jury, this court appreciates you for all of your hard work and dedication to these trials. The bailiff will escort you back to the jury room and you will be provided compensation for your time; you will then be escorted from the courthouse."
Junior whispered to Andrew.

"Your Honor!" Andrew spoke before Matthew hit his gavel against the desk.

"Yes, Mr. Brownstone?" he questioned.

"My client would like to address the court," Andrew spoke with confidence.

"Objection, Your Honor," Anayi intercepted.

"Your Honor, my client has just been found guilty by a jury who doesn't look like him at all," Andrew explained.

"He was found guilty on two of the four counts brought against him," Anayi argued.

"He's sat through this trial just like everyone else. You're telling me he doesn't have a voice?"

"Objection, overruled," Matthew spoke sternly. "Proceed."

Junior rose to his feet slowly and as he stood erect, he shook hands with Andrew.

Christian and Keisha anxiously looked on to see what their son had to say regarding the outcome of the trial.

"Your Honor, throughout my time in prison, and during this trial, I've been beaten on numerous times, demeaned, humiliated, and tormented. I've entered this courtroom numerous times with crutches, a black eye, and scratches on my face, and, not that I expect you do to so, but you haven't asked me once about it. You've spoken to my lawyer, but you haven't addressed me."

Christian shook his head slowly. He knew his son wouldn't be one to bite his tongue and with the unfair verdict being returned, he knew he would have something to say. He kept his hand on Keisha's hand.

"My most recent encounter was a few days ago, where I was brutally beaten by inmates in the prison. I and my cell-neighbor defended ourselves to fight off six of them."

Matthew raised his eyebrows but continued to look at his notepad. The jurors looked at one another as if they felt they'd made a mistake.

"Even to this moment, you have looked directly at me for a total of maybe four times. You have yet to truly look me in my eyes and determine my true character."

Andrew wasn't sure that challenging the judge was the best move for Junior, but he didn't want to cut him off yet.

"I already know that just based on who I am," Junior hinted towards race, "I was presumed guilty until proven innocent, and while I am grateful that justice has been served on two of the charges and completely for my best friend, I can't help but feel like justice wasn't served to the fullest extent," Junior spoke.

Andrew put his hand on Junior's shoulder as a cue for him to wrap it up. He was moving into hot water and didn't want Junior to get burned.

Junior nodded his head. "You're going to do whatever you have to do, and there's nothing I can do to change that. I've said all I wanted to say. Do what you will," he finished and returned to his seat.

Matthew nodded his head and continued.

"Mr. Tate, thank you for that commentary. The court will take it into consideration. For now, the jury is excused," he looked at the jurors. "Again, the court thanks you for your service." Matthew hit his gavel against the desk.

"All rise for the jury," the bailiff called.

Everyone in the courtroom rose to their feet, except for Junior; he didn't care about what was being said.

"You may be seated," Matthew announced to the court; everyone sat. "Ladies and gentlemen, we will be adjourning this case and will reconvene for sentencing in approximately two weeks. The defendants, Christian Tate, Jr., and Jake Warren will be remanded into prison, pending sentencing. We are adjourned." Matthew hit the gavel again and the bailiff brought the court to a stand.

Christian and Keisha were the first to approach Junior and Andrew, although Keisha knew her embrace would be short-lived.

She sobbed into his shoulder and Junior tried to maintain his composure, but he cried with his mother.

"Babe, I need for you to remain strong in there," she explained. "I am so sorry."

"Don't feel bad," Junior spoke. "I'm a soldier," he chuckled. Junior looked at his father and smiled. "At least my amazing father won the race for governor of this state."

Christian smiled on the inside but didn't let it show. He displayed a look of concern as he touched his son's shoulder.

"Junior, you've made me so proud. The way you've held yourself during this entire ordeal amazes me," he complimented his son.

Junior shook his head. "Pops, it's okay," he spoke softly. "I couldn't have made it this far without all of your help and support." Junior looked at Bianca. "I love you, B," he shed a tear. "And I mean this with every breath in my body: you don't have to wait for me. We're still extremely young. Live your life, babe."

"C.J., I'm not going anywhere," she spoke confidently. "I love you to the moon and back."

Junior reached over and embraced her and kissed her on the cheek.

"Make sure you come visit me."

"Hey!" Andrew interrupted. "This is *not* the end. Do you not know who I am?" he chuckled. "Or who your father is?"

Junior looked over to his father and back to Andrew.

"We will get you home before sentencing," Christian promised.

"Thank you all," Junior spoke as he teared.

Keisha embraced her son tightly and kissed him on the cheek. "I love you so much, baby," she couldn't control her tears.

The court's officer walked over to the family and Andrew saw him approach.

"Guys," he whispered.

Christian acknowledged Andrew's statement and tapped Keisha. Everyone gave Junior an individual hug.

The officer escorted Junior away from the group and to the back of the court. A moment passed before another word was spoken.

Christian embraced Keisha tightly as he spoke to Andrew. "So, what's your next move?" he inquired.

"Either look for holes to get the verdict overturned," Andrew gathered the folders and papers, "or I go for community service." Andrew stood erect. "As Junior stated, he's been beaten, tormented, humiliated, and demeaned while he's been in prison. If I can't get this overturned, the argument would be that we are fearful for his safety in prison. No judge in their right mind would be able to deny the motion after what Junior's been through."

Raymond shook his head. "History repeats itself."

"Who you telling?" Christian remarked.

18

Junior sat at the table with his hands on his head. He was still trying to wrap his mind around the verdict. Although he was found not guilty on two of the four charges, he was worried as he knew they would carry weight; especially with him being the son of a lieutenant and the charges being against an officer.

He knew Jake had been arrested, so he felt a little relief, but he couldn't help but feel nervous. He hadn't seen Jake since they'd arrested him in court.

Kanaan approached and sat next to him; he noticed Junior's anxiety.

"Don't even worry about today," he spoke in an assuring tone.

"Man, you're full of hope," Junior smiled. "How can you remain positive in a place designed to tear you down?"

"Man, it can only tear you down if you allow it," Kanaan responded. "Me? I like to keep myself occupied with reading, watching the news, working out, and bettering myself," he clasped his hands, "so when the day comes that I do get out of here, I'll be ready."

"It's just hard," Junior admitted.

"They didn't pin you with all four charges. That first charge alone would have had you looking at either life or the needle," Kanaan spoke. "We have so much that we're negative about when we should be focusing on the positives." Kanaan lit a blunt and inhaled on it. "We have our health, our integrity, your dad won the race," Kanaan exhaled. "Man, you better turn that frown around and fix your face before I fix it for you," he chuckled.

Junior laughed. "Now you sound like my pops."

"He's a smart man," he chuckled.

Junior and Kanaan shook hands and Junior rose to his feet. He saw a picture of his father on the television screen.

"Yeah, he's great," he replied.

***

"Did you find anything?" Junior asked Andrew as they sat in the waiting room of the courtroom.

"I found something," Andrew spoke. "Not sure how the judge will react to it, but it's worth a try."

Junior looked behind him and saw his mother, father, Bianca, Francesca, and several officers around to protect his father. Christian smiled at his son.

"All rise!" the bailiff called.

"Good afternoon, ladies and gents, we are here today for Christian Tate, Jr.'s sentencing," Matthew spoke. "Before we get into the sentencing, I've received word that the defense has a message for the court." He nodded towards Andrew.

"Thank you, Your Honor," Andrew spoke. "Your Honor, after the verdict, the defense has worked tirelessly to ensure justice was served." Andrew looked at Anayi and back to Andrew. "May we meet in chambers?"

Christian raised his eyebrows at Andrew and smirked.

"On what grounds, Mr. Brownstone?" Matthew questioned.

'There's something that needs to be presented to His Honor."

"My chambers," he announced as he rose to his feet.

Matthew walked to the back and Andrew and Anayi followed. An officer escorted Junior to Matthew's chambers.

"This better be good, Mr. Brownstone," Matthew sat in his chair.

"Your Honor, I have discovered audio logs from Officer Brian Whitley's body-cam and numerous written warnings from Governor Christian Tate to Officer Brian Whitley regarding unlawful stops," Andrew pulled pieces of paper from the folder; he laid them on the desk before proceeding. "These warnings weren't only involving my client, but numerous African American and Hispanic adolescents across the city."

Anayi leaned over the desk and looked at the papers. Matthew looked at the papers in shock.

"What does the prosecution have to say about this?" he questioned.

Anayi was silent.

"It says here Officer Brian Whitley has been reprimanded numerous times for unlawful traffic stops. Not only from Governor Tate, but from other higher-ups in the field."

"Your Honor," Andrew proceeded, "we also have audio footage that proves Officer Whitley knew my client and had malice intentions in pulling him over that night. Throwing racial and demeaning slurs towards his superior as well as Christian Tate, Jr."

Andrew pressed play on his recorder.

"I'm so sick and tired of Lieutenant Tate and his bullshit," Brian spoke over the recording. *"This porch-monkey son-of-a-bitch writes me up for a lawful traffic stop."*

"It's not that bad," Brian's partner spoke. *"It could have been much worse."*

"You say that, and shit could be worse, but I'm going to have the last laugh, I swear to God. I'm coming for him and that nigger son of his."

His partner could be heard chuckling.

"I'm serious," Brian uttered. *"I got tabs on the nigger. Let me drop you off at the station."*

"Your Honor, notice how all of this is spoken in a low tone; potentially so it wouldn't be captured by the bodycam," Andrew pointed out.

Matthew displayed a look of shock. Anayi shook her head at the discovery.

"The fucker is about to get on the expressway," Brian continued, and the sound of a holster locking could be heard. *"Shit's about to go down. Let's just hope no one is killed."*

"I've heard enough," Matthew uttered. "Bring in Officer Brian Whitley," he spoke to Anayi.

Anayi opened her mouth to speak and Matthew continued.

"No words," he spoke louder. "Get him in here, now!"

Anayi looked discouraged and nodded her head. She left the room.

Matthew looked at Andrew and Junior.

"Christian," he began. Junior held his head high. "I issue my deepest apologies to you. "In your closing remarks, you mentioned that I hadn't given you the respect you felt you deserved, and I take ownership of that," Matthew cleared his throat. "Especially in light of this newfound evidence."

Junior was silent but nodded his head.

"Your Honor, the defense requests that the court overturn the verdict and set my client free of all charges."

Matthew looked at the papers in front of him and looked at Andrew.

"Slow down, Mr. Brownstone," he uttered. "I am not in a position to overturn the jury's verdict. Mr. Tate resisted arrest and the second shot wasn't warranted."

"Your Honor, you just heard it yourself. Officer Whitley was harassing my client and even insinuated that he would be using his weapon. This was merely a few moments before the stop."

Anayi entered the chambers with Brian. Andrew glared at Brian and Brian kept his head down.

"Officer Whitley," Matthew called, "can you explain your auditory remarks on this tape?" Matthew replayed the audio.

With every word, Brian seemed to blush more.

"You've got some serious explaining to do."

■■

Junior put his pictures in his pocket and walked out of the cell. He ran into Kanaan.

"You're out of here," he congratulated Junior.

"Numerous fights and abrasions later," Junior chuckled as he did his signature handshake with Kanaan.

Kanaan pulled Junior in close. "Don't ever let me see you back in here," he spoke.

"How about you let me see you on the outside?" Junior laughed. "Behave yourself and get up out of here."

"Man, my time is coming. Keep your head on straight. In the meantime," Kanaan cleared his throat, "I'll be watching you ball out in college and then the NBA. Make sure you hit me up some time, man," he uttered.

"Let's go, Tate," the guard called.

"I got you," Junior spoke to Kanaan. "I'm gonna write you, bro, and I got you on the shoutouts as well," he laughed as he walked away with the guard.

"Be easy."

"You're out on a technicality," the guard spoke. "But your charge didn't go anywhere," he laughed.

Junior didn't utter a word to the guard. He didn't want to risk his chances of getting out of prison by saying something to the guard: it's what the guard wanted to happen. Junior and the guard got to the table and Junior signed his name and gathered his belongings before exiting the building. He ecstatically walked to his father's vehicle and climbed inside.

Christian gave Junior a long embrace before speaking.

"Welcome back, Son," he smiled.

Junior couldn't help but shed a tear as he reflected on all he'd been through. He was finally out of jail.

He looked out of the window as his father drove and noticed the direction they were driving in wasn't toward his house.

"Going to see Marcus?"

"Bingo," Christian smiled as he glanced at his son.

Junior smiled at his father and adjusted himself in the seat.

"How is it in office, Governor?"

"All is well, but nothing feels as good as being able to say my son is from behind bars."

"You did say I would be out," Junior uttered and smiled. "Crazy thing is, you didn't have to do a thing but support me through the journey." Junior looked at his father. "Thanks, Pops."

"Junior, I'm your father," Christian responded. "I will be by your side until the end of time; you don't have to thank me for doing my job as a parent."

Junior sat back in the chair and nodded his head. Christian continued the drive.

The ride was smooth, and Junior touched his ribs. Although the fight with Tim happened a month prior, he was still sore. But one thing he never counted on happening was making a friend while he was inside. He thought about Kanaan and how he'd had his back throughout his incarceration; he was truly a ride-or-die friend. Junior chuckled silently as he reminisced on everything that occurred.

Christian pulled into the parking lot and Junior nearly hopped out of the vehicle.

They walked into the building and were directed to Marcus' room.

Junior walked in with excitement; Marcus' focus immediately turned to the door.

Junior walked over and embraced Keisha tightly. He followed the embrace with a kiss on the cheek.

He embraced Natina and shook hands with Raymond. He kissed Bianca and didn't care who was watching.

Sierra smiled and held Marcus' hand.

"Bro," Junior spoke as he strolled over to the bed. He leaned over and tapped Sierra's shoulder to say hello.

"Welcome home, Junior," Sierra replied.

"Welcome home," Marcus spoke. "It's been a long time, huh?" he chuckled.

Junior chuckled at his friend. "Man so much has happened I don't even know where to begin."

Marcus smiled and laughed at his friend. "Tell me about what I missed while I was under."

"Met a real cool dude in prison. Name's Kanaan and he stuck by my side through whatever."

"Making friends in prison?" Marcus laughed lightly. "Nah, I'm just messing with you. I'm glad you had someone to keep you level-headed."

Junior chuckled. "Weird thing is, he was forty. That's a twenty-year age difference."

Marcus chuckled lightly and continued. "Man, I heard you were representing and standin' strong in court," Marcus spoke. He tried to speak loudly, but he was unable to do so.

"They tried to break me numerous times, but I'm a rider. I stand strong for mines."

"My nigga," Marcus chuckled.

A tear fell down Junior's face. "We just have to get you out of this bed. You know you have a scholarship waiting and you have things to do."

Marcus didn't reply to Junior's comment; instead, he just smiled and nodded. "Tell me what else is up. I know you have stories for days."

"You mean the fights?" Junior questioned with a slight scoff. He noticed that his friend didn't acknowledge his previous remarks.

"Yeah, man," Marcus sighed. "Tell me about those fights."

Junior laughed lightly. "I told you about Kanaan. Every fight that took place, he had my back."

Marcus smiled.

"The very first fight, he was coming for my family, and you know how that gets."

"Keep your head, bro," Marcus chuckled.

"I know," Junior uttered. "More recently, I damn near got a broken rib out of it, and I possibly would have been killed if Kanaan hadn't been there," he remarked. "And you know I'm levelheaded," Junior chuckled.

"And what's that mean?" Marcus laughed lightly.

"I stopped us from getting a charge. Kanaan was definitely going to kill them if I hadn't stopped them."

"Tell me about the verdict," Marcus insisted.

"You got the justice you deserve," Junior teared as he spoke. He held Marcus' hand tighter.

Marcus sighed. "I heard. And what about you? You deserve justice more than I do."

Junior chuckled. "That's my friend. Always putting others before himself."

Marcus cleared his throat. "Mine was open and shut pretty much," he remarked. "All I remember is you tending to Whitley and two officers shouting for me to exit the vehicle before I was shot down."

Hearing Marcus speak gave Junior chills.

"I was found guilty on two of the four charges brought upon me."

Marcus shook his head slowly.

"Some things will never change. So, how'd you get out?" he questioned.

"The judge insisted that he couldn't drop the charges right away," Junior uttered. "But he said I could get it eradicated and expunged after two years. He's allowing community service instead of jail time."

"System isn't designed for us. It's crazy because all we want is equality. They're lucky we aren't looking for revenge."

"If I was," Junior chuckled, "I would have aimed for the head and not close to the shoulder."

Christian heard and chuckled at Junior's comment. He knew his son was joking and was trying to get his friend to laugh. Christian looked at the machines as they monitored Marcus' health.

"Don't say that too loud in front of the Lieutenant-Governor, if that's a thing," Marcus laughed. "You might land yourself right back in there."

"After everything I've been through, I'm not even worried," Junior spoke confidently. "All you need to focus on, bro, is getting better."

Marcus looked around the room. "Seeing you in good spirits and hearing that all is well with you, is as good as it gets to me," Marcus spoke softly. "You're about to go to school on a full scholarship and ball out. That's where your focus should be."

"It is," Junior immediately responded. "But you have to be with me through it all."

"I will be," Marcus assured him. "Just keep riding and doing your thing bro. Hold it down in the meantime." Marcus uttered.

Junior didn't like the way his friend was talking; none of them did.

"We're ride or die, bro. Remember that," Junior remarked.

"Ride or die," Marcus spoke with a smile.

The heart monitor went from steady beeping to an elongated beep. Marcus' smile faded.

"Marcus!" Natina screamed as she walked closer to her son.

Raymond kept his hands on her shoulders and the tears fell from his eyes.

Christian hugged Keisha tightly and Sierra sobbed into Bianca's shoulder.

The alarm on the monitor began going off and nurses promptly entered the room.

"At least justice was served for one of us," Junior cried silently. "I'll hold it down for you."